# Every Witch Way but Hidden

Magical Misfits Mysteries - book 5

## K.E. O'Connor

K.E. O'Connor Books

# Chapter 1

## A sandy surprise

The soft sand under my paws made it tricky to move fast and not get eaten. But didn't everyone enjoy a challenge?

I whizzed past Sammy, who sat on a damp, seaweed-encrusted rock. "Are you sure you don't want to join in?"

He shook his head and backed up a couple of steps. "I'm not in the mood."

I glanced over my shoulder, my whiskers twitching with delight as my running mates, Archie and Mack, bounded behind me. "You're missing out."

"What am I missing? Who wants to get bitten by a ghoul?" Sammy's words were grabbed and carried away in the stiff breeze blowing off the sea.

My joy faded. Sammy had been grumpy for weeks. Every time I asked him what was wrong, he denied there was any problem. But my usually sweet-natured, bighearted companion was troubled.

"They're speeding up. Must be hungry." Archie blasted past me, leaving a trail of smoke. For an enormous hellhound, he was light on his paws.

I dug into the wet sand and pebbles and powered along, keeping a healthy distance from Adrienne and Joel. This had become a regular task, getting them to chase me so they burned off their hunt lust. It was one of many small compromises we'd made since discovering my witch's mother and her boyfriend were ghouls. But I'd do whatever it took to make Zandra happy. If that meant being chased by ghouls occasionally, then so be it.

The beach was the perfect place to be mock hunted, since Crimson Cove had become overrun with non-magicals who were here for the annual Reverence Festival. Few of them were brave enough to come to the beach as dusk neared, the temperature lowered, and the winds picked up.

Those who had braved the chilly conditions were far enough away not to bother us. But we'd brought along a bucket of fresh fish, in case we had to lure the ghouls away from the walking snacks dumb enough to get too close.

"I thought I was visiting you so I could have a rest." Mack drew alongside me, puffing out air through his broad snout. "Come for the week, you said. We can kick back with food and relax, you said. This is the opposite of relaxing. I'm a ghoul plaything!"

I grinned at my spiky honey badger friend. "We can relax soon. If you hadn't come with us, you'd have been bored stuck in the basement."

"I'd have been sleeping. That's not boring." Mack was a chunky, grumpy honey badger, who'd recently moved out of Crimson Cove to join a family of Griffin ranchers a few towns over. This was his first trip back, and I was excited to hear his news.

It was always good to celebrate a successful rehoming. Mack had lost a beloved vampire companion not so long ago, and it had taken him time to find the right path. But his glossy coat and bright eyes showed he was on the mend.

"There won't be much relaxing when the festival gets going." Archie slowed to join us. "Street entertainers, the Sundown Procession, the Crooked Swine effigy burning, and I've already seen Night Mare."

"Don't forget Skull Dugger and Cornard the Raven. They'll make an appearance."

Archie wagged his tail. "It's exciting. Remus is taking me to every show."

"It's a shame so many non-magicals learned about the festival," I said. "No-one can figure out how they got wind of the event. It's always been magic users only."

"Yeah, you've got a problem," Mack said. "I couldn't believe it when I arrived and saw them here. What's got them noticing Crimson Cove?"

"Something we haven't figured out yet," I said. "More and more arrive every day. It's as if we're corpse flowers and they can't resist seeking us out and inhaling our unique fragrance."

"You've got a problem with your wards."

"That's what I keep saying, but they've been triple-checked and there are no problems." I made sure we weren't within ghoul striking distance. "Something weird is going on."

"They could make celebrating tricky," Mack said. "Won't they freak out during the Serpent Dance? And how will you explain the Lord of Misrule reception? They don't still do blood sacrifices, do they?"

"No blood sacrifices." I checked over my shoulder again. "It's more civilized these days. And since everyone is dressing up for the events, it shouldn't be an issue. All the non-magicals will be in costume, so we can pretend we are, too. The vampires can come with their fangs out if they want to."

"They may figure out a talking cat, hellhound, and honey badger aren't so natural," Mack said.

"They're unlikely to hear us," I said. "Although I've had odd looks from non-magicals. Some of them seem to pick up a few words, so we must be careful. We'll keep out of their way to make sure there's no confusion. They're such fragile creatures."

"You should move them on," Mack said. "It must make it hard for residents to be comfortable using their powers in case they accidentally splat someone."

"We've had a few near misses," I said. "You heard about the werewolves visiting?"

"Who hasn't? Anyone get bit?"

"No. But the angels were freaking out for fear a non-magical would get caught in a battle they didn't understand."

"Let's run through the sand dunes," Archie said. "That should tire out Adrienne and Joel. Then we can go get something to eat."

Mack and Archie diverted toward the dunes, but I slowed. There was a family ahead of us, close to the water's edge, and none of them looked happy. There was an old lady in a wheelchair with a huge purse on her lap. A man stood behind her, holding the handles of her chair. A younger guy occasionally threw stones into the sea. And an attractive older woman argued with a skinny teenage male.

I didn't need to get closer to see they were non-magicals. Usually, I paid non-magicals little attention, but the stress radiating off them made my fur bristle, and the teen's voice was raised as he yelled at the woman.

"Come on, Juno! You'll get caught if you don't move," Archie shouted.

I lifted a paw in acknowledgement, my gaze raising to the sky. An owl circled the group. It was a huge brown bird with a wide wingspan. Odd. Owls hated the beach. They were raptors of the field or forest. What would bring such a magnificent creature to the shoreline? Perhaps it was curious about the arguing family.

It swooped high over their heads in a large, slow circle, occasionally beating its wings to stay on an air current.

The teenager threw his hands up then turned and stomped across the pebbles.

The woman made to go after him, but the man holding the wheelchair caught her arm and shook his head. They talked for several seconds before the woman's shoulders slumped and she looked out across the sea.

The teenager continued to march away, swinging his arms, his shoulders tight around his ears.

After completing another slow circuit around the family, the owl followed the surly young male.

I was yanked off my feet by my tail and came face-to-face with Joel. His lips were pulled back from his teeth, and his eyes were devoid of emotion as he raised me to his lips like I was his favorite treat.

An enormous, wet, slimy fish slapped into his face and bounced back against me, leaving a trail of scales and salty water across my silky white fur.

Adrienne whacked Joel with the fish again. "No! No biting. Juno not dinner!"

Joel snarled and attempted to take a chunk from my stomach. I hissed and batted him in the face with my murder mittens.

Adrienne kept whacking Joel with the slimy fish. "Put her down. Not food. Bad Joel."

Joel's snarling lessened, and the blackness in his eyes faded. He released his grip on my tail, and I fell to the ground, landing neatly on my paws.

I stank of fish and ghoul. Not the most fragrant of perfumes to take home to Zandra, but she sometimes smelled worse after a busy day at animal control.

"Juno! You okay?" Archie raced over, growling, flames flickering from his mouth.

I raised a paw to stop him from attacking Joel. "Fine. It was my fault. Joel wouldn't have bitten me, would you?" I looked up at the ghoul, who had a chastised expression on his face.

Adrienne stopped hitting him with the fish and rested a hand on his shoulder. "Better now. Got excited, that's all." She handed the sad looking fish to Joel as a consolation prize.

Mack joined us, his sides heaving in and out.

"That's enough running for one day. Or do you need to go farther?" I asked the ghouls.

"Good, thanks," Adrienne said. "No desire to eat you. Not from me, anyway." She nudged Joel as he chewed on his raw fish.

His gaze dropped to the sand, and he shook his head.

Joel wasn't a talker. Few ghouls were. Adrienne was the exception. She'd been an extraordinary woman when alive and was the same as a ghoul. She had rational thought, the ability to communicate in almost whole sentences, and she remembered her former life and the scattered love she'd always carried for Zandra.

"We should get out of here," Archie said. "That arguing family is headed this way. If they get a look at Joel's snack, they'll panic."

I glanced at the family again. The man was struggling to get the wheelchair to move, while the woman walked a few steps behind, her head down. The other guy was still throwing stones and looked like he was laughing to himself. He pulled a bottle from his jacket pocket and took a drink.

I turned back to see where Sammy was. He sat on the same rock, washing his face with one paw. Why hadn't he shouted an alarm when Joel was about to get me? And he hadn't bothered to come see if I was okay.

Things needed fixing with my Sammy. Everyone was entitled to a low mood, but his mood had lingered for too long. I had to get him to open up and confide in me. I was worried about him. I missed my sweet, supportive Sammy.

"Let's go," I said. "Adrienne, Joel, you coming back to Zandra's?"

Adrienne shook her head. "Dinner with Cannibal Bill. We've got offal."

"Delicious," Archie said. "You're so lucky."

Joel smacked his lips together.

Adrienne and Joel had landed on their feet when they'd moved in with Cannibal Bill. And they'd helped him build a larger unit for them to use as a home in the woods. It was an upgrade from the shed they'd started in.

It was the perfect compromise. They had a safe place to live. Cannibal Bill had company and made sure they were well-fed, and they could drop by and see Zandra any time they liked. So long as they were discreet. Not everyone accepted ghouls wandering around unsupervised.

"What costumes are you wearing to the Reverence Festival?" Archie said. "Remus got me half a dozen to try. I can be a vampire hellhound or an ogre hellhound. I'm leaning toward the Gorgon hellhound costume, though. It comes with a headdress covered in snakes that move. They're awesome."

"You could always come as yourself," I said. "You make an impressive hellhound. No adornments required."

He licked my head, almost knocking me off my feet. "Thanks. But everyone is dressing up. I don't want to feel left out."

"I'm not wearing a dumb costume," Mack said. "They can take me as I am or not at all."

"I might wear something. Even Zandra is maxxing her witchy look by wearing a pointy hat and carrying a broomstick. And it'll be nice we can be out in our natural forms and not scare the non-magicals. Even Adrienne and Joel can come as they are. So long as there's no biting."

Joel cast his gaze down again and nodded.

"No biting." Adrienne crossed her heart with a gray finger. The nail was painted pumpkin orange.

"We still need to be careful using magic," Mack said. "It's fine for the non-magicals to think we're in costume, but if any get blasted with a spell and die, that'll be the end of the celebration. You really have to figure out what they're doing here. What's so special about Crimson Cove that they can't stay away?"

"We're working on that. For now, we focus on the festival. We can figure out what the non-magicals are doing here another time."

# Chapter 2

## A holey mystery

I moseyed along the corridor in animal control, looking for my wonderful witch, Zandra Crypt.

After I'd eaten, made sure Adrienne and Joel got home safely, and said goodbye to the others, I was late getting to work. We were working the night shift, my least favorite of all shifts, but we all took a turn. Some creatures operated under the light of the moon, and that meant we had to be out at that time, too.

"It's not a problem!" That was Randal Nix, head super geek and tech mage, who was working on a huge system upgrade for animal control.

"It is if it means extra work for you. I'd never have said anything if I'd known it would give you another thing for your to-do list. Sorry." That was Zandra, and her tone suggested unhappiness.

"It's fine. It's part of my job. And I'm glad you mentioned it. I can take a look once the newest comm upgrade has bedded in."

"Forget it! I thought it would speed things up. You don't have to do it."

"I want to. Especially if it makes you happy."

There was silence. Then Zandra's sigh could be heard three rooms away. She'd been having tense, awkward conversations with Randal ever since their failed date.

I waited in the corridor to see if they'd continue bickering, but the silence remained like a tiny fish bone lodged in a back tooth. Uncomfortable and impossible to shift. I wasn't sure how to get them back on track. They liked each other, but seemed hesitant to attempt another date in case it car crashed again.

I couldn't see the problem of having another go, though. The timing had been off the last time, that was all. Zandra and I had been in the middle of assisting with a murder investigation, and Randal was dealing with tricky issues involving non-magicals frying his equipment.

And it was clear from all the blushing and stammering that they were still into each other. This relationship wasn't over yet. Not that it had really begun.

I didn't want my wonderful witch to remain single forever. Even though Zandra was prickly, she had a lot of love to give, and I wanted to ensure she found the right person to give it to.

The door behind me crashed open, and Sammy wandered in.

"Hey! I thought you were staying at the café with Sorcha and the others." I wandered over to rub faces.

Sammy dodged past me, snubbing my affection as he stalked into Barney's office. "It was boring there.

It's probably boring here, too, but I've got nothing else to do."

I jerked my head back as I followed him. "Sorry it can't be all fun and games at animal control."

"Yeah, whatever. It beats hanging out with all those idiots in the café while they stuff their faces and gossip."

"You could have stuffed your face, too," I said. "Sorcha always looks after you."

"When she's not nosing into other people's business like a lonely old shrew." Sammy hopped onto the desk and slumped on a pile of papers.

I climbed up beside him. "What's got this glum mood stirred up?"

He grunted and flopped onto his side. "I got out of bed on the wrong side."

"You've been doing that for weeks. Perhaps you should try another side."

He turned so his back faced me. "I almost got trod on by a dumb non-magical. Four huge buses pulled up, and this idiot tripped down the steps and nearly landed on me. The sooner we zap those losers and get them out of here, the better. A few blasts of magic will teach them a lesson."

"Or kill them! Sammy, we can't do that."

"They're better off dead. What kind of life do they have?"

I wrinkled my booping snooter. "They seem happy, despite having no magic."

"We're not happy with them invading Crimson Cove. They need to get back on those stupid buses and get out of here before someone makes them wish they'd never heard of this place."

I let out a gentle sigh as Sammy continued complaining. This behavior was unlike him. Sammy could be hesitant at putting a brave paw forward but always found strength to do the right thing, and he was never mean. I wanted to help him with his struggles, but there was nothing I could do unless he let me in.

Maybe I should pay him more attention. I was always focused on making sure Zandra was happy and safe. Perhaps I'd neglected Sammy. It was just like him not to complain if he felt unloved.

"You need to get that looked at." Glenda Ridgeback's sharp voice echoed along the corridor.

"It's just a scratch." Barney Hoffman appeared in the doorway, holding a bleeding arm. His hair was ruffled, and there was blood on his usually pristine white shirt.

"What happened?" I hopped off the desk and hurried over to him.

Glenda scratched her long nails through my fur. "Hey, cutie. Brave old Barney wanted to see action on the front lines. He got more than he bargained for, though."

Oleander Yokeley staggered along the hall, a cage balanced in his arms. Inside were three young, slender oxen-wolves. They were snarling, their eyes glowing red.

"You got them!" I said. "Nice job. They've been on the loose for weeks."

"We got a tipoff they were in someone's backyard," Glenda said.

"This injury is my fault." Barney inspected his shredded arm. "I'm getting rusty. I was so overwhelmed with paperwork that I decided a reminder of how important our work is would inspire me. Bring back the passion."

"Did it?" I gestured Barney to crouch so I could heal his injury.

"It reminded me what an amazing team I have. I'm so proud you go out every day and night to keep people safe and protect vulnerable animals." He lowered to his knees and held his arm out. "Thank you, Juno. You don't have to do this."

"Think nothing of it." I gently rested my paws on his arm and pulsed out healing magic. Barney Hoffman was a bear of a man, and he could be intimidating to those who didn't know him. But he had a heart as big as a full moon and always put his team first. Barney kept the worst of the bureaucracy away from us and always praised us when we did good work. He even put up with the likes of Oleander, who could be a jerk on his good days.

"You should retire," Sammy said from his prone position on the desk. "If you're getting injured, it means you're not up to the job."

Barney blinked several times. "I'm just out of practice, that's all. And that oxen-wolf surprised me. One was concealed in a hole."

Sammy muttered something rude under his breath, which I was glad Barney didn't hear. What was wrong with my snuggle buddy?

"What's going on?" Zandra appeared in the corridor and hurried toward us.

"We're doing all the hard work while you're taking it easy." Oleander stashed the cage in a nearby room and shut the door. "Why weren't you around to snag those creatures? Here for the easy ride, I suppose."

"You don't get to say that." Zandra shoved his shoulder. "We've got the night shift and are tracking the invisible creature that's been leaving half-eaten animals everywhere."

Oleander leaned against the wall and crossed his arms over his chest. "Still! I was looking for that thing three nights ago."

"Then look harder, since it's still out there," Zandra said. "Barney, you okay?"

"Much better, thanks to Juno. You need to be careful tracking that beast tonight. Its kills have been getting more frequent and larger. It must grow stronger with every feed."

I finished healing Barney then hopped onto Zandra's shoulder and nuzzled her ear. "I'll watch out for my witch. But its behavior is puzzling. Those animal corpses are popping up all over the place. Most animals have a territory they hunt in and stay in their lane to avoid trouble with other predators."

"It's not just that," Zandra said. "They're digging those holes, too. Some of them are deep. If they're making holes to put the bodies in, why don't they finish the job? They eat, dig a hole, but then leave the remains for everyone to find. Weird."

I licked her cheek, happy to be with my witch. "Maybe it's a ritualistic thing."

"It's a crazy ritual," Oleander said.

"It could be territory marking," Glenda said, "a warning to others. This is my turf, so stay out, unless you want to end up like this."

"Why dig the holes, though?" Zandra said. "And territory marking usually involves scent."

"You read that in a book?" Oleander said, his top lip drawn back.

"At least my witch can read." Although she didn't often. I was mildly ashamed Zandra found most books boring. But no one was perfect. Well, I was almost perfect if you ignored the tiny lies I occasionally told.

Glenda shrugged. "Beats me what the holes are about. Have fun with tracking that one. Make sure your nets are charged."

"We'll learn what's going on soon enough." Barney stood and inspected his healed arm. "I should change my shirt, then I'll get back to the paperwork. It's what I'm best at doing."

Glenda thumped him on the shoulder. "You did great out there. Any of us would have been surprised by that critter, too."

"Not me," Oleander muttered.

Glenda and Zandra glared at him, and he dropped his gaze.

"You coming to the main Reverence event this weekend?" she asked Zandra.

"Doubtful. I'll be catching up on sleep following these night shifts."

"You must come. It's a highlight of living in Crimson Cove. Have you ever been?"

"First time. Adrienne's told me about it, though," Zandra said. "It sounds fun."

"They have the best food stalls. Everything you can imagine. And people's costumes are out of this world. They work on them for months. And I heard a rumor you got a witch costume." Glenda winked at me.

Zandra shook her head. "It was just an idea. It's dumb. I'll be too tired to enjoy myself."

"We'll be there," I said. "We must celebrate death and rebirth. And Mack's visiting, and I promised him some fun. He won't want to miss out on the excellent food. Neither will I."

"It always comes down to food with you." Zandra pressed her cheek against my fluffy side. "Maybe we'll put in an appearance."

"You should." Glenda's smile was sharp. "Bring Randal, too. The guy's barely smiled since your dinner date damp squibbed."

Zandra's cheeks flushed. "Like I said, I'll think about it." She turned and headed along the corridor, away from the others.

"You should invite Randal. Get him to see everything magic has to offer. All that tech mage voodoo he uses misses the more primal side of our magic," I said.

"Uh-huh."

"You don't think he'll enjoy it?"

Zandra walked into the locker room. "I'm not certain I'm going. Let's go critter tracking."

After a check of the map to see where the latest animal remains and holes had been found, we headed outside, hopped into the van, and headed to the beach.

I was settled in my comfy bed in the passenger seat, my steady gaze on Zandra.

She glanced at me. "Something you want to say?"

"You should try again with Randal. He's a good guy. You just had a minor setback. Don't let that put you off."

Zandra flicked her gaze away. "I don't want to talk about it."

"You should talk to him about it. Randal likes you. He could be good for you."

"I'm too busy for romance. I thought I'd give it a go with him, but look what happened."

"You had a small misstep."

"I got dragged off to investigate a murder, and Randal almost fried himself alive, hurrying to finish work so we could eat dinner together. That's more than a small misstep."

"So pick a time when neither of you is busy."

"Never going to happen. Not with the increase in weird animal behavior." Zandra tapped her fingers on the steering wheel. "I'm leaving it for now. Randal's neck deep in the upgrade, and it's being slowed because of the non-magical interference. I don't want to be a distraction. He'll resent me."

"He'd welcome the distraction. It can't be all work and no play."

"It's going to have to be." We drove in silence for a moment. "Anyway, what's up with Sammy? He was rude to Barney. Sammy isn't rude to anyone. Even the people he doesn't like."

I shuffled in my bed, unable to get comfortable. "He's having a bad day. We all have them."

"Maybe he's hungry. You always have bad days when you're hungry." Zandra chuckled and tossed me a fishy treat from the bag she kept in the driver's door well.

I gobbled it down, my thoughts on Sammy. It was true, we were busy with this job, family issues, and the non-magicals, but we must find time for what was important in our lives, or what was the point?

We parked at the beach and climbed out of the van. It was almost dark, and all visitors had vanished.

"The most recent holes were dug near the dunes." Zandra tugged her dark hair off her face as it blew in the breeze. "We start there and look around."

I checked the information she'd brought with her, and then we headed to the dunes. The flesh-eating creature we hunted operated by night, and their kill rate was increasing, as were the number of holes they dug in the last week.

Whoever it was, they had to be stopped before they went too far and injured a person. And with all the non-magicals around, we had to be extra cautious.

"Here they are." Zandra peered at the ground.

I lifted my booping snooter and inhaled. The salty sea air and the sharp breeze almost masked the scent of blood.

"You got something?"

"This way." I trotted along the sand dunes, my head lifted. It took less than a minute to find three fresh holes and two dead, partially chewed on salt weaver plovers.

What held my interest was the abandoned shovel beside one hole.

Zandra stared at it. "A person is doing this? I thought we had a rogue familiar out here."

"It's unlikely any creature would need a shovel. These holes have only just been made. We must have disturbed them mid-dig." I swiveled my head from side to side to see if anyone was escaping the scene, but the beach was silent.

There was a shriek overhead. Sharp talons dug through my fur, and I was lifted into the air.

# Chapter 3

## Owl be back

I scrabbled my paws against nothing, trying to get purchase as the owl flew higher, its sharp talons digging into my skin. I twisted and yelped, attempting to land a paw blow so I could shoot the evil beast with a spell, but the monster had me in a death grip, with no plans to let go.

"Juno!" Zandra raced below us as the owl gained height. She shot out a spell, and it skimmed the fluffy devil's head.

The cruel-hearted creature squawked and rose higher, out of her spell range.

"If you're thinking I'll make a yummy snack, change your mind. This body has been around the block a few times, so I'll be chewy. And I bite back."

The owl's continual shrieking turned into what sounded like laughter.

I stiffened in its grip. "You can understand me?"

The claws dug in tighter.

I calmed myself and stopped fighting the owl. I drew in a breath. This owl wasn't a regular owl. "You have magic!"

The sharp taloned felon didn't reply.

"I saw you with a group of non-magicals on the beach. Why are you with them if you have powers?"

The owl squawked.

"Don't play dumb owl with me. I feel it. You're hiding it well, but it's there. Why conceal your ability?"

Another of Zandra's spells zapped close to us, and the owl changed direction and headed out across the water.

I glanced down, grimacing at the icy waves. "Why grab me? Do you see me as a threat?"

The owl kept flapping, heading away from the shore.

"Do you have something to do with those holes on the beach? Are you the one leaving the half-eaten corpses around Crimson Cove?"

There was more flapping and more squawking.

"You're not fooling me. I demand answers. You don't come to this town and get away with such bad manners. You're up to something, and I intend to find out what it is."

The owl turned in a large circle over the sea, and its grip slackened.

"Oh, no you don't. Don't you dare—" Then I was howling, my paws raking through the air. That wretched creature had dropped me!

I didn't have time to cast a spell to soften the blow as I crashed into icy, salty water and went under, my eyes stinging and my belly smarting.

I spun under the waves, no idea which way was up. My fur grew heavy and threatened to drag me under, but I held my breath and kept fighting. My fury at that despicable owl would ensure I'd survive, so I could obliterate the feathered monster.

Once I stopped spinning, I allowed my natural buoyancy to take me in the right direction. My head popped above the waves, and I sucked in a breath.

A wave tumbled me, and I went under again. I hated the sea. It looked beautiful, but swim in it and get a mouthful of the salty muck, and it wasn't so much fun. Although sea fishing was always an enjoyable pursuit.

I took a moment to orientate myself. Reassuring lights shone on the shoreline, so I attempted a dignified paddle in that direction. I hated to call it a doggy paddle, but that's what I did. In this form, the breaststroke was beyond me.

"Juno! Where are you?" Zandra stood on the water's edge, peering into the darkness.

I swam toward her, murderous thoughts rolling around my head. When I got my paws on that owl, I'd make it sorry.

It had something to hide, and we must have been close to discovering its secret since it grabbed me and tossed me into the sea like a sullied oyster.

Zandra spotted me. She waded into the sea up to her waist and scooped me from the waves, clasping me to her chest as she returned to the beach. "I thought you were a goner when that owl grabbed you. That thing came out of nowhere."

"There's more to that owl than meets the eye." I plastered myself against Zandra to get warm.

"Did it try to eat you?" Zandra held me in one arm as she gathered wood, made a hole in the pebbles, and cast a fire spell to ignite the kindling. Then she piled on more wood to build the flames.

"I don't think it wanted me for dinner." I shivered as a sharp breeze fluffed my soaked fur. "It wanted us to stop looking at those holes."

Zandra took off her jacket, which was mainly dry, and briskly rubbed me. "Do owls normally dig holes like that? I've never seen behavior like that from a raptor. Although, I'm no bird expert."

"That was no ordinary owl." I got close to the flames, my steaming fur slowly drying. "That despicable creature had magic."

Zandra kept rubbing me. "Did it tell you what it's doing here?"

"It played dumb. But it's not the first time I've seen it. It was on the beach when I was running with Archie and Mack. The owl was hanging out with a group of non-magicals. It was circling their heads. Then it followed a stroppy teenager when he stomped off after an argument."

"You're sure it was the same owl?"

"Positive." I picked a lump of seaweed off my side and flicked it away.

"And it has power?"

"It understood what I said. And it wouldn't have been able to restrain me if it had no magic."

"Maybe it doesn't realize it has magic," Zandra said. "Sometimes, when familiars go rogue, it messes them up. Or it has memory loss if it's been mistreated. Maybe it became confused and attached itself to this family because it thinks it knows them."

"It knows what it's doing, the hateful thing." I hopped onto Zandra's lap to absorb her body heat.

She petted me. "I know you're not loving the owl right now, but people don't normally keep them as pets. But they make decent familiars. Something could have gone wrong with the owl's bond. It happens. We see it all the time in animal control."

I considered that, putting aside my loathing for the feathery abomination. "If the bond warped, it could have sent the creature insane. That's why it's digging those holes and leaving all those corpses."

"What about the shovel?" Zandra said. "Owls don't use shovels to dig."

"It can't be working alone. The creature has an assistant. Maybe it's using the non-magical family to help them."

"What's it looking for?" Zandra wrung the ends of her soggy hair to remove water. "Who has an owl familiar in Crimson Cove we could speak to about odd raptor behavior?"

"Doesn't Voss Black have a bird? I've seen a raven sitting outside the pizza parlor."

"Yes! We should visit tomorrow. See if he knows anything about a rogue owl familiar causing problems. Although, if there was anything like that going on, someone should have reported it to animal control."

"Not everyone does the right thing," I muttered. "Once we know where its lair is, we can destroy it."

"Juno! The owl could need help."

"That owl almost killed me. It didn't have to throw me into the sea."

She hugged me tight. "My heart almost stopped when it let you go. But I knew you could swim."

"And I knew you'd save me if I got in real trouble." I placed my damp front paws on her chest, and we touched foreheads.

"Want to call it a night?" Zandra said. "You're still soggy. And you don't smell too sweet."

"No, let's keep working. We can look around the beach for fresh holes and clues this owl could be involved."

Zandra pulled out a bag of thankfully dry fishy treats from her jacket pocket and fed me some. I gratefully accepted them. Being catnapped by an owl worked up an appetite.

I didn't know what the owl's game was, but one thing I was certain about. That owl would be sorry it ever met me.

***

Despite working the night shift, we were up early the next morning and heading to the new artisan pizza parlor in town. The crowds were already out in force, since there were daily activities in the lead up to the fun at the weekend at the Reverence Festival.

I sniffed my fur and wrinkled my booping snooter. I still smelled faintly of the sea, despite allowing Zandra to give me a head-to-tail bubble bath and then a thorough brush before bed.

"Hey! Be careful. You almost trod on my cat." Zandra shoved a guy as he stuffed a giant hotdog smothered in cheese and onions into his gaping mouth.

"You walk your cat?" He shook his head. "This place is so weird. I love it! Does it do tricks?"

Zandra glowered at him until he backed away and hurried off. She placed me on her shoulder. "You'll be safer up high. Fewer idiots will step on you."

I purred softly. I had no issue with being settled in one of my most favorite spots in the world.

There was a queue out the door of the pizza parlor, and it wasn't even close to lunchtime. I suppose pizza for breakfast was a legitimate meal. Zandra lived on cold pizza slices for her first meal of the day before moving in with Vorana.

We got several dark looks and rude mutters as we bypassed the queue and went to the counter. Voss Black dashed around, serving pizzas and taking orders. He was newish to Crimson Cove, but everyone loved his fancy pizzas with homegrown herbs.

He nodded at us. "Hey! Having fun at the festival?"

"We're working," Zandra said. "You look like you could do with a hand."

"Tell me about it. I had no clue we'd get so many visitors. I got a sign in the window for an assistant, but no luck so far. I don't suppose..." He gestured his head at the pizzas.

Zandra smirked. "If you knew how bad my cooking skills were, you'd never invite me behind the counter."

"Just a thought. Skull Dugger is coming through soon, and everyone's out to see him. And the crowds are hungry. I also heard a rumor Night Mare is on the prowl." He winked at us, his green eyes alive with laughter. "He'll need feeding, too."

"I won't keep you. I need to talk birds." Zandra glanced at the waiting crowd. "You have experience with ravens, right?"

Voss gave a knowing nod. We all knew to keep the language non-magical, so as not to confuse those without it. "Sure. I have Sid."

"Has Sid seen any owls around?" Zandra said. "There's a lone bird causing trouble. It grabbed Juno off the beach last night."

"Huh! No kidding." Voss slid several pizzas into the stone oven at the back then returned to the counter. "You okay?" He reached over and tickled me under my chin.

I could only nod, since a talking cat did all kinds of strange things to non-magical brains.

"I've seen nothing. I'll check with my contacts and let you know if anything useful comes up." Voss washed his hands then got back to his pizzas. "What's the owl done that's got it on your radar, other than grabbing Juno?"

"We're figuring that out," Zandra said.

"Weird it was at the beach. Owls don't hang out in that environment. Maybe it's sick." Voss rolled out dough and spread his secret blend of tomato sauce and herbs across it.

Pizza was never my first go-to option for fast food, but what was cooking in the stone oven smelled delicious.

"We wondered if it was unwell, or... unattached?" Zandra said.

"Could be. When the crowds die down, I'll check in with Sid. He doesn't miss much when he's on the wing."

"Thanks. We'd appreciate that."

There was a gasp from the crowd, and I looked behind me. Night Mare crashed through the door, causing everyone to surge against the counter. He was a magnificent, giant horse with sharp teeth, horns where his ears should be, and spikes glittering through his mane of jet black hair.

He reared up and stamped his hooves on the ground, causing the crowd to rear back again and squeak. Phones or cameras were raised as laughter flickered, and they took pictures of what they believed was someone wearing an incredible costume.

Night Mare was all too real. He was an ancient, primitive magical character, who had two desires in life: food and fornication. Not terrible choices.

"Feed me," he growled, his words a low rumble in his deep chest.

Voss bowed, and so did Zandra and me. We knew to respect the old ways. You didn't mess with a creature like Night Mare and get away with it.

"I've been waiting for you, sir." Voss pulled out six huge pizza boxes. He opened one and presented an enormous cheese and meat spectacular. "Does this meet your approval?"

Night Mare hovered over the box. His gleaming nose descended on the pizza, and he inhaled it. "Acceptable. More."

"Whoa! How did he do that?" a non-magical whispered. "One second, the pizza was there, and the next, it was gone. Does he have a compartment for the food?"

"The special effects are out of this world at this event," another non-magical said. "I'd love to touch him."

"You shouldn't," Zandra cautioned. "You don't want to break the illusion."

If any non-magical touched Night Mare without his permission, they'd lose fingers. That was the best-case scenario. Night Mare snapped bones and swallowed skulls when riled. He even flattened villages when his mood was sour enough.

Sensibly, the non-magicals didn't touch him. They may not comprehend magic, but the primal parts of their brains alerted them to danger and stopped them from doing anything too foolish.

Night Mare hoovered up three more pizzas. He grabbed the rest, and they vanished from sight. Then he reared up, slamming his hooves onto the floor again. There was a flash of light and a blast of noxious smoke, and he was gone.

The non-magicals stared at the spot he'd been with open mouths.

"Night Mare needs to lay off the theatricals," I whispered to Zandra. "There's only so much we can get away with before this lot realizes it can't be special effects."

Zandra nodded, looking impressed by Night Mare's performance.

"Where did he go? Find him!" The crowd shoved out of the pizza parlor, heading outside.

"There he is!"

"Let's follow him."

Night Mare was on the other side of the street, tossing his spiky mane and rearing up, kicking out with gleaming hooves to ensure no non-magicals got too close.

The crowd swelled as everyone converged toward him, bedazzled by his spectacular form and determined to get a picture. Among the non-magicals were Crimson Cove residents. They were in costume or their natural magical form, and sparkle and magic flitted through the air. But the locals were being restrained to ensure no non-magicals got harmed by an errant blast of power.

"I love seeing the old guard in action." Voss leaned against the counter, a smile on his long face. "It's good to be reminded of our origins. You two want pizza while it's quiet? I'm sure the crowds will be back, so I don't have long."

"Sure. What's wrong with that guy?" Zandra approached the door.

I stopped studying the pizza menu and looked out the window. My stomach flip-flopped, and all thoughts of a seafood medley pizza for breakfast vanished.

As the crowd had chased after Night Mare, they'd left a body on the ground.

# Chapter 4

## Body dump

"Hold the pizza order." I leaped off Zandra's shoulder and bounded to the slumped figure. As I grew near, I recognized him. It was the teenager from the beach.

"Hey! Are you okay?" Zandra hurried after me.

I sniffed around him and recoiled. "He's very much not okay. I smell blood."

"I see blood!" Zandra reached down and checked for a pulse. Her gaze flickered to a red stain on the front of his white T-shirt. "He's been stabbed."

No one in the receding crowd noticed what was going on, as Night Mare enthralled them. He led them along the street in a clatter of hooves and guttural braying, away from the body.

"This only just happened," I said. "Someone in the crowd must have attacked him and used the chaos as cover to strike a killing blow."

"Should we bring him back? Try to heal him?" Zandra hovered a hand over the chest wound. "There's still time if we hurry."

"Wait! You can't use magic on him. He has no power."

Zandra hesitated then pressed a hand on his arm. "There's nothing there. He must be a visitor from out of town."

"I've only ever heard bad things happen when you use magic to reanimate a non-magical," I said. "It's too risky. He'd come back broken. Unstable. And he'll attach to you."

She tugged on the ends of her hair. "What about a healing spell?"

I rested a paw on Zandra's hand, her anxiety seeping into me like poison. "He's gone. If it was another magic user, I'd work with you to bring him back, but non-magicals are too vulnerable. The power of such a spell would backfire, and you'd be arrested for breaking magical law."

Frustration crossed her face, then she nodded. "You're right. But who did this?"

"I don't know, but I've seen him before. On the beach. He was with a group of non-magicals. Possibly his family." I looked around and spotted an old lady in a wheelchair sitting by a bench. She gazed at the crowd, a bundle of knitting on her lap and a large red purse wedged beside her. "He was with her."

A screech overhead made me tense. The hateful owl was back. It swooped over us, its screeching higher pitched and more agitated.

Zandra crouched, and magic flickered on her fingers.

The bird swooped lower, but it wasn't interested in me or Zandra. Its gaze was fixed on the body.

"It's distressed," I said. "Somehow, that bird is connected to the victim."

"Stay with the body. I'll talk to the old lady, see if I can find out who he is. Or was." Zandra jogged to the old woman and kneeled beside her.

The old lady looked at her then smiled, waved, and kept staring at the crowd.

I ducked, glaring at the owl as it continued to screech. Even though I'd never forgive the bird for dropping me into the sea, I felt sorry for it. It had lost a companion and was grieving.

I waved a paw in the air. "Stop shouting! Did you see what happened to your friend?"

The bird swooped around us one more time then shot off, leaving a splintered cry drifting on the breeze. It sounded as if its heart had been shattered.

Zandra ran back to me. "I couldn't get the old woman to understand what's happened. She wouldn't even tell me her name. She mainly growled and kept mumbling about Night Mare and someone called Adam."

"Maybe this is Adam." I pointed at the body.

"Perhaps. She just laughed when I said he'd been hurt and I needed to find his family. You said he was with more people the night you saw him?"

"Yes. I think the wretched owl has gone to get them."

Zandra glanced skyward. "It's weird the owl is hanging out with non-magicals. This guy has no hint of magic on him. It must be really sick to get so confused."

I looked at the body, and unease shivered through me. A non-magical murder in Crimson Cove was a giant problem. We weren't equipped to deal with their deaths. The regular police couldn't get interested in our town, not with the wards so ineffective at deflecting non-magicals. Our magic was at risk of being exposed to the world if word got out about this.

"Hey! What's going on? Is that guy okay?" Voss appeared in his store door.

"He's been attacked," Zandra said.

Voss hurried over, wiping his hands on a white cloth. His eyes widened, and he stopped walking. "Is that blood?"

"We think he's been stabbed," I said.

"Is he..."

"He's dead and a non-magical," Zandra said.

Voss licked his lips. "Not good. What you gonna do?"

"We need to get Angel Force involved."

"We could consider a concealment." I studied the body. He wasn't a large teenager. Kind of scrawny. He'd be easy to hide.

"Juno! This was someone's son. Someone's grandson if he's with the old lady. He'd be missed. There's no way we cover this up. His family will want to know what happened."

"I'm no fan of concealing a crime, but Juno has a point," Voss said. "A non-magical murder in town will draw the wrong attention. And things are already shaky, with the wards enticing in non-magicals."

I glanced at the crowd, grateful Night Mare was being so entertaining. It would be simple to hide the body and pretend this never happened, but we had to face this uncomfortable situation. "Voss, could you send Sid to summon the angels?"

He winced then nodded. "You're right. We report it." He turned and dashed back to the pizza parlor.

Zandra looked at the old lady in the wheelchair again. "She shouldn't be on her own. Someone should be taking care of her."

"Maybe this guy was. He got carried away in the crowd, though. Night Mare is enchanting." I circled the body, taking in the scene to see if I'd missed anything. I inspected the hole in the victim's T-shirt. It was small, suggesting a thin blade had been used, but it must have been long and sharp, since there was so much blood.

I slowed and inhaled deeply. My toe beans tingled. Under the whiff of fresh blood, I smelled concealed magic. Deeply familiar magic.

A screech overhead had me crouching. The evil owl was back. And not far behind it was some of the group who'd been on the beach with the victim.

A middle-aged brunette woman in straight-legged denim jeans and a lightweight red sweater arrived first. She dropped to her knees and grabbed the young man's hand. "What happened? Adam? Wake up! Adam!"

"We're not sure." Zandra glanced at me and shifted from foot to foot. "We were in the pizza parlor when we saw him on the ground. It looks like he's been stabbed."

The woman stared up at Zandra for a second, no comprehension in her eyes. "Impossible."

A tall, dark-haired man arrived next, similar in age to the woman. "Julie, what's happening?"

"It's Adam. They're saying he's been stabbed." Her hand hovered over the chest wound.

The guy lifted Julie off her knees, his expression tight as he stared at the body. "Come away. You shouldn't see that."

"Who did this?" Her gaze lifted to Zandra. "You saw it happen, but you didn't stop it?"

Zandra raised a hand. "We didn't see what happened, just after he'd fallen."

"We? Who were you with?"

Zandra's cheeks flushed. "I meant me. I mean, I'm with my cat. This is Juno."

Julie barely spared me a glance. "You must have seen more than that. Why aren't you helping? Where's the ambulance?"

I bit my tongue. We always helped if we saw someone in trouble, but we'd been too late to stop this murder. And if the young man hadn't concealed his magic, we'd have done more to bring him back.

I wrinkled my booping snooter. Except, it wasn't his magic I'd sensed. I wanted to investigate, but with the family looming over us, a cat sniffing around the body wouldn't go down well.

"I just wanted to make sure he was okay." Zandra fidgeted with her hair.

"Of course he's not okay. Look at him!"

"Julie, come away. This isn't good for you." The man put an arm around her shoulders. "Sorry. This is a shock. Adam was supposed to be sitting with his gran. He shouldn't have taken part in the festival. We told him to behave."

"Is that the lady in the wheelchair?" Zandra said. "I've been to speak to her. She... err... well, she growled at me."

"That's my mother, Edith," Julie said. "Adam was supposed to stay with her. Why does he always disobey me?"

"I couldn't get her to understand what was going on," Zandra said.

Julie sighed. "You wouldn't. Where's Eric? Eric!" She looked around, seeming to expect the mysterious Eric to appear in a flash of magic.

"I sent him a message as soon as I heard something had happened to Adam, but you know what he's like," Simon murmured.

"I'm coming. Over here!" Eric appeared, weaving along the street. I also recognized him from the beach. He'd been throwing stones and drinking from a bottle.

"Hurry! Something's happened to Adam."

Eric stumbled over, his eyes bloodshot and his chin unshaven, although his skin had an odd glittery sheen to it. He was younger than Julie by a good twenty years. Maybe a son? "What's going on?"

"Adam's dead," Julie said.

Eric's mouth fell open, and he stared at the body. "Good one. This is a joke. He's always doing things like this." He kicked Adam's toe. "Get up! He's wearing a fake blood pack. Don't let him fool you."

"It's not a joke," Zandra said. "I've checked, and there's no pulse. I've sent someone to bring the... Police."

Eric rapidly blinked and ran a hand down his face. "You sure? He's the world's biggest joker. He once held his breath underwater for two minutes. I was convinced he was drowning. I jumped in to save him, and I can't swim."

"I'm sure. It's best you don't touch him." Zandra pressed Eric back as he leaned over Adam. "There could be evidence."

"Where's the ambulance? Did you call one?" Julie said.

"Help is on its way. But there's nothing you can do for him. I'm really sorry."

Although Julie appeared shocked, there were no tears. That was interesting. I hopped onto Zandra's shoulder and leaned against her ear. "What do you reckon?"

"I reckon we should get out of here before this gets any more awkward," she muttered out of the side of her mouth.

The sensible thing was to make a quick escape. We didn't want to get tangled in a non-magical murder. But the scent I'd identified compelled me to stay. I jumped down and sniffed around Adam. I had to know where it was coming from.

"Get away from him. Don't touch him." The dark-haired guy swung a kick at me.

I hissed and backed away. I took another sniff, and an intense tingle of familiarity hit me. I knew that magic. There was no way I could mistake it for anything else.

It was mine.

How had a non-magical gotten his hands on my ancient power? Was it the reason he'd been stabbed? Someone discovered Adam was messing with a power he couldn't control and stopped him before he did something dangerous.

I kept an eye on the kicker while I inspected the body. Adam couldn't contain the magic, so it had to be in an object he carried.

"Get that thing away from my nephew!" The man aimed another kick at me.

Zandra lifted me into her arms. "You kick at her again, and you'll lose that leg!"

The man gaped at her.

Zandra cleared her throat, holding me against her chest. "I mean, my cat's just curious. She means no harm. You don't have to kick her."

"It's okay, Simon. Check on Edith. She's talking to herself again," Julie said.

Simon patted her arm. "Of course. Eric, check on your gran. And bring her over here."

"Bad idea," Zandra said. "You don't want her getting upset when she sees Adam."

"The old girl lost touch with reality years ago," Simon said. "This'll mean nothing to her."

Zandra looked doubtful but didn't protest as Eric stumbled toward the old lady.

All the while we'd been talking, the owl continued to screech and circle overhead.

"And you can shut up!" Simon grabbed a stone and hurled it at the owl.

"Don't! That was Adam's pet. It must sense something is wrong." Julie glared at Zandra. "Where's this help you promised?"

"They're coming!"

A vibration traveled through Zandra and tickled my paws. The angels wouldn't fly here for fear of drawing unwanted attention, so they must be on foot. A blur of white in the distance confirmed Finn, Bertoli, and Cythera were on their way.

My tail twitched, and I snuggled against Zandra. If Cythera was leading this case, they meant business.

"Look! There they are," Zandra said, "our police."

"Your police dress in white?" Simon said. "Hardly practical."

"We don't have much crime in Crimson Cove. It's a peaceful place."

Julie looked at Adam and snorted. "You call this peaceful?"

Simon grabbed another stone and flung it at the screeching owl.

I leaped out of Zandra's arms and bit Simon's hand, making him howl. The owl was an irritant, but there was no need for that.

"Juno!" Although Zandra attempted a scolding tone, her eyes sparked with anger. She hated animal abuse as much as me.

I gave Simon's hand a good scratching before jumping off and leaping out of his reach. That would teach him to throw stones at defenseless creatures and try to kick me.

"Did you see that? It bit me for no reason." He held out his bloody hand. "It could be rabid!"

"Err... yeah. Sorry. Juno can be temperamental. I'll leave you to it." Zandra rapidly backed away then glanced at me and nodded.

"You can't leave! That thing attacked me. I could be infected."

"With terrible manners and no respect for animals," I muttered, unable to help myself.

"Sorry?" Zandra couldn't have sounded less sorry.

"You can't leave. You saw what happened to Adam. The police will need to speak to you." Julie stepped toward Zandra.

"They know me. We sometimes work together. Just give them my name, Zandra Crypt." She kept backing away.

Julie's eyebrows flashed up. "Crypt? I know that name."

"It's common around here. And I'm happy to help, but I've already told you everything. I'll make a statement if needed."

I raised a paw and gestured at the screeching owl to let Zandra know I had a mission in mind before we regrouped.

She nodded again then turned and hurried off before Julie could restrain her or the angels question her.

I dodged away too and waved at the owl. At first, the stupid creature didn't notice me as it circled and screeched, but after several increasingly frantic paw waves and a loud hiss, its gaze turned to me.

I inclined my head toward an alleyway then dashed away from the complaining Simon and his bitten hand. I only had to wait a moment behind the pizza parlor before the owl swooped overhead and settled on a metal pole jutting out of the wall.

My gaze settled on the tense looking creature. "Okay, owl. We need to talk."

# Chapter 5

## A feathered ally?

The owl fluffed its feathers, staring at me with huge, unblinking eyes.

I stared back.

The competition to see who'd blink first went on until my eyes watered.

"We have no time for games. You know something about this murder," I said.

The owl said nothing, although its beak clacked from side to side.

"What are you doing hanging around a group of non-magicals?"

It squawked, and more feather fluttering ensued.

"You can't squawk your way out of this. You understand me, and you have magic."

The owl shrieked again.

"Less squawking and more talking. That young man is dead. Did you see what happened to him?"

The owl finally blinked and hunched low on its perch. It fussed under one wing before sighing. "I should have seen, but I got distracted."

"Okay. Now we're getting somewhere. Greetings. I'm Juno. Familiar to the wonderful witch, Tempest Crypt. And you are?"

"Lucian Proudfeather."

"How are you connected to that family?" I paced while Lucian hunched on his temporary perch.

"That's not important."

"Are you the reason Adam's dead?"

His shriek almost ruptured my eardrums. "No! I'd never hurt him. That's not why I'm here."

"Then why are you following them? And why should you have been looking out for Adam?"

There was more feather fluttering. "I already said. Not important."

It was, but this owl was reluctant to open up. "That young man has magic on him. What do you know about that?"

Lucian narrowed his eyes. "Why do you want to know about his magic?"

"I know what he carried should have killed him the second he touched it. Is that why he was targeted?"

"It's not that. It's got nothing to do with that. You don't understand. And you don't need to. It's not your business."

"A stabbing that takes place in the town I live in, and a victim who is covered in magic familiar to me, makes it my business."

Lucian stepped closer. "You're familiar with the magic?"

"More than you."

I couldn't deny it any longer. A non-magical had gotten his hands on a piece of my magic. How?

There were few who could hold such power and not be driven mad.

Lucian soft-squawked. "You're nothing special. A basic witch's familiar."

I slashed out a murder mitten. "You're a foolish bird brain if that's what you believe. You must have heard of the Crypt witches."

"So what if I have? I'll figure out what happened to Adam, and I don't need your interference to do so."

"But you've got it. And you've got Angel Force involved, too. Soon, non-magical law enforcement will be here. Think you can keep your secrets, then?"

Lucian snorted. "They don't need to be involved."

"Why not? Is there something special about Adam? There must be if you're hanging around him. I need answers."

"What you need is to stay out of this. Unless you saw what happened, you're of no use to me."

I drew in a breath, wanting to yell, but it would do no good. This owl was angry, but not far beneath that anger lurked fear and sadness. Lucian had cared for Adam, and now he was gone.

"Don't blab to your witch that you know about my power," Lucian said. "The more people who know about me, the harder it'll be to figure out what happened."

"You're keeping a low profile so you can investigate?"

"I always keep a low profile. It works best for the family."

"You still haven't told me why you watch over them. Do they have magical ancestry? Were you left to them by a magic user and you feel obligated to carry out their last wishes?"

"Juno! I need a hand out here." Zandra sounded close to the alley.

I turned to call out and let her know I was dealing with a difficult owl. Lucian launched off his perch and flapped away. I glared at the retreating owl. I wasn't done with him, but my witch needed me, so I'd tackle the feathery hoodlum another time.

I trotted along the alleyway and met Zandra at the entrance.

"There you are. I've been watching from a distance, and the angels are in full-on flap mode. Cythera has brought a file with her and is checking protocols for how to deal with a non-magical murder. It's going badly. She yelled at Bertoli and even scared the family."

"At least the angels have protocols to figure out what to do when a non-magical dies here." I walked beside her back to the crime scene. "I just spoke to the owl, Lucian Proudfeather. He's being unhelpful."

"Did he say sorry for dunking you?"

I wrinkled my booping snooter. "It wasn't mentioned."

Zandra appeared to hide a smile. "I'm sure he is."

"Let's stay back from the scene. We don't want the family coming after you again," I said.

Zandra nodded, and we stopped in a doorway to watch the action from a safe distance.

Adam's body had been covered, and his family moved away. Several angels were with them. Finn was speaking to Julie, but when he saw us, he nodded and headed over to join us.

His expression was grimly determined as he glanced at the family. "They're saying you found the body," he asked Zandra.

"Juno found him first," she said.

"But, of course, saying a magnificent magical talking cat discovered their deceased son wouldn't have gone down well," I said. "We'll stick with the line it was Zandra."

Finn had his notepad in his hand and jotted down a couple of lines. "Good call. Did either of you see it happen?"

"Adam was in a crowd of people who were chasing Night Mare after he invaded the pizza parlor. I only saw Adam when the crowd moved on," Zandra said.

"He was attacked during the crush. Everyone was excited to follow the freaky horse. That's all they were focused on. It was the perfect opportunity for whoever did this to strike without being seen," I said.

"There was plenty of pushing and shoving so people could get close to Night Mare." Zandra jerked her chin up. "You could always ask him if he saw anything."

Finn tugged at his collar. "You want me to bring in the demonic night creature of oppression and ask him if he saw anyone get stabbed?"

"Maybe he did it. Old Horse Face enjoys splashing the blood around," I said. "Although I'd expect there to be hoof prints on the body if he was involved."

Zandra snorted out a laugh. "And you know that how? You two best buddies?"

"Oh, you know. I read. You should try it sometime." I'd met the various incarnations of Night Mare over the decades. His form shifted, but his blood lust never slackened. "Although I've never heard of him stabbing anyone."

"I imagine he's more a stomp and bite kind of demon." Finn flipped through his notepad. "I'll leave that decision to Cythera. Maybe she'll want to handle him."

"Please, if they meet, let me watch." I leaned back and pressed my front paws together.

"Juno! Be nice." Zandra shook her head at me.

"I'm purrfection. But Night Mare and Cythera are opposites. Their clash would be spectacular."

She arched an eyebrow. "Moving on. What about the crowd? Anyone see anything?"

"We're asking questions to see if we can get anything useful, but I think you're right," Finn said. "In the crush, it would have been easy to stab Adam and conceal the blade without anyone noticing."

"Any idea what weapon was used?"

"We'll have more details after the autopsy, but it looks like it was a thin blade. The wound could have been inflicted fast, so Adam wouldn't have realized he'd been stabbed for several seconds. He may have felt a sharp pain, but thought it was a muscle spasm. He may even have walked a short way before realizing he'd been attacked. Poor guy bled out fast, though, so the knife nicked something important."

"How's the family doing?" Zandra said.

"It's hard to tell. The mother, Julie Smith, seems shocked but stoic. She's more panicked than upset and keeps asking for discretion. The older guy, Simon, is Adam's uncle, and the younger one is his older brother, Eric, who's been drinking. Or taking something. He's got dilated pupils and keeps saying he thinks it's all a joke."

"There's also an owl involved," I said. "He's called Lucian Proudfeather, and he's being cagey about why he's hanging around the non-magicals. Somehow, he's linked to them. You need to find him and talk to him."

Finn tilted his head. "An owl with powers? He can't be their familiar. What's going on?"

"Lucian's not talking. All he'd tell me was he was supposed to be guarding Adam when he got stabbed. Lucian's planning on figuring out who did it, but he doesn't want help."

Finn tipped back on his heels, his wings fluttering. "This complicates things. Cythera is already in super stressed mode while she figures out how to make this work. Throw in an owl with magic, and she'll blow a gasket."

No one spoke as the family and the other angels fluttered around, trying to look like they knew what they were doing. Several times, the old lady in the wheelchair reached up as if to grab an angel's wing. Could she see them?

"Maybe there's more to this murder," I said. "Mind if I take another look at Adam once the family has left?"

"Sorry, Juno. Not for a while. And I'm not sure when you'll get a chance," Finn said. "Cythera insists we do this by the book. That literal book in her hands. It's the Complete Handbook to Managing a Non-Magical Murder. It has fifty chapters!"

"This is important. I sensed something odd about Adam." I glanced up at Zandra. "He's carrying magic, and I wondered if that was the reason he was targeted."

"You think a resident killed him because he carried something he shouldn't?" Zandra said. "We may not love non-magicals, but we don't harm them. We take an oath to protect them if we encounter them or keep out of their way and put our magic on slow simmer so they don't get hurt."

"Maybe Adam didn't realize he carried something with power. I should take a look again to ensure I didn't make a mistake." I tried to dodge around Finn, but he held up a hand.

"I'll see if I can get you in for another look, but no promises. And not here," Finn said. "With non-magical law enforcement getting involved, it's essential personnel only. No magical cats allowed."

"I'm essential! I was the first on the scene. The first to identify Adam had magic on him."

"Are you sure? I sensed nothing magical about him," Zandra said. "What did you feel?"

I focused on the covered body. "It's hard to say."

She cocked her head, sensing I concealed something.

"Maybe it's nothing, but I must be sure. Perhaps Adam tinkered with dark magic without realizing how deadly it could be," I said. "You know what these young men are like. They're fearless and believe they're immortal."

"The autopsy will show us if there's anything unusual about him," Finn said. "Wait until we get the report. Don't worry, Juno. I know you don't think much of the angels, but we've got this figured out."

Zandra's expression was full of questions as she watched me, but she didn't press me for more information.

I still hadn't figured out how to tell her about my past. But every time I discovered one of my missing magical pieces, it drew me closer to revealing all.

I loved our relationship and didn't want things to change. What would happen when Zandra knew the truth about me?

We stayed out of the way as Finn went back to work.

"No tears," Zandra said. "None of them are upset Adam is dead. Bit weird."

"This whole situation is weird."

"That magic you sensed, you mean?"

I nodded. "And the owl familiar who's not a familiar. Maybe Lucian was after the magic Adam stumbled upon. He was tracking the family because he wanted a chance to take it."

"You think the owl did this? What did he do, sweep into the crowd and stab Adam with a talon?"

"I wouldn't put anything past that sneaky owl. And those talons are sharp." I tensed as Cythera strode over.

Her nose wrinkled, as if she smelled something unpleasant. "We need this place shut down."

"Greetings, Cythera. You mean the murder scene?" I said.

Her gaze flickered to me, and her forehead wrinkled. "No! The town. We can't have any more non-magicals arrive until this is resolved. Make it happen."

Zandra looked down at me and shrugged. "You want us to do that? How?"

"Figure it out. Take my angels and use whatever resources you need but don't let a single non-magical into Crimson Cove. Any that arrive, you make leave."

Zandra gulped as Cythera turned on her heel and stalked away.

I leaped onto Zandra's shoulder and nuzzled her ear. "Cythera must be desperate if she's asking for our help."

"Yeah, I guess. What should we do?"

"Get to work."

# Chapter 6

## If your name's not down

"No one is allowed in." Zandra stood with her hands on her hips, staring down a bunch of non-magicals who'd been failing to push through our blockade for twenty minutes. How they hadn't gotten their heads blown off was a mystery I'd never solve.

"You make it sound like there's a plague. We just want to look around. We've been hearing great things about this place," a non-magical with a wispy ginger beard said. "Let us in. You're not police. You can't stop us."

"It's not a plague. It's a gas leak. You'll get sick if you come in," Zandra said. "Turn around and walk away. Find another town to spend the day in."

"We want to come here," a skinny girl with a long blonde ponytail whined. "All our friends said it's amazing. They won't stop talking about Crimson Cove this and Crimson Cove that. It's not fair."

I stepped forward, wanting to ask where they'd gotten the recommendation. No non-magical should know about this place. But I couldn't risk talking. It would confuse them.

We'd been quick to act after Cythera gave the order to stop any non-magicals entering Crimson Cove. Angel guards were set on all main roads into town, and I guarded the road that ran past Finn's animal sanctuary along with Zandra, two angels, Archie, Sage, Vorana, and Remus, who'd shown up with two vampires who didn't object to daylight.

We'd been busy ever since we set up the blockade. The non-magicals were persistent. They wanted into Crimson Cove, and nothing we could say would turn them away.

"Juno! There's a rat!" Archie whispered in my ear. He bounded toward a group of non-magicals making their way along the road, causing them to scream and scatter.

The rat, which was actually a Chihuahua, squeaked a bark and raced away. Archie grabbed the poor thing within twenty strides, flipped it in the air, and opened his mouth.

I leaped and knocked the creature away from his giant jaws, landing on his booping snooter and bouncing off.

The Chihuahua had the audacity to growl at Archie then high-tailed it back to its owner, who stood with her mouth open, clutching her precious rat-dog to her chest.

"No eating the non-magicals' creatures," I hiss-whispered. "They'll give you indigestion."

"Where'd it go?" Archie's head whipped around as he looked for the Chihuahua, who'd wisely hidden under its owner's jacket. "Huh! How did the rat get over there? And did you just drop-kick me in the head?"

"It was more a swinging front kick. And that rat is a small dog. It needed saving."

"That's a dog? Are you sure?" Archie lifted his booping snooter and inhaled. "It smells ratty. And it might have broken wind. Or was that you?"

"No! And hush! You're drawing attention to us. Remember, some of these non-magicals have been hearing us when we talk. Keep the conversation to a minimum and look as animal-like as you can. No glowing eyes or fire. Got it?"

Remus sauntered over. He wore a fetching scarlet suit. The matching top hat added a flare of exuberance to his attire. "Did you kick my hound?" A hint of fang appeared as he rested one hand on Archie's huge head.

I lifted my chin. "He was about to eat a Chihuahua."

Remus sniffed. "Archie must be hungry. Like my vampires. How much longer do we need to be here? Border patrol is demeaning."

"Until we have no more non-magicals barging their way in."

"Remus! I almost ate a dog-rat," Archie said. "Juno said it wasn't, though. It was a dog-dog. I'm not sure. What do you think? It's over there. Can I eat it?"

Remus petted Archie. "Sadly, my magnificent ball of furry perfection, Juno is correct. That's a tiny version of what you are. It wouldn't have tasted pleasant. You missed nothing."

Archie still didn't seem convinced but was mollified when Remus fed him a handful of treats from his scarlet purse.

I studied Remus's vampires. They looked hungry, and their fangs kept appearing. They studied the non-magicals as if deciding on what meal deal to get from a fast-food restaurant. "Your vampires should leave if they can't control themselves. We don't want a bloodbath on top of the murder."

"They have restraint. But all this tasty flesh is even trying my patience. And they smell delicious." Remus smacked his lips together. "Can I take a few home for my hive? They won't feel a thing after the first bite."

"I want to stay on border patrol." Archie raised a paw. "This is fun. And I'm learning about new types of dog. You always tell me to learn something new every day. And did you see the way those non-magicals scattered when I ran? I could do that some more. I could chase them away."

"Then they'll call in their police about a wild animal on the loose," I said. "It's a nice idea, Archie, but we must handle this situation delicately. With more and more non-magicals trying to get in every day, it feels like we're losing control of our town."

"I'd never let that happen," Remus said. "If the non-magicals become too burdensome, I'll instruct my vampires to have a feeding frenzy. That'll get rid of them."

Archie rumbled out a bark. "Can I help? It's okay for me to eat non-magicals, right?"

"No! No eating creatures that can't defend themselves," I said. "Remember the rules."

Archie hunched lower to the ground. "You eat mice."

"Have you ever tackled a mouse? They don't flop down and let you bite them. That's what a non-magical would do. There'd be no fun in that."

Remus shrugged. "You've gotten sensible, Juno. You used to be so much fun."

"I'm protecting my town and my witch from unwanted attention." I glanced at Zandra, who was moving on more non-magicals with the help of an angel. "That'll always be my priority."

"It's our priority, too." Archie stood and puffed out his broad chest. "We won't eat anyone. We'll just think about it lots."

Remus petted Archie's head. "Any more news from the angels? I expected the non-magical police to have arrived by now. I enjoy admiring their uniforms."

"Let's ask Finn." My gaze was on the sky. Finn approached the non-magicals from behind, so they wouldn't see him on the wing, and landed behind a tree. A few seconds later, he strode toward us.

"Can we get in yet?" a non-magical yelled. "We've been waiting for over an hour."

Finn raised his hands, an easy smile on his angelic face. "Bad news, everyone. It'll take at least forty-eight hours to make the town safe again. I suggest you go home. Come back in a few days when the leak is fixed. You don't want to walk around the streets. The place smells like rotten eggs, and it's making some people sick."

"What kind of gas are we talking about? I'm a heating engineer. I can take a look if you like." The guy with the wispy beard was going nowhere fast.

"That information is above my pay grade. We've got the experts working on it."

The crowd continued to grumble, although several broke off and wandered to their cars.

"Any progress with Adam?" I said to Finn as Zandra walked over to join us.

Finn scratched his fingers through his sandy blond hair. "Yeah, but it's odd progress. We moved him to the mortuary and did a basic visual scan of the body to locate anything unusual."

"What did you find?" My whiskers twitched.

"The stab wound is strange," Finn said. "It's a small hole, but the wound is rotting. That shouldn't happen for days. Or not at all if he's properly stored."

"Which makes the injury sound unnatural," Zandra said.

"Did I hear correctly a knife was used?" Remus said. "That's also unnatural. Why stab someone when you can use a spell and go nowhere near your prey?"

Finn shrugged. "I can't answer that. I'm just telling you what we've found so far. There's no sign of magic on Adam."

"You're sure?" I said. "Nothing else odd has shown up?"

Finn shook his head. "The cause of death has been recorded as a stabbing."

"The wound decay suggests magic was used," I said. "Could a spell have been used to infect him with something to ensure he didn't survive?"

"It's possible. We're running more tests, but so far, nothing weird has shown up on the magic front."

Finn checked the non-magicals were still behaving. "I should warn you, though, Cythera sent the details to the higher angels to see what we should do. Even with the handbook, we're not equipped to handle a non-magical murder. No one in the team has ever dealt with the police from the other side."

"Have you made contact with them?" Remus said.

"We're still waiting on orders from up high before doing that. Cythera knows they need to be involved, but she's looking for a get-out."

"She's panicking," I said. "It's only natural. The less attention that lands on Crimson Cove at the moment, the better. Until our wards are repelling non-magicals again, we're vulnerable. So are they."

"What shall we do while you wait for a response from the higher angels?" Zandra said.

"Keep patrolling, and keep people out," Finn said. "There's nothing else we can do for now until the test results are back."

"What about the Smith family?" I said. "They're being questioned?"

"We took brief statements, but none of them were at the scene when Adam was stabbed."

"The lady in the wheelchair was watching Night Mare."

"I spoke to Edith," Zandra said. "She was away with the fairies. If she saw what happened, she has no memory of it."

Finn nodded. "Julie Smith, that's the mother of the victim, said Edith has dementia. Her eyesight is bad, too, and she refuses to wear glasses."

"I'm glad Edith saw nothing," Zandra said. "It's better than being woken in the night after a nightmare about seeing your grandson stabbed."

Finn shuddered. "We'll talk to them again soon, but I don't see how any of them are involved. Cythera believes it was a robbery gone wrong, or Adam had a fight with someone and they saw a chance to get revenge."

"She's thinking a non-magical did this?" I said.

"Cythera's not really thinking at all. It's why I came here. I needed a break from the chaos and negativity she kept flinging my way." A trace of demon energy flickered across Finn's white wing feathers. "My boss can suck the joy out of the world at times."

"She's an energy vampire," I said.

Remus gently hissed. "Vampires don't drink energy."

"That's not what I heard." I twitched my whiskers at him. "But you're always fun. You're not a mood hoover. Neither is your hive."

He inclined his head. "And my parties are all people talk about. They always want to come back for a repeat performance."

Zandra hip-bumped Finn. "Stay here as long as you like. I'm not having much joy moving people on, and we need more muscle."

He grinned. "I prefer charm to muscle, but happy to stay and assist."

I nudged Archie once Remus, Zandra, and Finn had moved back to the blockade. "Go get Sage. We have a kitten impossible mission to undertake."

His eyes grew wide, and his tail thrashed. "I love it when you put a plan together." He raced off, and within a few minutes, I was gathered in a huddle with Sage and Archie.

"What's going on?" Sage said. "I'm about done with the non-magicals cooing over me and telling me how brave I am with my wheels. They keep wanting me to walk around while they video me for their socials. It's humiliating."

"It's also distracting them," I said. "And that's what we need. But right now, we have a body to look at. Follow me."

Sage grunted but made no complaints as she trundled away after a quick check Vorana was safe and happy.

"You want to break into Angel Force and look at the corpse?" Archie strode beside me.

"We need to look at Adam's body with no interruptions or family members nearby," I said. "My brief inspection of him wasn't enough."

"Enough for what? What are you hoping to find?" Sage said.

"Answers. Keep up."

We entered Angel Force, and I was happy to see the place almost empty. There were three angels at their desks, and Cythera was nowhere to be seen.

"I'll apologize for what I'm about to do later, but we can't afford to let anyone get in our way," I said. "Back me up if I need it. Angels, Cythera sent me to tell you you're needed on the front line. The non-magicals are restless. Go to the main road and make sure none of them get through."

Without questioning my order, they finished what they were doing and dashed out. Sometimes, I loved the angels for being so biddable.

Once they were gone, I checked no angels were tucked away in any offices or break rooms then gestured the others to follow.

"I smell corpse! This way!" Archie raced across the open-plan office and along the corridor that ran the length of the building.

I followed him with Sage, who kept grumbling.

"Problem? You always say you want to be more involved in these kitten impossible missions, yet when I invite you, you moan."

"It's not that. But you're up to something again. This has nothing to do with the murder."

I huffed out a breath. Sage was too intuitive for her own good. "It could be connected. When I found the body, I smelled my magic on him. My stolen magic."

Sage stopped walking and stared at me. "That's what killed him?"

"No! Well, I hope not. But what if Adam was killed because he held some of my magic? There are many who'd sacrifice a lot to get their paws on such power. Adam may not have been aware of what he carried. He came to Crimson Cove with my magic. Another magic user spotted what he had and took it."

"Which makes you responsible," Sage said.

"I didn't steal my own power, and I didn't give it to that unfortunate young man. But I need to know what he has."

"You want it back, I suppose."

"Of course. It's mine, and it was taken against my will. And it's better for it to be with me than some unfortunate creature who can't control it. Are you in or not?"

"I'll help. But if this gets us in trouble—"

"It won't. We'll be done in a few minutes. No one will know we were here."

"What do you want me to do?" Archie stood by a set of double doors, wagging his tail and huffing out smoke.

"Guard duty. Alert us if any angels return." I headed into the mortuary with Sage. There was only one body in the room, and after removing the cover, I confirmed it was Adam.

"Look at the wound." Sage backed away, her booping snooter wrinkled. "It stinks."

I hopped up and inspected Adam's pale, bony chest. There was a hole by his heart, and black tendrils of icky looking magic spread out from it. "There's nothing natural about this. Magic killed him. Although Finn said nothing about the wound looking this bad."

"Whatever infected him must have been fast acting."

I sniffed around Adam, pausing at his wrist, where a multicolored, corded bangle with a metal clasp rested. "This bracelet! It contains my magic."

"Then grab it and let's go." Sage bumped the table with her wheels. "Unless you think it'll explode like the last time you found your power."

I tentatively rested a paw on the bracelet. The second I touched it, I sensed my power. I flicked it up and slid it over my head. The magic recognized me and thrummed warmly against my skin. No explosion this time.

My eyes slid shut, and I swished my tail. This felt right. I was getting back to the way I should be. I'd missed this.

"Err... Juno. What did you just do?"

I opened my eyes and looked at Sage, who'd backed even farther away. "What do you mean?"

"The dead guy isn't your average non-magical anymore."

My attention shifted from my magic to Adam, and I froze. I was sitting on a goblin's chest.

# Chapter 7

## And you are?

Sage hissed at me and headed for the door. "So much for no one knowing we'd been poking about in here. Why'd you turn him into a goblin?"

"I didn't!" I stared at Adam. There was no doubt about it, he was a full goblin. His pale skin was shiny green, and his ears had elongated, along with his arms and legs.

"How will we explain this?" Sage tried to get the door open with a front paw. "This was supposed to be a quick in and out mission."

"I'm thinking. Stop panicking."

"It's that bangle you took. Put it back on his wrist. Turn him back, and let's get out of here."

"I can't! It contains my magic. If I give it to Adam, I'll lose it again." And I refused to do that.

Sage skittered around the room, her wheels bashing into cabinets and tables. "Then you're explaining to the angels how you turned a corpse from a non-magical into a goblin."

"I will. I'm still figuring out how to break the news to them."

"Is everything okay?" Archie called from the other side of the door.

"We have a Juno situation again," Sage said.

"This isn't my fault."

The door slammed open, and Archie trotted in. He looked around the room. "Who's that? I thought we were here to look at a non-magical."

"We were. This is the non-magical. Or rather, he was. Then Juno got her fluffy paws on him and poof! He's now a goblin." Sage pointed a paw at Adam.

Archie tilted his head from side to side. "I'm not the smartest hellhound on the block, but that's not a non-magical. Why'd you turn him goblin, Juno?"

Sage rested back on her wheels and stared at me.

"I'm not sure what happened, but when I removed his bangle, he changed into this."

"Your magic did that to him?" Archie said.

"No. I didn't disguise him as a non-magical. And I don't know why he carried a bangle with my stolen magic in it. When I took it off, this was the result." My ancient magic was spectacular, but why had it been used to do this? And how had someone manipulated it so well? Adam's disguise had fooled all of us.

"I was convincing Juno to give Adam his bangle, so we could get out of here and no one would know what we've been up to," Sage said. "But she's being stubborn."

"There's nothing stubborn about wanting to keep something that's mine." I studied Adam for a second. "Maybe my magic unwittingly held his disguise in place. For whatever reason, he chose the form of a non-magical, but a nudge from my ancient power dislodged things when I removed the bangle."

"Who'd willingly hide themselves as a non-magical?" Sage said.

"The only person who can tell you that is lying on this slab." I settled on the white cloth that had covered Adam's body, since sitting on cold flesh was always an unpleasant experience. "This discovery brings up a bigger issue. Is Adam's family hiding their true form, too? Or did a young goblin insert himself into a non-magical family and allow them to raise him?"

"A changling! Was he swapped at birth, and the parents don't know they're raising a goblin?" Sage said.

"That practice has been outlawed for hundreds of years," I said. "Besides, it's fairies who swap babies, not goblins."

"It might be illegal, but it still happens," Sage said. "And it's not just the fairies who do it."

I turned in a circle and curled my tail around my paw. "What if the whole family is in disguise?"

"Why do that?" Archie sniffed around the room. "And if you had to pick a disguise, wouldn't you go for something cool, like a vampire?"

"Not everyone thinks vampires are cool," Sage said. "They can be troublesome oinks. Vorana had to deal with a frisky vampire not so long ago who refused to believe she wasn't interested in him. I had to show him my claws more than once before he got the hint and flew away."

"Remus is amazing, though. Best vampire in the world." Archie's tongue flopped out of his mouth.

He wandered to the corpse and took a sniff. "That wound looks nasty. Smells rank, too."

"Because magic was involved in this murder." I studied Adam again. "Could this disguise be the reason Adam was killed? Someone figured out who he really was and didn't approve of him concealing his true form?"

"So, they killed him? Some magical types can be snobby," Sage said. "Werewolves are the worst, but they wouldn't be interested in some goblin hiding with a non-magical family. Or a family of goblins in disguise. It would mean nothing to them, although they wouldn't approve of the deception."

I sank onto my belly, my gaze on the dead goblin's face. "It's not just werewolves who despise liars. Many years ago—"

"Where in tootin' tarnation is everybody?" A sharp male voice boomed through the open-plan office.

"Archie, you're supposed to be guarding the door. Whoever that is, it doesn't sound like an angel." I crouched over the body.

Archie hustled back to the exit. "I got bored. You sounded like you were having fun, so I came to investigate."

"Check who that is," I whispered. "Maybe they'll leave if they don't see any angels around."

Archie poked his head out the door and quickly recoiled. "It's some guy wearing a swishy cape. And he's armed."

"With what?"

"All kinds of weapons. I saw wooden stakes." Archie growled. "He'd better not be here for my vampire. I'll bite his head off if he goes for Remus."

A quick glance around the room revealed the double doors were the only way out. There wasn't even a window to shimmy out of. "We'll stay quiet and wait for him to leave. Then we'll escape."

"I'd suggest we hide, but Archie is impossible to conceal," Sage said.

"Remus tells me I'm excellent at hide and go seek. Sometimes, he doesn't find me for hours. I can hide if I have to."

"Unless you want to squeeze into a cold store where they keep the bodies, let's wait this out." I hopped off Adam, cracked the door open an inch with one paw, and looked through the gap.

The stranger was tall and muscular, with dark features and a grim-set face. He wore an impressively swishy black cloak that stopped just below his knees. When he moved, it revealed two straps across his broad chest loaded with weapons.

He paced the office one way then the other. He tried to get through the locked door into the cells but gave up when it didn't budge. Then he turned and headed toward us.

I rapidly backed away. "He's coming. Be prepared."

"What for?" Sage said.

"Anything! We don't know why he's here, but he's not come to deliver good news with that attitude and those weapons."

"He's bad news," Archie grumbled. "Shall I bite him?"

"Let's see if he leaves us alone before we decide what to do to him."

Sage grumbled to herself, but the faint flicker of magic across her fur revealed she was ready for action.

The door thumped against the wall, and the caped crusader stood in front of us. His gaze narrowed as it settled on the corpse. Then he groaned. "What in the pickled baloney third circle of hell is this?"

I stepped forward. "Greetings. I'm Juno. These are my companions, Archie and Sage."

The guy glanced my way. "You three are in charge of Angel Force?"

"We provide expert assistance in times of need. We're their go-to consultants."

"What happened to him?" The as-yet-unnamed guy strode to Adam.

"Unfortunately, he was stabbed. Do you know him?" I kept a safe distance from the man, although he made no move toward the weapons strapped across his chest.

"This shouldn't have happened." He inspected the stab wound. His forehead wrinkled as he concentrated on the injury.

"We're as shocked as you. But sometimes, terrible things happen to good people."

"I don't mean the stab wound. I mean, why the heck in all blazes does Adam look like this?"

"You mean his goblin form? I'm uncertain. I'm assuming that was his natural form, and it's not some kind of trickery."

The guy slid me a look, telling me to watch my step. "Maybe. Why the interest?"

"I was the first on the scene after Adam was stabbed, while Night Mare entertained the crowds. I went to see if he was okay."

The guy grunted. "He loved anything to do with that old horse. I knew something like this would happen if they showed up here. I told them to stay where they were, but they thought they knew best. Some people can't be told."

"They? You know the whole Smith family?"

He ignored my question as he wandered around the body, moving his hands over Adam but not touching him. "I'll need a statement from all of you. Let's start with you, since you're the chattiest." He pointed at me.

"Perhaps common decency would get you that statement."

The guy grunted again.

"Why should I give a statement to someone who hasn't told me who they are?" I said. "For all we know, you could be the stabber. You have enough weapons strapped to your chest to perform the task."

"I didn't kill him. That's not my job." He adjusted a strap and flicked a blade out to inspect. "I need information and fast."

The fur on the back of Archie's neck rose. "It's good manners to introduce yourself. Remus taught me that. You're rude."

"Who I am isn't important. Give me the facts, then I'll take Adam and get out of here. You won't need to think about him again."

I hopped onto Adam's chest and lifted my hackles. "This young man goes nowhere. You're a stranger, and you have a sucky attitude."

"It stinks worse than that chest wound," Sage said. "You try to take the body, and you'll answer to us."

"Juno said we had to leave. How was I to know she wasn't telling the truth?" An angel's voice filtered through the door.

"I'll have words with that wretched cat when I get my hands on her. Never listen to her. She can't be trusted." Oh, goody. Cythera was here, too.

The mysterious guy grimaced. "That's all we need. Bureaucrats to slow things down even more. Get off the body. I have time if I'm quick." He shooed at me with his hands.

"You'll need the okay from the angels before you take Adam." Although I sounded calm, inside I was panicking. I hadn't figured out a plausible story for why we were in the mortuary and how I'd turned Adam into a goblin.

"Where is the cat?" Cythera said.

I concentrated on washing my face with a paw and waited for the inevitable showdown. And I was interested to see what Cythera would think of Mr. Swishy Cape and his weapons. Maybe she knew him. Although he didn't seem like the company Cythera would normally keep.

Mystery Guy pulled open the door. "Hey! I've got what you're looking for in here."

There was a second of silence, then rapidly approaching footsteps grew near.

Cythera appeared in the doorway. She glared at me then focused on Mystery Man. "Who are you?"

He lifted a shoulder. "Johnny Smithe."

"You have the same surname as Adam," I said. "You were related?"

Johnny hissed air through his teeth. "Nah. I have a silent 'e' at the end of my surname. No relation."

I narrowed my gaze. That was a fake name. What was he hiding?

Whatever it was, Cythera definitely didn't know him. "What are you doing in my mortuary, Johnny Smith with a silent 'e'?"

"Business. I heard about the murder, so I came to find out what happened."

Cythera's gaze flicked to me, and she scowled before gesturing at the angel standing behind her. "This is Angel Force business. Take Juno and her companions to a cell."

"You can't arrest us!" I said. "We've done nothing wrong."

Cythera opened her mouth to say something, then her gaze settled on the body. She strode into the room. "What have you done with Adam?"

I wriggled my booping snooter. "That's an interesting story."

Cythera turned so fast, her wings almost knocked me flying. "Juno! What did you do to him? You don't play hide and go seek with a corpse."

"I knew you remembered my name!" I reared up and waggled my front paws. "And I did nothing. Well, nothing bad. This has only just happened. Somehow, Adam changed from a non-magical into a goblin. I was working out why when Johnny arrived."

Cythera's hands fisted. "That goblin is Adam?"

I nodded. "Now you're catching up. I'd stopped by to see how things were going. Adam changed, and then—"

"Because of something you did! You always have to interfere. Not this time. Take them all to a cell. They can stay there for a few hours and think about what they've done while I deal with Johnny."

Archie tipped back his head and howled, the sound vibrating the glass and making the instruments in the room vibrate.

In the blink of an eye, Remus flashed into view. He bared his fangs at Cythera, his eyes black, and his expression fierce. "Have you harmed my hound?"

Cythera took a step back. "No! There's no need for you to be here. This isn't vampire business."

"Archie made it my business. Move away from my hound unless you want your wings detached from that glittery frame." Remus loomed closer to Cythera.

Archie's idea was an excellent one. I tugged on my bond to let Zandra know I'd appreciate her joining me and stopping Cythera from going supernova while she only had half the facts.

Zandra tugged back to let me know she was on her way. There was another blast of magic, and she appeared. She walked over and scooped me off Adam, nuzzling her nose against my ear as she took in the scene. "What have you gotten yourself into this time?"

Cythera crossed her arms over her chest. "I don't appreciate your interference, either. You should be guarding the roads while I deal with this situation."

"It's getting late, and there are barely any non-magicals around." Zandra settled me on her shoulder. "What are you doing to Juno?"

"And Archie?" Remus said. "He's under my protection. If you've harmed him, there'll be trouble."

"Cythera wants to put me in a cell." Archie whined and lifted a paw. "My friends, too. We've done nothing bad. We're helping."

Remus hissed. "And why would that be? Cythera, explain yourself."

Cythera's wings extended and fluttered as they stared each other down. She was the first to break eye contact, her wings sagging. "They're interfering in an active investigation, and they've clearly tampered with the corpse. This is not Adam."

"I only had a brief look at the body," I said. "There was no malicious tampering. And this is Adam."

"You were sitting on his chest when I walked in! That's tampering and disrespectful."

Zandra petted my side. "Juno didn't do that to cause trouble. It's hard when you're small and want to look at a body on a trolley."

"Unacceptable! I'm sick of that cat flouting the rules because they don't suit her."

"I flout to help, not hinder," I said. "Cythera, we're on the same side."

Her expression remained sour. "They're claiming they didn't move the victim and replace him with this goblin. I don't know what ridiculous game this is, but it ends now."

"That didn't happen," I said. "We moved no bodies."

Zandra tugged at the bangle around my neck. "What's this?"

"I'll tell you later."

She raised her eyebrows but demanded no more answers.

Cythera rallied her rage and shifted it to Johnny. "You've yet to explain yourself. Are you another of Juno's sidekicks?"

Johnny smirked. "We've never met."

"So you're here because..."

He took a few seconds and stared at the body, the muscles in his jaw working from side to side.

"You're not leaving this room until I get answers," Cythera said.

Johnny lifted a hand. "Sure. I owe you that. The cat and her friends aren't lying. That goblin is Adam Smith."

"How can that be?" Cythera said. "The stab victim was a non-magical."

He rolled his shoulders. "On the surface. Adam was in witness protection, like the rest of the family. I'm their case worker. I got them new identities, fixed up their disguises, and checked in with them to make sure they were doing okay." He pulled out a badge and showed it to Cythera.

"You could have told me that at the start," she said. "And why give a fake name when we first met?"

"What's your real name?" I said.

"Gideon Cairns. I use Johnny Smithe to blend in. Witness protection is kept low-key for a reason. The fewer people who know about us, the better." He tucked his badge away. "The family went the unusual route of picking a non-magical disguise.

And it made sense. Magic users rarely move to an area with no magic. It's been working for five years, but they've struggled, especially Adam. He found it hard to keep his power hidden."

"I sympathize," Zandra said. "We've been dealing with a non-magical issue in Crimson Cove. We're all holding back on using too many spells."

Gideon nodded. "I noticed the infestation. Can't be pleasant." He looked at the body. "I don't get why his disguise broke, though. It should hold even after death."

Sage gave me a pointed look, but I stayed silent.

"I'm interested in what Juno and her friends did to remove Adam's disguise," Cythera said.

"We meant no harm. We were curious about Adam," I said. "We didn't know he was hiding his true form."

"Did you find him like this when you got here?" Gideon said.

"He changed after we arrived. We were figuring out what happened when you marched in and tried to take Adam." I glanced at Cythera. "We stopped him."

Gideon sneered at me. "Thanks for nothing, cat. I was helping you out of a sticky situation by letting them know my role."

"If we hadn't been here, you'd be down a corpse, Cythera. Rather than threaten us with cell time, buy us a celebratory dinner. I always favor fish."

Cythera seemed unimpressed. "You broke into the office and interfered."

"To help!"

"To tamper!"

Remus smoothed a hand down his velvet jacket, the blackness in his eyes gone. "There's no need to lock Archie and his companions in a cell. I'll tutor him in the proper behavior around corpses. The others, too."

Cythera grunted out her displeasure then waved a hand in the air. "Go! Get out of here. Don't come back anytime soon."

I wouldn't stick to that recommendation. I was deeply curious about this case and wanted to know more about why a goblin family had ended up in witness protection. Goblins were fearsome creatures who adored a bloody battle. It must have been an intense situation for them to retreat so dramatically.

"Come on," Zandra whispered. "Let's leave while we can. And then, we're talking."

# Chapter 8

## Broken engagement

Sorcha Creer concealed a yawn behind one hand as she set down the last plate of food. "Sorry, I can't keep my eyes open." She settled in a seat at the table in her café, joining me, Zandra, Vorana, and Sage for a late dinner.

"You feeling okay?" Zandra said. "You look worn out."

Sorcha glugged down coffee. "Just working too hard and not getting enough rest. I'll be fine. I can't remember the last time I had a day off, though."

"You should get an assistant to help," I said. Sorcha usually looked radiant, no matter how much sleep she managed. She was part-vampire, so I was surprised she struggled with tiredness. Most vampires could go for days without sleep and feel no ill effects.

Tinkerbell, Sorcha's unpleasant sort of familiar, strode through the café, pointedly ignoring us, and jumped onto the window ledge.

"So, what's the gossip?" Sorcha said. "I saw Voss earlier, and he said you were there when that guy got stabbed."

"We were," Zandra said. "What seemed like a simple stabbing has turned into something complicated, thanks to Juno's snooping."

I nosed the green garnish off my poached salmon. "I've made things less complicated."

"How do you figure that?"

"We don't need to get the non-magical police involved. Goblins don't fall under their jurisdiction."

"Goblins!" Vorana's eyebrows shot up. "I thought a non-magical got stabbed?"

"Juno discovered he was in disguise," Zandra said. "Although I still haven't figured out how you did that. I got zero magic when I was around Adam's body."

"You should tell them the truth," Sage said. "It's wrong to lie to your witch."

I slid her a glare. "I was getting to that." I still wore the bangle around my neck, and my magic throbbed happily, although I had yet to test its power to see how stable it was.

"I knew you weren't telling me everything," Zandra said. "What is it?"

"Juno made a discovery," Sage said.

"I'll tell the story!" I didn't want Sage to get me into trouble. "I had a feeling about Adam. I couldn't understand why anyone would stab him. So, I looked at the wound."

"What did you find?" Sorcha said.

"Black tendrils radiating from the entry point. And I sensed magic on Adam when we discovered him in the street."

"How is that possible?" Zandra had abandoned her food and stared at me. My witch's stare could pierce most armor, mine included.

"That's why I was so curious about him. I identified some magic attached to a bracelet the victim wore. I gave it a gentle tug, and that's when he transformed into his goblin form."

"You mean, the bracelet you haven't taken off since you found it?" Zandra tugged at the multi-colored threads around my neck.

"It didn't seem right to put it back on Adam. The magic may have backfired. And then Gideon arrived..." I took a big bite of salmon, so I had an excuse not to talk.

Zandra narrowed her eyes and pursed her lips. She knew I was still concealing something from her.

"So, the non-magical stab victim is a goblin," Sorcha said. "Weird. Why was he killed? Any idea?"

"It had something to do with his disguise," I said. "Someone figured out who he was and didn't approve of him concealing himself."

"We shouldn't gossip about this too much. We have to keep this between us, given the family's situation," Zandra said.

Sorcha and Vorana leaned forward at the same time.

"What else is there? It sounds juicy," Vorana said.

Zandra stabbed some french fries. "Promise you won't blab?"

"Hearts crossed and yank out our eyes with a blunt spoon if we do," Sorcha said.

Zandra grimaced. "Your word is enough."

"You've got it," Vorana said. "What else is special about Adam?"

"Adam and his family were in witness protection. Some guy called Gideon showed up and laid claim to the body. He revealed the family has been in disguise as non-magicals for over five years."

Sorcha and Vorana poked their tongues out and made noises of disgust.

"Interesting choice of disguise." Vorana bit into her burger.

"It's a clever choice. None of us would ever nose into a world without magic. It was probably the best choice, if not the easiest," I said.

"Which suggests they were in mortal danger if they went that route," Sorcha said. "And that danger caught up with Adam."

"Apparently, the family was struggling not to use magic. We all know what that's like. You get a buildup if you don't discharge your power, and things can go wrong," Zandra said.

"They came here to let off steam without drawing attention to themselves?" Vorana said.

"Maybe. Angel Force plans on talking to the family as soon as possible. With this new information, they need to move fast. The rest of the family could be at risk if there's someone targeting them," I said.

The café door swung open, and a horde of non-magicals poured in. They were mainly older ladies, but a couple of families were mixed in with them. Leading from the rear was Gus Bainbridge, the guy whose coach broke down near Finn's animal sanctuary not so long ago.

Sorcha groaned. "How did they get in? I've just strengthened the wards around this place to keep them out, but they have no effect. I've had three groups of them in today. They're so messy."

"That's why you're tired," Vorana said. "Need a hand?"

"Would you mind? I can't deal with them all on my own. I'm wrung out."

"Sure. Zandra?"

"I'm useless in the kitchen. I'd be more of a hindrance."

"My witch is perfect in every environment, except the kitchen," I said.

"We can handle them between us." Vorana hopped from her seat and headed to the counter with Sorcha to deal with the non-magical customers.

Gus's usually cheerful expression was flat as he paced the café, his hands stuffed into his pockets and his head down.

He slowed as he reached our table. "I know you. You're involved with the animal sanctuary, aren't you?"

Zandra raised a hand. "Sure. I'm Zandra. This is Juno."

"Of course. I'd never forget such a cutie." He scratched the top of my head, his expression remaining pensive.

When he didn't move on, Zandra glanced at me and shrugged. "Everything okay?"

Gus puffed out a breath. "No. Have you heard about the stabbing?"

"We were there when it happened."

"Oh! That's good. Well, not good for you, but you know what I mean. You tried to help Adam?"

"We did what we could. You knew him?"

"He was part of my coach tour. It's the first time we've opened to families." Gus shook his head. "I told the boss we should stick to the oldies. They're less frisky. Well, most of them are so long as they don't get their hands on the sherry, but she wanted to expand the business and make more money."

"How well do you know Adam's family?" Zandra said.

"Not at all. They seemed okay, though. Kept to themselves. Not friendly but not rude. The mother was nervy, though. She kept checking to make sure they were all comfortable. You know what parents are like." Gus turned and looked at his party of golden oldies. "I saw Adam's brother sneak alcohol on board the coach. I should have stopped him, but he wasn't being loud or causing problems, and we all need something to take the edge off now and again."

"Did Adam say he was worried about visiting Crimson Cove?" Zandra said.

"Nothing like that. He was your typical, surly young guy. Barely said two words, and when he did, they were mumbled to the ground. He seemed nervous, too, I suppose. But I could be reading into things. You get paranoid after something like this."

"Gus! We need your help," one of his old ladies called out.

"Duty calls. I'll have to bring another party to the animal sanctuary. We had so much fun on our last visit. See you around." Gus hurried to the counter.

I twitched my booping snooter. "That's a problem. I assumed the Smith family traveled here alone. If everyone on the coach tour knew Adam and his family, the goblin issue makes things tricky. We should mind wipe them so they forget the family."

"That would make things even messier. It's too dangerous to mind wipe everyone, and there'll be records kept that they came on this trip." Zandra picked up a french fry. "Let Angel Force deal with this. I want to talk to you about the stolen bangle."

The skin on the back of my neck itched. "Um... What about it?"

She waggled the french fry at me. "I didn't sense any magic on Adam. How were you able to sense it when I couldn't?"

I spent a second inspecting my salmon. "I don't know. I just did."

"Juno! What aren't you telling me? We've had the no secrets talk before. Do we need to have it one more time?"

The cafe door opened again, and my eyes widened. Sammy sauntered in with what looked like a date. A pretty, slightly fluffy tortoiseshell female missing a back leg hopped beside him. And from the look on her face, she was smitten.

"Who is that?" My tone sounded accusatory, and rightly so.

Zandra glanced over. "I haven't seen that cat before. A new friend?"

"She's not my new friend. Not if she keeps looking at Sammy like that." My fur bristled.

Zandra raised her eyebrows. "Are you two in an open relationship? They do look kind of friendly."

"Of course we're not. Well, we haven't defined our relationship, but I'm not seeing anyone else. Neither should Sammy. He knows better. Is this what he's been doing all this time? No wonder I've had trouble reaching him." My toe beans began to sweat.

"I thought he'd seemed distant recently. Have you been arguing about something? Maybe he thinks you're on a break."

"No! I wondered if I'd been a little neglectful, which was why he was giving me the cold shoulder, but this is unacceptable." Sammy hadn't even glanced my way as he'd settled on the window ledge to look out with his new companion by his side. Tinkerbell had even made room for them, and Sammy and Tinkerbell hated each other.

"Do you want to see what's going on?" Zandra said. "Maybe she's a new familiar in town and Sammy is showing her around."

I grumbled to myself as I glared at them. They sat too close to each other to be simply friends. And when Sammy licked her cheek, I almost fell off my seat. "I should go over. Say something."

"Introduce yourself. I'm sure it's a misunderstanding. Sammy would never do anything to hurt you. He's so sweet on you it makes my teeth hurt."

I didn't realize how deep my feelings were for Sammy until I saw him with somebody else.

Finn barged into the café and ran to the table. "I need help. Cythera is about to kill Gideon."

# Chapter 9

## Angel rage

"Who started the fight?" Zandra held a half-eaten slice of pizza as we dashed out of Bites and Delights with Finn.

"Cythera tried to pull rank, and Gideon stood up to her. Things got thrown, and nothing any of the angels said calmed the situation. Cythera even ordered us to arrest Gideon. But, honestly, he's done nothing wrong, other than tread on her toes and flash around his credentials. He keeps saying his priority is to protect the family, and he needs to take Adam's body."

Although I listened to Finn, I still watched Sammy and his new friend as I passed the café window. He barely spared me a glance. And when our eyes met, he behaved as if he didn't know me.

I slowed and turned back. I had to speak to Sammy. Something was terribly wrong.

"Juno! Keep up," Zandra said. "We'll need you if Cythera doesn't back down. You may have to chew through a wing to get her to see sense."

I didn't want to leave Sammy, but I had to help Zandra. Why was he behaving like this?

Was I making too much of the situation? Was Sammy just being his usual friendly self? No. He had been behaving differently. He'd been late for several dates and had grown increasingly rude to people he considered friends. When I had a moment, I'd speak to him.

"Juno!" Zandra gestured me to follow her.

With a sigh and my thoughts a tangled mess around Sammy, I headed to Angel Force. Why couldn't these pesky angels sort out their own mess?

A blast of white magic slammed open the entrance doors before we reached them, and Gideon flew out and landed on his back, sending up a cloud of dust as he slammed down.

Cythera stalked out and stood over him. "This is my office. You follow my rules. Since you can't do that, you're no longer welcome."

"You weren't kidding," Zandra said to Finn. "I've never seen her this angry."

"I keep telling her she needs to take a break," Finn said.

Gideon rolled smoothly to his feet, his jaw set, and his eyes narrowed. "I'm the witness protection expert. You don't understand who you're dealing with."

"Because you won't tell me anything useful. You claim you're keeping the information secret to protect them, but how am I supposed to know what level of protection to offer while they're here?" Cythera's wings were out and swooping up and down. "What's so special about the Smith family that you insist my troop of angels guard them? If I take my patrols off the streets, crime will increase. And we have all the non-magicals to deal with. You ask too much without giving anything in return."

"You don't need to know it all. I tell you what to do, and you agree to do it. Problem solved."

Zandra winced, and I grimaced. That was the perfect way to make Cythera despise you. She always needed to think she was in charge, even when she wasn't. Life was simpler that way.

"That's not how things work around here." Cythera extended her wings.

"You want us to separate them?" Zandra said, as angels piled out of the building to watch the ruckus.

"You might have to. I don't mind taking on Cythera in a fight if you two deal with Gideon," Finn said.

Gideon and Cythera stared each other down.

While they attempted to out-alpha each other, I looked back at the café. I needed a plan to win Sammy back. Although I wasn't sure why I had to win him back at all. When had our relationship gotten so complicated?

"How about we take this inside?" Finn bravely placed himself between Cythera and Gideon. "We're gathering a crowd. And it's not just angels watching. You don't want non-magicals to see you."

"I wasn't the one who brought the debate out here," Gideon said through gritted teeth. "I'm doing what's best for the Smith family. You don't know how important they are."

"Then share," Cythera said. "You're slowing things down by keeping unnecessary secrets."

Gideon hunched his shoulders. "I'll share if you agree to follow my orders."

Heat flashed up Cythera's neck and onto her cheeks. "And as I keep telling you, I'm in charge around here."

"Then do the adult thing and recognize when you have someone with more experience in front of you. I don't want trouble. I'm here to ensure no more members of the family are killed."

There was more glowering, wing fluttering, and fists being clenched. Cythera turned on her heel and stalked into the building.

"Well, that's progress. Shall we?" Finn gestured at the door.

Gideon shrugged and brushed dust off his pants. "I was trying to make progress before Cythera went psycho. She needs to relax."

"She's had a stressful few weeks," Finn said. "It's all the non-magicals. She's usually much calmer than this."

Zandra smirked, and I decided not to comment.

We all went inside. The place was a mess. Angels were picking up scattered papers and righting toppled chairs.

Cythera waited in the open-plan office for us to arrive. Her foot tapped on the ground. "Well, who are they?"

"They're goblins," Gideon said.

"We discovered that, thanks to a small, fluffy interference who doesn't understand when her presence isn't wanted." Cythera glanced at me.

I bit my tongue. She knew my name. She was just being stubborn by not using it.

"Yeah, that's a mystery," Gideon said. "How did you break through the magic disguise? It was supposed to be unbreakable magic. It goes through seven levels of testing before anyone is given it. What are you, some kind of super juiced magic slinger?"

"Juno is special," Zandra said. "She's not your regular familiar."

"That's because I'm attached to a wonderful witch," I said. "You should all bow before her, or her magical brilliance will blind you."

"Less of that," Zandra muttered. "We both have power, though. Maybe the combination of our magic and bond meant your concealment spell broke."

"It still shouldn't happen." Gideon ran a hand down his face. "We have the highest level of magic users working with us. Those who go into witness protection are targets for shady characters who wouldn't think twice about killing them. We have to make sure the disguise lasts for as long as they need it."

"Could Adam's murder have disturbed the magic?" I fluffed my neck fur to conceal the bangle.

"That shouldn't have made a difference. I just don't get it."

While they discussed how the magic got disrupted, I snuck to Bertoli's desk. I pulled off the bangle and placed it in his bottom drawer. I'd deal with it later, when there was less attention on me.

"You've yet to answer my question," Cythera said. "Why is this family so important?"

There was a tap on the main door leading into the office. Julie appeared, and she wasn't alone. Simon stood beside her, and just behind them, Eric pushed Edith's wheelchair.

"We came as soon as we got your message," Julie said. "Is it safe?"

"You couldn't be safer." Gideon strode over and shook her hand. "I know this must be a tough time for you."

"We want to know what's going on. And we need to see Adam. We've yet to mourn him appropriately." Her gaze flashed around the office, taking us all in.

"Of course. I'm so sorry this happened to him. We let you down. We promised you'd all be safe under our care."

Julie's expression grew pinched. "You said we shouldn't come to Crimson Cove. But Adam pleaded. And I thought, if we were discreet and blended with the others in a large group, no one would notice anything odd. Crimson Cove is getting a name for itself, so I figured, with all the other non-magicals visiting, it would be fine for us to have a short break. How did someone recognize him?"

Cythera sighed. "It's a question I'd love answered. Gideon, you were about to tell us who the family really is."

His gaze went around the room of watching angels. "Do you trust everyone here?"

"My team is reliable. You have nothing to worry about."

Gideon looked our way. "What about these two?"

"I'll vouch for Zandra and Juno," Finn said. "They've helped us on some tough cases recently."

"And you have my paw-felt word, the family won't be at any risk because of us."

Gideon nodded slowly, his attention returning to Julie. "Would you have any objection to revealing yourselves to the angels?"

"If it'll help." Simon settled a hand on Julie's shoulder. "I'd actually like a break from being under the weight of this disguise. Especially while we mourn."

Gideon reached inside his jacket pocket and pulled out four small bottles containing orange liquid. "This'll temporarily disable your disguises. Only for an hour. It'll give you time to complete the mourning rituals. Once it wears off, you'll be back in your non-magical forms." He handed around the liquid.

Julie went to lift Edith's over-sized purse off her lap so her hands were free, but the old woman clung to the purse and hissed at her, digging her less than clean nails into the leather.

She sighed, left the purse where it was, and helped Edith drink her potion first, before downing her own. Eric and Simon swallowed theirs in a single gulp. They all shuddered, and their disguises faded to reveal four goblins.

Cythera drew in a sharp breath and dropped to her knee. "Welcome, your Highness. It's an honor to have you in Crimson Cove."

Julie nodded. She wasn't a conventionally attractive goblin, with an overly long face and high, pointed ears, but she carried herself as a woman with great power and influence. Her spine was straight, her shoulders back, and her piercing orange gaze was firm and focused as she examined everybody.

"You see now why I needed discretion?" Gideon said.

"Who are they?" Zandra whispered to me.

"The Wrunard family. They're the last in line of the oldest recorded goblin family. Their lineage goes back to the first goblin king, Zil Wrunard."

"I've heard of them," Zandra said. "Don't they own some goldmines in the Riltare Valley?"

"We own all of them," Julie said, "as well as substantial tracts of land and castles. Unfortunately, we've been unable to make use of our assets since we were hidden. Witness protection allows minimal contact with our workers, and to draw down funds would attract the wrong attention."

Cythera remained on her knee, and the other angels, who'd all copied her gesture of submission, stayed glued to the ground.

Julie gestured them to stand. "Please, there's no need. I have become settled in my non-magical form."

"Should we keep calling you Julie, or Your Highness, or Queen Dixia?" I said.

"Use our non-magical names to avoid confusion. Queen Dixia sounds almost alien to me." Her attention moved to Cythera. "I would like to see my son. We must perform the mourning ritual to ensure a smooth passage."

"Of course. Right this way." Cythera stood and hurried off with the family.

Zandra puffed out her cheeks. "They're all goblin royalty?"

Gideon nodded. "Simon's brother married the queen. Eric and Adam are her offspring. They're princes. Although Eric acts more like a feral dog. Edith is the Queen Mother, Ixithia."

"It makes sense why they had an owl protector," I said. "Lucian was Adam's guardian?"

Gideon curled his top lip. "He was supposed to be. But some use he was. And I see he's vanished. No doubt licking his wounds and feeling sorry for himself. Useless owl."

"We'll need to interview them all again," Finn said. "They were only spoken to briefly after Adam was stabbed. This information about their true identity changes things."

"That won't happen until tomorrow," Gideon said. "The family is fragile. They can't be pushed. Not at a time like this."

"They may forget useful information if we leave it overnight," I said. "It's best to interview people as soon as possible. Memories fade."

Gideon arched an eyebrow. "You a master interrogator, too?"

"If needed. I've been around enough criminal types to know the information you gather early in a case is the most crucial."

"I agree with Juno," Finn said. "It won't take long."

"No interviews until tomorrow." Gideon crossed his arms over his chest. "Cythera put me in charge of this case, and now she knows who we're dealing with, she won't argue with me about protocol."

Finn didn't look happy about being told what to do by Gideon but didn't protest.

Cythera returned without the family. "I've left them to mourn."

"Have you got somewhere secure they can stay overnight?" Gideon said. "And I'll need a full contingent of angels to guard them. Can you make that happen?"

Cythera bristled under Gideon's brusque tone but nodded. "Of course. My angels are some of the best. Now I know who we're protecting, I'll do everything in my power to keep them safe."

"You may think your angels are the best, but Adam was killed on your watch."

Cythera's hands twitched. "I had no idea a family of ancient royal goblins in witness protection were in Crimson Cove. If I'd been informed by your department, I could have done something."

"You're not laying this disaster at my door. If you can't keep control of the local population, this is your fault. Adam died because your angels were negligent in their duty. And they were negligent because of you."

"Here we go again," Finn muttered.

Cythera and Gideon batted insults and rebuttals back and forth while we watched. It was oddly entertaining.

"Let's get out of here, shall we?" Zandra said to me.

Finn grabbed her elbow as she turned to leave. "You're abandoning me? What if they don't stop this time?"

"You could come with us," I said. "Let them fight it out. I expect they'll be best friends by morning."

He tipped back his head and groaned. "No, I can't leave them. You get out of here. Let's just hope we still have a building left standing tomorrow."

"Good luck," Zandra said.

I glanced at Bertoli's desk as we passed it. Although I was tempted to take the magic with me, I needed time and no distractions so I could focus on it.

One puzzle at a time. Although, right now, I had too many puzzles and not enough pieces to fit them all together.

# Chapter 10

## Owl avenger

*Tap, tap-itty tap. Tap, tap, tap.*

I slid open one eye to discover Lucian Proudfeather perched outside the basement window, his feathery face pressed against the glass.

When he spotted I was awake, he waved a wing at me.

I rolled off the bed, trotted up the basement steps, and went out into the dawn light. "Greetings, you unpleasant, familiar-grabbing owl fiend. Why are you here?"

Lucian ruffled out his feathers in a showy display. "I need your help."

I settled on the porch and washed my face. "Why should I help you? I haven't forgiven you for dropping me into the ocean. I still smell like the sea."

He gave a gentle squawk. "Adam's killer must be found."

"You mean, Prince... what was his true name?"

"Oh! You found out about their disguise?"

"Of course. Gideon revealed their true forms to us."

"Prince Lork. I called him Pork for fun. Well, when no one else was around. Any other time, he was plain old Adam Smith." Lucian clacked his beak up and down. "Will you help me find his killer?"

"Angel Force and witness protection have the situation in hand. And with two alphas in charge, it's not a situation I wish to involve me or my witch in. Cythera and Gideon came to blows last night."

Lucian flapped his wings, hopping from one foot to the other. "Please! I don't trust the angels or Gideon. Someone revealed the family was coming here. That's why Adam died."

I tilted my head. "You think there's an informant putting your family at risk?"

"It's a theory I'm working on. There are others. The family has been to other magical towns and nothing like this happened, so perhaps it's a local angel."

I studied Lucian as he hopped and ruffled. "You're doing this out of guilt, aren't you? You were supposed to look after Adam, and you took your eye off the ball."

Lucian fluffed his feathers again. "There's truth in that. Adam hated me watching him. He said it creeped him out. So, I started going off for short periods of time to give him space. I'd always return and check on him, and there were never any problems."

"Until there was, and now he's dead." I stared at the sagging, sad-eyed owl. "You made a mistake."

"One that cost a young goblin his life. I must undo that damage and make amends."

"And are you sorry?"

"That Adam is dead? Of course."

"I meant, are you sorry for grabbing me off the beach and tossing me into the sea?"

"Oh! Well, you were interfering in my private business. And I didn't know you at the time. How was I to know you could be an ally?"

"You could have asked."

Lucian lowered his head. "Then I'm also sorry to you. Juno, I really need your help. I can't do this alone. You know Crimson Cove. And you're powerful."

"Wait here." I trotted back inside, down the basement stairs, and jumped on Zandra's chest.

She grunted and caught hold of me. "It's too early for games. What are you doing?"

"Are you fluent in feisty owl?"

※·····≫ ≪·····※

Two hours later, the three of us were back at Angel Force, and I was pleased to see the building still standing. It suggested Cythera and Gideon had resolved their differences or at least figured out how not to kill each other.

Lucian stayed outside, giving us time to work an angle to get an in on this investigation.

Finn met me and Zandra by the reception desk. "I need to give you fair warning. Cythera is snippy.

Even apple donuts with powdered sugar and pink sprinkles didn't make her smile."

"Gideon got the upper hand, then?" I said.

He shrugged. "She won't talk about it. This way. I've been working on her to get you all on board. It may take an angel miracle, though."

We followed Finn into the open-plan office and over to Cythera's office. He tapped on her door.

"No!"

Finn knocked again. "I know you're busy, but I've got the support I mentioned. We should brief them."

Cythera yanked open the door. She muttered what might have been a curse under her breath. "No! This isn't the support we need. Go away!"

"It makes sense to have Zandra and Juno involved in this case." Finn hurried in behind Cythera as she strode across her office.

"I agreed with Gideon to use only key personnel. You now know how important the family is. Zandra and her fluffy menace are untrained. They're amateurs. And trouble making amateurs at that. The cat stamped all over the prince's body!"

"We're amateurs who've solved more cases this year than you have in your lifetime," I muttered from my position on Zandra's shoulder.

She grunted an agreement but froze when Cythera pinned us with a glare.

"They're the only ones who can communicate properly with Lucian Proudfeather." Finn glanced over and winked at us. He'd gone for the owl angle because it gave us leverage to be involved in this case.

"The owl guardian is a potential witness in this murder." I hopped off Zandra's shoulder and settled on a bundle of important looking papers. "And Lucian is suspicious of everyone. He doesn't like to talk about his involvement with the Wrunard family."

"Then why is he talking to you?" Cythera yanked the papers from underneath me and blew fur off them.

"We have a bond. We understand each other. He's the family's protector. Just as I protect Zandra."

Zandra smirked at me but made no comment.

"Why can't the owl talk to me?" Cythera said. "Surely, it must trust me."

"Lucian takes time to trust. And he sometimes reverts to owl speak. I can translate. He also..." Should I mention this, or would Cythera blow a gasket?

"Yes? What is it?"

"He's worried there could be a leak in Angel Force. That's how the killer knew where Adam was."

Cythera's face went red, then white, then grayish-beige.

"We should also consider Lucian a suspect," Zandra said hurriedly. "All we have so far is his word he was nowhere near Adam when he died. If we lure Lucian into our confidence, he could let something slip."

Gideon strolled into the room, a sugared donut in one hand. "Lucian's been with the family since they went into witness protection. He's always been reliable, but recently, his standards have gotten slack. I wondered if he'd become jaded and was considering assigning him to a fresh case. But Adam liked him. They liked each other. The owl didn't do it."

Cythera sank into her seat. "And there are no leaks in Angel Force."

"The information didn't come from my side." Gideon tore a chunk off the donut, and a glob of the apple filling dropped onto the desk.

"Let's not get into that now." Finn swiftly wiped away the donut filling with a tissue before Cythera noticed and got mad again. "We focus on what happened to Adam and get any information we can. The family will arrive any minute, so we can interview them and have Lucian sit in, too. Well, watch."

"Very well," Cythera said after a moment of consideration. "The witch, owl, and cat can be involved as observers, but only in a 'silent until spoken to' role."

I nodded, knowing that would never happen. I had a sassy mouth, and Zandra's tongue was sharper than a miffed honey badger on a rampage, but if Cythera didn't know that about us by now, she'd never learn.

"I'd like to talk to Lucian and find out what went wrong that day," Gideon said. "Maybe it's time he was retired. Some magical creatures lose their edge when they get to a certain age."

I winced. Poor Lucian. He was in for a rough ride. "I'll bring him in. He's waiting outside." I hurried out of the building and gestured to Lucian, who'd perched on the top of the Angel Force building.

He swooped down and joined me. "What did they say?"

"We're in. And they're about to interview the family."

"Can we sit in? I'm great at knowing if someone isn't telling the truth. There's one family member I'm particularly interested in."

"No, but the angels have one of those rooms with a one-way mirror. That's where Zandra and I go when we're involved in cases."

Lucian tilted his head from side to side. "That happens often?"

"More often than it should. Since we moved to Crimson Cove, we've gotten involved in a variety of curious cases."

"That must make life interesting."

I headed back inside Angel Force, with Lucian hopping beside me. "Interesting and busy. I never have enough time to do everything." Like see Sammy and figure out what he was playing at with that pretty, three-legged female.

"I get it. My job is never off the clock. I always sleep with one eye open to make sure no threats come for the family."

"Having your eyes open didn't help Adam."

Lucian squawked at me. "Don't rub it in. I know I messed up."

"Lucian! You're here, too."

We turned back to the main entrance to discover Julie pushing Edith in her wheelchair. Simon was also with them. They were back in their disguises and looked the picture of non-magical normalcy.

Lucian bobbed his head. "Your Highness. I hope you aren't angry with me for vanishing, but I needed time to myself after what happened to Adam. I feel terrible."

She blinked once. "I imagine you must. You had a strong bond with my son. He cared for you."

"Adam will be greatly missed."

"He will. By all of us."

"Pretty bird. Come have a treat." Edith held out her hand. A wizened apple core rested on her palm.

"I'll pass, but thanks," Lucian said.

"The angels are interviewing you, too?" Simon said. "They asked us to come back first thing this morning to give statements. Though I can't imagine we have any useful information. As you know, Adam was always going off and doing his own thing. He found it uncool to hang out with his family members."

"He was testing his independence," Lucian said. "He didn't even want me hanging around most of the time."

"I should never have indulged him," Julie said. "Adam was my last hope."

I flicked my tail in the air. "Last hope?"

She sighed. "For grandchildren, to continue the family name."

"You have another son," I said. "That'll be a small comfort, but your lineage can continue through Eric."

"Unlikely. Eric is troubled," Lucian muttered.

"He's more than troubled. He's lost to uncontrollable addictions." The skin around Julie's eyes tightened. "For many years, I've considered myself to have only one son. Adam's gone. This is the end of the line for us."

Lucian squawked and flapped his wings.

"There's still time." Simon placed an arm around Julie's shoulders. "Eric may turn things around. And you're young. Perhaps there are more infants in your future if you find the right person to look after you."

She shrugged his arm away. "I can't think about that now."

A flush whispered across his cheeks. "Of course. I just wanted to give you hope."

"No more babies for you," Edith said. "Too dangerous. We're all dead. Tee hee."

"Not now, Mother." Julie glanced at Simon. "Are you sure she took her meds this morning?"

"She did." He leaned down to Edith. "You're just having a funny turn, aren't you?" He spoke so loudly, my ears hurt.

Cythera appeared and curtsied. "Welcome. Thank you for arriving so promptly."

"I want to deal with this quickly and discreetly," Julie said. "And where is Gideon? We need to figure out our next move."

"He's here. We'll take your statements, and then you can spend time with Gideon. I trust your accommodation was suitable?" Cythera ushered the family into the main office.

"Very suitable. Thank you for giving up your apartment to us."

I wriggled my whiskers. Cythera was bending over backward to accommodate this family. She must think they were something else if she'd opened her home to them. I'd never had an invitation to Cythera's place. What was it like? All white and clinical like her office, or was she a secret pastel paint aficionado? Or maybe she had black walls and a passion for heavy metal.

"It was no trouble. My angels reported a quiet night. There were no security concerns," Cythera said.

"And we appreciate that," Simon said. "Just as we would appreciate this happening quickly. We have a lot to deal with."

"Bury the body then make up the lies," Edith said.

Julie sighed. "Is there somewhere I can put my mother? She needs quiet. Preferably a darkened room. She's been nervy since Adam died. She can't comprehend what happened, but she's aware something is different. Adam was always so patient with her when she babble-talked."

"Of course. We can put her in an empty interview room and dim the lights. Would that be suitable?" Cythera said.

"Ideal. Thank you. She'll sleep when no one is around."

Ten minutes later, Edith had been left in a quiet room with an armful of Julie-approved snacks, and Julie was settled in a separate interview space.

I sat in the room next door with Lucian and Zandra. "What's your opinion of the mother?"

"I'm not a fan," Lucian said. "She has a Commonwealth to rule but can't because of her situation. It's made her bitter."

"Bitter toward Adam?" Zandra said.

"Bitter toward the world. I keep out of her way. Her sharp tongue stings."

"Is she the family member you're interested in? You think she did it?" I said.

"Maybe. I'm still working through my theories. I want to hear what she has to say before I go into attack mode."

Cythera, Finn, and Gideon joined Julie in the interview room. After Cythera ran through the formalities, she began her questioning.

"Tell us about your relationship with Adam."

"He was my son."

"Were you close?"

No emotion flickered across Julie's carefully composed face. "He was a wayward goblin testing the limits of his independence. I loved him, but we had moments when we screamed at each other. I'll admit to not always liking him. But he was still my son. The future of the family rested on his shoulders."

"That must have been a burden for Adam," I said.

"There were never any screaming fights. Julie barked orders, and Adam jumped to avoid the conflict," Lucian muttered.

"I've seen them argue," Gideon said. "It was never anything serious. Adam was just your typical high-spirited guy, proving a point."

Julie nodded. "Exactly. They're all the same at that age."

Cythera ignored Gideon's comment. "When was the last time you fought with your son?"

"It's been a while. Adam withdrew from the family recently. He was barely speaking to any of us."

"That's true," Lucian said. "Adam spent most of his time in his bedroom."

"Doing disgusting teenage things?" I said.

"No. Well, sometimes he could be gross. He messed around with magic, though. They weren't supposed to use it where they lived because it was a risk to non-magicals, but he struggled to stick to that rule." Lucian preened his chest feathers. "They entered witness protection when Adam was thirteen, so he hadn't developed many abilities before they went into hiding. He was curious about what he could do."

"An ancestor of Zil Wrunard would be powerful with the right training," I said.

"Adam could have been something special. Now, we'll never know."

"Where were you when you learned what happened to Adam?" Cythera said to Julie.

"In my bedroom at the place we'd rented. I had a headache and needed to be somewhere quiet. Mother had been difficult that morning, trying to get out of her chair and slapping anyone who helped her. All the noise from the crowds only made her worse. I left Mother with Adam and told him to watch her."

"Did anyone see you at your accommodation?" Finn said. "Maybe a neighbor you spoke to?"

"No. I haven't seen any neighbors since we arrived. We rented a small, private house on the edge of town. You could check, but I didn't see anybody when I walked back there and went inside."

"Julie has no alibi," I murmured.

"Was there anything you can think of that was troubling Adam?" Cythera said.

"If there was, he wouldn't talk to me about it. The mother is always the last to know."

"Julie's not telling the whole truth," Lucian said. "When they argued, it was always because Adam wanted to go back to a normal, goblin existence. He was done hiding. Julie denied him and said it was too much of a risk for the family. She accused him of being selfish. Him! He was a good guy. Well, a slob, but he was a teenager. All teenagers are slobs."

"If you don't mind me saying, you don't seem sad about losing Adam," Finn said to Julie.

"I mourn in my own way." The first flicker of emotion crossed Julie's face since the interview started. It wasn't sadness. It was anger. But it was gone in a flash. "For years, I've suppressed my true nature to stay alive. It's changed me. I'm desperate to protect my family, though. I'd do anything to keep them safe, even subduing my power. I struggle sometimes to feel anything. Most of the time, I feel numb."

"Don't believe her. There's fire in that goblin queen. The family name is everything to Julie," Lucian said. "Once they die, the name will be gone. Usually, goblin females have a vast number of offspring, but Julie has always struggled. It took her ten years to conceive Eric."

"The gran was right when she said it was too dangerous for Julie to have lots of infants. Julie can't have more offspring?" I said.

"It would be a risk, but one she'd consider taking if it meant the family could thrive. Although to do that, they'd need to fix things so they could return to power."

"Julie is planning a return to the goblin community?" Zandra said.

"I guarantee she is. I've overheard her talking about it with Simon." Lucian's eyes were narrowed as he studied Julie. "Maybe this is her way of doing it."

"How would killing Adam get her back where she wants to be?" I said.

He plucked free a loose feather. "If Julie mentions a certain goblin rival, I'll bet good vermin she killed Adam."

"Why?" Zandra said.

"Because Adam is the reason they're in witness protection," Lucian said. "He witnessed a rival goblin murder somebody. Adam's testimony put them behind bars."

"If this rival was jailed, why did the family have to enter witness protection?" Zandra said.

"Because her loyal followers are still out there. We're talking someone high up in the goblin community. Ever heard of Razia Obelong?"

"The Blood Soaked Queen of Xanitz?" I said. "Everyone's heard of her."

"I haven't," Zandra said.

I gave her some serious side eye. "That's because you don't study."

She smirked at me. "I may know nothing about her, but Razia's nickname tells me all I need."

"Razia Obelong isn't fun to be around. She was supposed to remain behind bars for the rest of her life but got out on a technicality three months ago. Since then, Julie has been plotting."

"Razia must want revenge for what happened to her," I said. "Shouldn't she be the prime suspect in this investigation?"

"Razia isn't involved. The more I hear, the more convinced I am it was Julie. And if she mentions Razia, I'll know it was her."

We returned our attention to the interview. Cythera had been asking Julie for the names of anyone who saw her when she returned to her accommodation, but she wasn't forthcoming.

"Who do you think did this to Adam?" Finn said.

Julie looked down at her clasped hands. "I assumed it was a random attack. You hear stories of non-magicals getting over-excited and causing problems."

"Magic was used to kill Adam," Finn said. "It was disguised as a stabbing, but there was nothing random about this attack. I'm assuming you saw the wound?"

She paused, and her tongue traced her bottom lip. "If it was a targeted attack, I can only think of one person."

"Wait for it." Lucian crouched, his eyes gleaming. "She's about to show us her guilt."

I exchanged a glance with Zandra. I wasn't so certain of that.

"Who would that be?" Cythera said.

"Razia Obelong."

Lucian squawked and flew at the glass. "I knew it! That goblin fiend is guilty. She's using Razia as a cover for her own dark deeds. She killed Adam!"

# Chapter 11

## Raging feathers

I leaped at Lucian as he scrabbled and pecked ineffectively at the glass. "Stop that! It won't do any good."

"It was her!" He snapped his beak at me. "Julie killed Adam to open the door for their return. I never trusted her. She was always sneaking around and looking for a way home. She cares more about her reputation than her children." He thumped his wings so hard against the glass, Finn and Cythera looked over.

"Julie strikes me as smart. She wouldn't kill her only hope to further the family lineage," I said. "She admitted she'd written Eric off as a future heir. With Adam gone, she loses it all. The family name will die out."

"Goblins are long-lived. If she can get back to rule, she'd have another three hundred years to command her people. And she'd continue to search for a solution so she could bear more offspring."

Zandra bit her bottom lip, exchanging an alarmed look with me as Lucian spiraled. "If you're right, maybe Julie sacrificed Adam to get in Razia's good books. She got rid of him to ensure the rest of her family could return to the goblin realm."

Lucian whacked his wings against the glass. "Julie's devious enough to do it. She always has her eye on the prize. If she could restore her family to prominence, it would mean everything to her."

"But killing her son..." I shook my head.

"We need to tell the angels about this." Zandra attempted to place a comforting hand on Lucian, but he snapped his beak at her.

I stepped between them, so the feisty owl couldn't focus his rage on my witch. "I suppose Julie could have snuck into the crowd, stabbed Adam, and crept off when everyone followed Night Mare."

"We have to confront her," Lucian said. "I'll tell her what I know, so she'll have to reveal the truth."

"It doesn't always work like that," Zandra said. "But we'll watch and see if she slips up. And I'll tell the angels to keep an eye on her, too."

Lucian seemed only mildly mollified, but at least he stopped beating his wings and head against the glass.

Cythera and Finn wound up the interview, and after Cythera had sufficiently groveled and curtseyed, they all left the room.

Finn popped his head around the door. "Everything okay? I heard noises."

"Lucian has a theory about Julie," I said.

"I'll be glad to hear it. But later. We're interviewing Simon next. He'll be brought in soon. Lay off the thumping, though, or Cythera will kick you out."

Lucian shuffled away from the glass, grumbling to himself.

"Let's hear what Simon has to say," I said to Lucian. "Maybe he'll know about Julie's plans. They seem close."

He made a gross noise like he was hacking up a vole carcass. "He'd like to get close to her. The guy gives me the serious creeps."

"They're related!" Zandra wrinkled her nose.

"Not by blood, and that's good enough for him. Julie married Simon's brother, but he died six years ago during a skirmish. Simon stepped in to offer a shoulder to cry on, and he never left. And I know what he wants."

"Julie?" I said.

"The power that comes with her rule. Simon loves the finer things in life. And he loves to spend. It broke him when they were forced into witness protection and given a budget to follow. He went from sipping fine wine from gold chalices to plastic cups and bargain basement cartons of plonk. And he's never gotten over the shock of being given an allowance and having to report his spending."

"So, it would benefit Simon if Julie returned to power and took him with her," I said.

"It would. But Julie is smart. She keeps her enemies as close as she can."

"She considers Simon an enemy?" Zandra said.

"Julie considers everyone an enemy. Even her family. And the husband who died in the skirmish, there were rumors she landed the killing blow."

Zandra whistled air through her teeth. "That's darkly impressive."

Finn and Cythera brought Simon into the interview room, and they settled in.

Although Gideon had remained in the room, he seemed content to sit back and listen. Although his eyes were half-closed, he was paying attention. There was a guy who missed nothing, especially when his neck was on the line because a client he was supposed to protect had died.

Cythera ran through the formalities before starting the questioning.

"Describe your relationship with Adam."

Simon's smile was tinged with sadness. "I considered him more like a son than a nephew. After my dear brother died, we became much closer. I'd like to think I gave Adam a steer as he developed. It's what young men need to help find themselves. Without a mentor, they can lose their way."

"Was Adam happy with you taking on the role of his father?" Finn said.

"Why wouldn't he be? Everybody needs a role model."

"Don't be fooled by Simon. He's charming, but it's surface level," Lucian said. "He knows the right words to say, but there's never any sincerity behind them."

Simon sat forward in his seat. "Losing my brother was devastating, and I wanted to make sure Julie and her family were supported."

"He's good at looking like he cares," Zandra said. "I'd believe he meant that if you hadn't told us what he was like."

"He'd get into bed with anyone for the right deal," Lucian said. "It's always about what he can squeeze out of a situation to make his life cushier."

"Were you aware of Adam having problems?" Cythera said to Simon. "People bullying him or trouble at home?"

"Nothing like that. He was a quiet young man. Usually respectful. He found it hard to make friends in the non-magical world and took time to adjust. We had to cut all ties when we went into witness protection. I'm uncertain Adam ever fully adjusted." Simon splayed his fingers on the table and studied them. "I'm not sure any of us did. Adam always asked questions about what life was like in the goblin community. He had some memories but never got to experience life as an adult goblin."

"It was a difficult time for all of you," Cythera said.

"It was. Thank you for acknowledging that. Of course, I'm grateful we're safe, but we gave up a lot. Adam withdrew at times. He spent a lot of time in his thoughts, most likely wondering what his life could have been like if he hadn't seen Razia slay her victim. Those few seconds changed so many lives."

"What do you think happened to him?" Finn said.

"I can't answer that. It was one of those senseless acts that'll never be resolved."

"Make no mistake, we'll resolve it," Cythera said.

Simon shifted in his seat. "I hope you do. This is a stressful situation, and we want it resolved. It's likely we'll have to relocate. It would be impossible to return without Adam. Questions will be asked. And even after all this time, our enemies search for us."

"Maybe that was the plan all along," I said. "The family needed a change, but witness protection wouldn't help them."

Lucian nodded. "It takes something monumental like this to force them to move you again. Keeping witnesses protected isn't cheap."

"Killing Adam to move house is extreme," Zandra said.

"It wouldn't just be a different house. They'd start again. New location, new identities. Maybe this time, they'd choose a disguise that allowed them to use magic. Of course, they'd be limited in what they could use, but some power is better than none. And it would give Julie a foot back into the magic community."

Zandra was quiet for a few seconds. "Simon sounds like he hasn't adjusted well. He keeps coming back to what a struggle it's been for him."

"And if he figured out Adam's murder would mean witness protection would move them, it's another person to keep on the suspect list," I said. "So far, these interviews aren't helping weed anyone out."

"Could you confirm where you were when you learned what happened to Adam?" Cythera said to Simon.

"I'd taken a break from the Reverence Festival. It was fun but busier than I thought it would be. We're so used to spending time on our own that noisy crowds are alarming." He sighed, and a wistful look crossed his face. "It's not like the old days. Back then, we were never left alone. Someone always wanted to speak to us or invite us to a party."

Lucian snort laughed. "Simon loves being the center of attention. He's never happier than when he's in a room full of people who are captivated by his far-fetched stories. Crowds don't bother him. And they never wanted to speak to him. It was always Julie."

"So you left the festival, and where did you go?" Finn said.

"For a walk. I vaguely headed toward the house we've been renting. I knew it was quiet. It's a small no-through road, so you don't get anyone passing by."

"Did you see Julie?" Cythera said.

"No, she left the festival before me. She must have already gone into the house by the time I walked past. Anyway, I did a circuit of the road and then wandered around. I wasn't paying much attention to where I went."

Finn jotted some notes. "What did you do after your walk?"

"I was heading back to the festival when I saw Lucian sweep overhead and go to the Angel Force building. He was screeching like he does when something is wrong. So, I followed him. That's when I heard the terrible news and went to find Adam. I found Julie crouching over his body."

"That's another one without an alibi." Zandra glanced at Lucian. "Could Simon have done it?"

"We shouldn't discount him. But I still think it was Julie," Lucian said. "Simon always complained about their accommodation and how little there was to do in the area."

"His creepy interest in Julie gives him a second motive," I said. "He wanted to remove a problem teen and leave the way clear to target Julie without Adam getting in the way."

"If that's true, Eric could be vulnerable," Zandra said.

"Doubtful. Most days, Eric can barely stand because he gets so wasted. He has no clue what Simon wants from Julie. And even if he did, he wouldn't care. Eric only thinks about himself and how fast he can get to the bottom of a bottle before opening the next one."

"Can you think of anybody who'd want Adam dead?" Cythera said to Simon.

He blew out a breath and stared at the ceiling. "I don't like to speak ill of much-loved family members."

"He's totally going to," Lucian said. "Let's see who he pins it on."

"Someone in the family had an issue with Adam?" Finn said.

"Eric and Adam had been fighting. Those fights escalated, and it sometimes got bloody."

"I wasn't aware there was a problem between them." Gideon dropped his seat back onto all four legs from his corner lounging position.

"When they were in public, they behaved. But the second the doors were closed, they bickered." Simon shrugged. "I suggested to Julie they needed a sterner hand, but since they lost their father, she's indulged them. Not that I blame her. She's suffered so much. But those boys didn't like each other."

Finn made more notes, his pen tapping up and down when he'd finished writing. "You think the fighting escalated to murder?"

"It's a suggestion. Eric's the only one who's been violent toward Adam. And Eric is troubled. He drinks, and he experiments with substances. They've warped his mind."

"It wasn't Eric. If he'd tried to murder Adam, he'd have fallen over his feet and stabbed himself with the knife," Lucian said.

"Surely, the gran would have seen another family member with Adam," Zandra said. "They'll interview her, too, won't they?"

"There's no point. Edith received a head injury she's never recovered from. She used to be a powerful goblin, but since that attack, her memory is gone, and she spends her time in a make-believe world. It's probably best," Lucian said. "She'll remember nothing about Adam dying. We can tell her he's gone to study abroad and she won't question it. Eventually, she'll forget him."

"Bad luck plagues this family," Zandra said.

Lucian ruffled his feathers. "Goblins live brutal lives. Many of them don't get past their one hundredth birthday."

"Thanks for your time, Simon. We'll speak to Eric next," Cythera said. "Or perhaps we should talk to Edith. She must need to rest soon."

"When you speak to her, be kind. It takes little to agitate her," Simon said. "Test the water to see if she's lucid before you ask questions; otherwise, you'll just get babbled at. That can be frustrating."

"Of course. Let's bring in Edith. Then we'll talk to Eric."

"I'll be interested to hear what Eric tells you," Simon said. "I spoke to Adam several times to see if there was anything I could do to help, but he wouldn't open up. He was upset his brother had turned on him. There were jealousy issues going on."

Lucian shuffled on the ledge. "If they fought, it was never when I was around. I spent most of my time shadowing Adam, and other than the usual brotherly banter and rough play, there were no problems between them."

"Everyone around here is telling us half-truths," Zandra said.

"I'm sick of it," Lucian said. "And I won't stay with them. They're liars, and one of them killed Adam. I'd rather sleep in the dirt than spend any more time with that family."

I glanced at Zandra, and she rolled her eyes then nodded.

I patted Lucian's wing. "I have a better idea."

# Chapter 12

## Abrupt endings

"We got nothing from the gran." Finn closed the door and leaned against it.

"Edith wasn't helpful?" Zandra had her feet on the window ledge, while I lounged on her lap, and Lucian perched on the arm of the chair.

"She didn't want to leave the room, so we questioned her in there. She kept talking about the festival then threw a candy at Cythera and called her a feathered freak."

"Don't take anything Edith says personally." Lucian twisted his head in a most unnatural angle, almost flipping it so his skull faced the floor, and tapped the side of his head with a talon.

"Cythera wasn't offended, but we wasted time. And given Edith's poor mental health, even if she saw something, she wouldn't be a credible witness."

"On to Eric?" Zandra said.

"He's being brought in. Although we're having trouble finding him. He was supposed to stay in the visitor area."

Lucian chuckled. "I know where he is."

Finn raised an eyebrow. "Care to share?"

"He's off getting high or drunk. Find the nearest inn, and you'll find Eric."

Finn pushed away from the door with a sigh. "Give me ten minutes."

I discreetly studied Lucian while grooming my tail. He was being helpful by illuminating this less than perfect family unit, but was he doing it to keep the spotlight off himself?

Lucian jumped up and down a few minutes later. "Eric's here! I can smell the booze."

Eric stumbled into the interview room ahead of Finn. He tripped, steadied himself on the table, then chuckled.

"Take a seat." Cythera's tone made her displeasure at his booze-soaked appearance clear.

Eric staggered around the table while Finn brought him a coffee. "Thanks, man. Rough day."

"And it's just getting started," I muttered.

"We'll keep this brief." Cythera perched on the edge of her chair. "For the record, confirm your relationship to Adam Smith."

"Who?" He hiccupped. "Kidding! I was Lorky's older brother. I mean, Adam. Although it's good we don't have to keep the stupid secret around you. You angels are all cool about this, right?"

Zandra winced. "Cythera will hate him for messing around."

"What kind of relationship did you have?" Cythera said to Eric.

"We were bros. I already said." Eric put a hand to his mouth and looked around the room.

"Uh-oh. I know that look. They need to stop the interview and get Eric a bucket." Lucian tapped the glass.

"Are you okay?" Finn leaned closer to Eric. "You don't look so good."

Eric kept his hand over his mouth. "Just need a minute."

"They need to move him, or they'll regret it," Lucian said.

There was a knock on the interview room door. An angel walked in with papers in his hand.

Eric lurched to his feet and shoved past him.

"Stop him!" Cythera ordered. "Don't let the suspect get away."

The angel dropped the papers and ran after Eric.

Eric whirled around and threw a wild punch, one hand on his stomach. He lurched back, turned, and brought up everything he'd drunk all over Bertoli's desk. Then he tripped over a waste container before dropping to the floor.

Cythera walked over and stared down at him. "Put him in a cell to sleep it off. We can't interview him in this disgusting state."

Finn and the other angel dutifully obliged.

"And someone clean this mess up!"

Since the interview with Eric had turned into a comedy scene from a silent movie, we had plenty of time to arrange Lucian's temporary accommodation. He was moving into our basement room.

It didn't take long to complete the task. Owls had few personal belongings. Once he was settled, and I'd introduced him to Mack, we all took a long nap, ate lunch, and spent the afternoon reading or pondering murder.

"This'll do nicely." Lucian was settled on the window ledge, peering at the darkening sky. "And thanks. After what I did to you when we met, you didn't have to fix my accommodation issues. I've slept in plenty of trees when there's been no other option."

"We all make mistakes. Everyone deserves a second chance," I said.

"So long as you don't poop on the floor, you can stay as long as you like," Zandra said.

Lucian squawked. "I'm a clean bird. Never make a mess."

"Dinner is ready," Vorana called from the top of the basement steps. "And Finn's arrived."

"Perfect. I'm starving," I said. "Let's go eat."

I headed up the stairs with Lucian, Zandra behind us.

Finn sat at the table in Vorana's kitchen, helping himself to the freshly made bread rolls and covering one liberally in butter.

He smiled as we entered the kitchen. "I figured we could talk murder while we ate."

"Always a perfect dinner conversation topic." Vorana arched an eyebrow. "Just keep it gore free. I don't want to be put off my food. And don't worry. I won't gossip to anyone. I know how sensitive the case is."

"Even Sorcha?" Zandra said.

"Um... she doesn't count, right? We trust her. She already knows about the goblin in disguise thing, doesn't she?"

Finn wrinkled his nose then nodded. "If word gets back to Cythera any of you know the inside scoop about this case, I'm denying everything. None of the information came from me."

I climbed onto my usual seat next to Sage, and Lucian settled on the back of the chair.

"No Mack for dinner?" Vorana counted the number of seats around the table.

"He's out with Archie. They're having a sleepover at Remus's. Mack's not a bird fan."

"His loss," Lucian grumbled.

"Behave yourself, bird," Sage said. "I know what you did to Juno."

"That was a misunderstanding," I said. "All is forgiven."

"I wouldn't be so easy to forgive if some feathered demon dropped me into the sea and left me to drown. My wheels would rust."

Finn's eyebrows flashed up. "What happened, Juno?"

I slid a glare at Lucian. "A story for another time."

Vorana served plates of beef stew and dumplings, and everyone settled at the table. I had a side of dried herrings, which I shared with Sage and Lucian.

"How's Eric doing?" Zandra said.

"He's sick to his stomach and still hung over. We're keeping him in overnight and interviewing him tomorrow morning," Finn said. "That way, he can't get his hands on more booze and mess himself up again. I don't know how he got so drunk so fast. He was out of the office for half an hour."

"Eric has made getting wasted an art form," Lucian said.

"He's a suspect?" Vorana said.

Lucian shook his head.

"He could be. Once he's sober enough, he'll be questioned." Finn took a bite of dumpling.

"Everyone's gossiping about what happened at the festival. There's even talk about canceling the remaining events out of respect for Adam," Vorana said.

"Don't do that." Lucian leaned close to my plate of herrings, eyeing the largest piece. "Adam talked about coming to Crimson Cove for weeks before we arrived."

"How long have you been in town?" I said.

"Six days. The family wanted a proper vacation. Adam was looking forward to it. It would break his heart to know his murder canceled the festival."

"People thought it would be disrespectful to carry on celebrating," Vorana said. "There's a candle lighting event for him outside the pizza parlor, if any of you want to go. It's just before Skull Dugger does another session of terrifying everyone."

"Adam had a picture of Skull Dugger that he hid in his sock drawer, where he thought no one knew about it. He'd want that old critter to dance around the candles and rattle his bones." Lucian shuffled closer to my plate. "Keep things as they are."

"We should check with the family," Finn said. "If they're fine about it, then we carry on."

"Magic fascinated Adam. All kinds," Lucian said. "He'd barely used any since entering witness protection."

"How do they manage?" Vorana said. "If I don't use my powers regularly, I feel sick."

"Once a year, they were driven to a secure location where they could discharge their magic."

"Only once a year?" Zandra shook her head. "That's rough. And it's not the same as casting an amazing spell or seeing your power in action." She threw a chunk of meat for Lucian before he attacked my delicious herring.

"It must be so hard for all of them." Vorana cut into her food. "It's what we're meant to do."

"They went through tough times, especially to begin with," Lucian said. "But the less they used it, the easier it got. Although not for Adam. He was always reading about magic online, joining forums, and talking about it. He got reprimanded by witness protection because he said too much and people got curious about him."

"Any other suspects?" Vorana said.

"Plenty. We've already interviewed Adam's mother, Julie," Finn said. "She doesn't have an alibi."

"It's more complicated than that," I said. "Lucian has theories."

Vorana and Finn looked to Lucian for more details.

"Julie is a devious, power-hungry queen goblin, intent on getting back to her rightful place. She'll do whatever it takes to achieve that. Including killing her son. Adam was the reason they had to go into witness protection."

"Wow! A queen."

Finn made a shushing noise at Vorana. "Forget you know that."

She zipped her lips. "Got it. What else?"

"Julie comes off as composed but calculating," Finn said. "It's possible she killed Adam hoping to get back what she's lost. I don't think it's as simple as that, though. There's also Simon, Adam's uncle."

"A creepy, smarmy loser, intent on getting into Julie's bed," Lucian said.

I pressed a paw on my herring to stop him from taking the whole thing. "Simon also has no alibi, but I couldn't see a motive until Lucian revealed Simon has the hots for his sister-in-law."

"So, they're both suspects?" Vorana said.

"Julie is my only suspect." Lucian caught more food Zandra threw. "She did it."

"Not necessarily. There's also the drunk brother, who I just couldn't deal with this evening," Finn said. "The office smells of sour booze from where he puked."

"At least he wasn't sick over your desk," I said.

"Every cloud, Juno, every cloud. We tried to interview Adam's Gran, Edith, but it wasn't easy. We pulled her medical records to learn more about her condition. She's been diagnosed with memory loss, possible dementia, and mobility issues. Since she can barely get out of her chair, I don't see how she could have snuck into the crowd, stabbed her grandson, hidden the knife, and then behaved like nothing happened. And why would she?"

"Edith may be away with the fairies, but she's harmless. The same for Eric," Lucian said. "You can rule them out of this."

"You don't think Eric made a drunken mistake?" I said.

"No, and he drinks for a reason," Lucian said. "Eric's magic got warped from being suppressed. Witness protection does what it can to give them an outlet, but he was growing into significant power when they were told they had to stop using. It made him crazy."

"Crazy as in he got tempted to pick up a weapon and stab a member of his family?" Zandra said.

"More having delusional thoughts and seeing things that aren't there," Lucian said. "I often catch him talking to himself."

"Maybe one of those delusions convinced him Adam was unsafe to be around," Vorana said.

"No. He's just a drunk who dabbles in substances that mess with his mind. He's shown no maliciousness toward Adam."

"We'll figure out where Eric was tomorrow," Finn said. "Only then will I consider him harmless and off the list of suspects."

Lucian gulped down another piece of meat Zandra tossed him. "And don't buy the line Simon strung out about Eric and Adam hating each other. After their dad died, the brothers grew closer, rather than farther apart."

"I know a smooth talker when I meet one," Finn said. "Simon charmed Cythera, but I didn't like the guy. He stays a suspect. Especially with his lack of an alibi."

"I'll be back in a sec." Vorana stood from her seat, hurried into the hallway, and returned with a book. "What's the name of the goblin family?"

"Wrunard," Finn said.

Her eyes widened a fraction as she skimmed through the index pages. "I've heard of them. They were huge in goblin royal circles. Superstars."

"Which, of course, you won't share with anyone else," Finn said. "As far as we're all concerned, we have no knowledge the Wrunard family is in Crimson Cove."

"Cross my heart. The information stays between these walls. But they have a long history of violence. Hundreds of years of goblin clans fighting for power." She flicked through a few pages. "They often clash over hidden stashes of stolen treasure, usually gold, with each clan saying it belongs to them."

"They're always fighting," Lucian said. "All the clans loathe each other. They may form temporary alliances so they can beat another clan, but the second they achieve their goal, the gloves are off, and they attack each other. It's how goblins roll. You should focus on Julie. She did this. She wants back in with the goblin elite. Sacrificing her son would be a small price to pay."

"Not a small price, but we're not discounting that theory. We're still gathering evidence," Finn said. "After Gideon gave us more information about the family, we now know we need to speak to Razia Obelong."

"Oh! I know that name, too," Vorana said. "There's a chapter dedicated to her in this book."

"The Wrunards and Obelongs have been going after each other since the clans began," Lucian said.

"Razia must have issues with Adam," Finn said, "since he's the reason she lost everything and was put away."

"She's a suspect, too?" Vorana said.

Finn tore the last of his roll apart. "She is. And we'll get around to her."

"You're scared!" Lucian squawked a sharp laugh. "You don't want to go up against Razia because of her reputation."

He shrugged. "I wouldn't say scared, but I'm sensible. We all know how her clan operates."

"Poisonings, beheadings, making people vanish, and throwing their enemies into deep water while they're wearing concrete boots," Lucian said. "They're nasty."

"Exactly. We handle interactions with Razia carefully," Finn said. "Cythera is determined not to aggravate the goblins."

"You need to poke them a little," I said. "What if Razia is involved with what happened to Adam?"

"Talk to her, but she's not," Lucian said. "A public stabbing isn't her style. If she wanted Adam, she'd have stolen him in the middle of the night. There'd be no clues left, and no trace of his body. This doesn't have Razia's signature attached to it. Focus on Julie."

"We are," Finn said. "And I'm not tackling Razia alone."

I swished my tail. "Of course not. That's why we're here. When do we meet her?"

# Chapter 13

## Sibling rivalry

I was being watched. Although I was still half-asleep, snuggled against Zandra's warm back, there was a prickling down my spine. I opened one eye to discover Lucian staring at me.

"What's up with you?" I wriggled to the edge of the bed.

Lucian blinked. "What do you mean?"

"Have you been watching me the whole time I've been sleeping?" I hopped off the bed and performed a full body stretch before checking my glorious white fur looked perfect. It did.

"I wasn't watching you. I sleep with my eyes open."

"Shush. Not so loud." I checked Zandra hadn't been disturbed. "Have you ever been told that's creepy?"

Lucian ruffled his feathers. "Most people don't notice because they're asleep, too. It's a habit I learned when I joined witness protection. We were taught skills to keep our magic users alive. And before you say anything, I know those skills failed Adam."

"You shouldn't beat yourself up. We all slip."

"Most slips don't result in the person you're supposed to be looking after getting murdered, though, do they? I'll lose my job over this." Lucian hunched on the window ledge.

I gestured my head to the stairs, and he swooped off the ledge and followed me, so we could continue the conversation without waking Zandra.

"Do you enjoy your job?"

"I used to. I never figured I'd be sent on such a long assignment. Normally, we're given someone to watch for a few months to ensure they settle and do nothing dumb, like expose their location." Lucian landed and hopped beside me. "Because the Wrunard family is so high profile, the powers that be decided they needed a full-time watch for life."

"That must have been tough, considering the location they sent you." I was happy to see plenty of dried food in the bowls on the floor. Vorana left it for Sage, who liked to graze during the night. I pointed at the bowls. "Help yourself."

"I'll wait for the tasty treats. Your landlady's food smells divine."

"It's a perk of living here." I eyeballed the food but decided to do the same as Lucian.

I went to the window and looked outside for any exciting rodent events unfolding in the backyard. It was peaceful. That was unfortunate. Dawn was an excellent time to find rodent gifts for Zandra.

Lucian joined me, and we watched the dawn break in silence.

"If you don't mind me saying, you've got interesting power. I sensed it when I grabbed you off the beach. Where does it come from?" Lucian scanned the yard, too.

"Here and there."

"It's old."

"Perhaps."

"Don't want to talk about it, huh?"

"It's not that. My power differs from other familiars." I didn't know Lucian well enough to share my history, but I wasn't surprised he'd sensed something different about me. "I'm interested in the magic Adam carried on him."

"His goblin magic?"

"No, the magic on his bangle. It contained someone else's magic. Know anything about that?"

Lucian swiveled his head and stared at me, unblinking. "I knew I recognized your signature. It was on that bangle. That was your power?"

"Maybe. What do you know about it?"

"Did it belong to you?"

I huffed out a soft breath that steamed the window. "Not the bangle, but the magic is mine."

"How did it get into a piece of jewelry?"

"It's a question I can't answer. Where did Adam get the bangle?"

"I forget. Maybe I will have something to eat." Lucian fluttered to a bowl.

I followed him. "You used to watch Adam. You must have seen where he got it."

Lucian gulped down a huge mouthful of game-flavored mix.

"Did he steal it? Was he gifted it? Did he take it from someone? Find it lying in the street?"

Lucian kept gorging. Anyone would think he didn't want to answer me. "Why do you want to know?"

"Because, as you pointed out, the magic in that bangle is mine. It should never have left me."

Lucian tossed back more dried food. "I'll answer your questions if you answer mine."

I twitched my booping snooter. I was curious about where that bangle had come from, but sharing my story with too many people made me vulnerable.

Lucian paused from eating. "I'm good at keeping secrets. This is the first case I've messed up. Don't worry about me blabbing."

"It's not that. I'll share what I can, but my story involves falling foul of a deceitful goblin who did something to my power. If he ever found out where I was, he'd come for me."

"Goblins are a vengeful lot. I get it. And I'd gain nothing by sharing your story."

I settled next to the food bowl, scooped out a few pieces, and ate them. "I once had a different form, great power, and looked after many. That power attracted jealousy."

"What were you, some kind of queen? I could see you ruling a nation. You've got that haughty way about you."

"You're not far off."

Lucian stopped eating. "No kidding! Should I bow or something?"

"Not tossing me into the sea again is enough to show your servitude."

He click-cackled a laugh. "You got it. Although I see why a goblin wanted to take you down a peg or two."

I gave a delicate sniff. "Perhaps I was full of myself at times. One day, an enemy struck when I least expected it. I was changed into this form, and my magic was taken. At least, most of it. My enemy broke my magic into pieces and hid it. I've recently found some of it and am putting it back together."

"So you can rule again, just like Julie wants to?"

"Perhaps." I wasn't sure what I'd do once my magic was back. Things would have to change, though.

"This goblin put your magic in the bangle Adam stole?"

"Ah! He stole it?"

Lucian tilted his head to one side. "Adam had light fingers. And I sometimes helped him get into places. There was no malice behind it. He was just a high-spirited teen who got bored."

"That high-spirited teen stole something of mine."

"Maybe it dropped into his pocket. I didn't ask questions about where all the stuff came from."

"Do you remember when this bangle conveniently fell into his pocket?" I said.

"I do. He got it from a group of traveling performers who passed through the Wrunard estate."

"Adam stole the bangle before he went into witness protection?"

"Oh, yeah. The stealing stopped when they moved. Nothing much worth stealing where we moved to. And no challenge to take from a non-magical."

"So, this group of performers came through..."

"Yep. They traveled in brightly painted wagons. Adam went into one and found the bangle. It's really yours?"

"Yes. Well, I've never seen the bangle before, but the goblin fiend must have infused my magic into it. I believe my power was too strong for him, so he was unable to conceal it in a single source. Or maybe he did it to make my life difficult and prevent me from returning to obliterate him."

"That's the plan?"

"It's a plan. I'm working on several."

"How many pieces did your power get broken into?"

"You two are up early." Zandra shuffled into the kitchen and headed to the coffeemaker.

"Just checking our visitor is settling in." I caught Lucian's gaze and shook my head, hoping he'd get the hint not to keep talking about my stolen magic.

"Sleep well?" Zandra said to Lucian.

"Like the dead."

"With his eyes open," I muttered.

"Great. I got a message from Finn just as I woke. They're interviewing Eric this morning, and he wanted to know if we'd sit in."

"Absolutely," Lucian said. "Although we get a proper breakfast first, don't we?"

Zandra grinned. "Vorana never allows us to leave the house until we've got full bellies. She'll be down soon. Even when we're in a hurry, she'll have emergency muffins ready to go."

Lucian hopped to the bottom of the stairs in the hallway. "I'll wait here. Make sure she doesn't forget."

Forty-five minutes later, we were fed, groomed, and walking through the doors of Angel Force.

Finn raised a hand when he saw us. "We're using the usual interview room. Eric is waiting for us. Gideon is already in with him."

We settled in to watch the interview. Eric looked asleep, and Gideon sat in a chair, his gaze fixed on nothing. We only had to wait a couple of minutes before Finn and Cythera arrived.

Eric was partly slumped on the table, his stubbled chin resting in one hand. There were bags under his bloodshot eyes, and his hair needed a wash.

Finn gave him a steaming mug of black coffee. "How you feeling?"

"Like I've been sat on. My head is pounding."

Finn also gave him a bottle of water. "Get hydrated, and when you feel able, get food inside you. It'll help soak up the toxins."

Eric grimaced. "Can I have my flask? I'll feel better with a hair of the dog inside me."

"Not happening. Let's get this interview going." Finn ran through the formalities. "Tell us about your relationship with Adam."

"Well, he was my younger brother. Kind of annoying, but we got on fine."

"There was quite an age difference between you, wasn't there?"

"Yeah. That bugged me. He'd always want to hang out with my friends and get in the way."

"Did you ever argue about that?"

Eric scratched his stubbled chin. "Sure. Adam used to sneak around and watch us. Sometimes, I caught him and taught him a lesson."

"You hit him?" Cythera said.

"Nothing serious. Just to let him know to stay out of my way. You know what little brothers are like."

"Let's talk about you for a moment," Cythera said. "Your behavior suggests you have addiction issues."

"No way! I only got ill yesterday because I ate something dodgy. I went to that café where the sick looking vampire works."

"Your illness isn't because of food poisoning. This office still smells of the booze you violently ejected from your mouth," Cythera said.

Eric waved a hand in the air. "I only drink for fun."

"You drank to excess yesterday. And food poisoning doesn't make you attempt to strike an angel."

He shifted his jaw from side to side. "Wouldn't you fight back if you were in my situation? Witness protection was the only option to keep us alive, but it's not much of a life. And why do we have to live in a non-magical town? We can't be ourselves. It gets tough. So, I have a few drinks to make things easier. Sometimes, I go overboard. I'm sorry for punching your angel. Is he okay?"

"He'll be fine. Is that all you use?"

"Sure. Nothing else."

"Is Eric telling the truth?" I asked Lucian. "You've said he dabbles in strange things."

"He'll try anything to get high. But the angels are wasting their time by considering Eric as a suspect. I've already told you he's not involved."

"There's been a suggestion that you had a problem with Adam," Cythera said.

Eric pulled himself upright. "What kind of problem?"

"Your fighting had grown in intensity, and you wanted Adam out of the way."

Eric almost knocked over his coffee as his hands flew up. "Who told you that? He was annoying, but I'd never want him dead. He was one of the few people who knew what I was going through. The only person I could talk to about magic, or rather, our lack of freedom to use it."

"You see. He has no motive." Lucian tapped his beak on the glass.

"I wouldn't say that," Zandra said. "Maybe their fighting had gotten bad. And if Eric got high on something and lost control, he could have lashed out. He made a mistake, and it ended his brother's life."

"Yeah, but that action would have been spur of the moment. Adam's killer snuck into a crowd with a concealed knife and stabbed him when no one was looking," Lucian said. "That's not the behavior of someone high as a kite with rage issues."

"The owl makes a valid point," I said.

"Is that why you're questioning all of us again?" Eric said to Cythera. "You think one of us did it? That makes no sense."

"Can you think of who else would target your brother?" Cythera said.

"In case you hadn't noticed, we're in witness protection. We're not here for fun times and hijinks."

"You believe Razia Obelong could have done this?"

Eric hesitated. "You know about her? We're not supposed to talk about why we're in the system."

Cythera slid a glance at Gideon. "Witness protection has been kind enough to keep us informed."

Gideon lifted one shoulder. "My cases take priority over keeping all the agencies informed. You understand."

"So I can talk about her?" Eric looked at Gideon.

"It's fine. Say what you need to say. But stick to the facts. No one wants to rattle Razia's chains unless absolutely necessary."

Eric tipped back in his seat, his gaze on the ceiling. "It makes sense it was Razia. We know they recently released her. Adam snitched on her when she kidnapped Solomon Minsk and kicked him off the roof. That was why we had to go into witness protection. Razia is back for revenge. And she got it."

"Eric sounds resentful about being in witness protection," Zandra said. "Could that be the reason he went after Adam?"

"He sounds tired. He's no killer. What Adam saw changed their lives," Lucian said. "And not for the better, so there's bound to be resentment."

"Have you asked Razia what she's been up to since she got out?" Eric said.

"We'll be talking to her. We've made contact to establish her alibi," Cythera said. "If she had anything to do with this, we'll ensure she pays."

"Good. Because it wasn't me. As annoying as Adam was, I'd do anything to get my idiot brother back." Eric scratched his fingers through his hair. "Can I have my flask now?"

"One last question," Cythera said. "When we first spoke to you, you couldn't remember where you were when you heard the news about Adam. Are your memories any clearer now you've had time to think?"

"He was probably too drunk to remember," Lucian said. "Eric started early that day."

"It's still hazy." Eric picked at his thumbnail. "I wasn't anywhere near Adam. Isn't that enough?"

"We need someone to corroborate where you were," Finn said. "We don't care what you were doing. We just want to discount you from the suspect list."

Eric said nothing.

"Do I need to remind you of the seriousness of this situation?" Cythera leaned forward, her wings fluttering. "A murder has been committed, and there's a suggestion you had problems with your brother. If you don't want to be a suspect, you need to remember where you were."

Eric continued giving them the silent treatment.

"If you keep concealing where you were, we'll think you're hiding something," Finn said.

"I'm not. It's just... the fun places always get shut down when you official types learn about them."

Finn glanced at Cythera. "What fun place are you talking about?"

"The slime place."

"What's that?"

"You've got one of those amazing places where you get covered in snail goo and are reborn. It's addictive." Eric grinned. "I had no idea you had one in Crimson Cove, but then I heard someone talking about how he was taking people there. I latched onto the party and struck gold."

"Who would ever choose to get covered in snail goo?" Zandra wrinkled her nose. "People are weird."

"Depending on the snails in question, it's a lucrative black-market operation," I said. "They must have some rare giant rainbow snails from the Island of Gwentic. They evolved unusual magical powers because they were separated from the mainland. They excrete their power through their slime. Other magic users learned about the effect the goo has on them, so the snails became targets and are forced to share their excretions."

"Are the snails willing participants in this slime venture?" Finn said to Eric.

"It's hard to know. I mean, they're just snails."

I jumped up and paced the room, my tail thrashing from side to side. "Every creature should be free and happy, not trapped by a deranged individual intent on exploiting their gifts, no matter how gooey."

"Easy, Juno." Zandra reached down to pet me. "Not everyone thinks that way."

"Then they're idiots. No animal abuse, regardless of the size, type, or appearance of the creature. Ever!"

Zandra tugged on her hair. "Agreed. Do the snails suffer during this... goo procedure? I know nothing about snail goo extraction."

"It weakens them," Lucian said. "Eric found a snail goo place about a year ago when he snuck off for a day of misbehavior. He wouldn't stop talking about it, despite Julie threatening to disown him. The last I heard, it got closed because the snails got sick and died."

"Where is this snail place?" Cythera was on her feet, glowering at Eric. "We're not having rare magical creatures manipulated in Crimson Cove."

I clapped her enthusiasm. "Go, Cythera! I had no idea she was an animal lover."

"She's a rule lover," Zandra said. "And Eric just admitted to a huge rule break by revealing there's an illegal business operating under Cythera's nose."

"If I tell you, you'll close it." Eric's bottom lip jutted out. "I planned on going back when I got out of here. It's so relaxing. I could spend all day covered in snails and their goo. Bliss."

"Write down the address."

Eric grumbled to himself as he scribbled the details. "I don't know the exact address. That's as good as it gets. Like I said, I followed a group in. I paid my money, and no one asked questions. I'm sure the snails don't mind. After all, they're only snails. They don't have feelings."

Cythera snatched the address details. "Go be with your family. And don't go looking for any more trouble. This interview is over."

Finn hopped up and hurried Eric away.

Cythera shoved open the door to the room we sat in and thrust the piece of paper at Zandra. "You heard that?"

"Every word."

"You need to check it out."

Zandra was already nodding as she read the information. "We plan to. Nobody exploits an animal on our watch and gets away with it."

Cythera lifted her chin then nodded. "For once, we agree. Now, go!"

# Chapter 14

## Slimy surprises

"If this is true, it's outrageous. Those snails are so rare, they're on the critically endangered list." Barney Hoffman thumped closed the book he'd been looking through. "There are fewer than five hundred left. It's a disgrace people still exploit them."

After learning about Eric's snail exploits, we'd gone into animal control and updated Barney. As always, he'd put the animal's needs first, abandoned his paperwork, and we'd researched the snails.

"Has this happened in Crimson Cove before?" Zandra said. "It seems like a niche business opportunity. Not just anyone could get their hands on these snails if there are so few of them."

Barney's cheeks were tinged red as he placed the book back on the shelf and returned to his seat. "I've heard rumors of a black-market trade in snail goo but never here. It's shocking. I can't think of anyone living in the area who'd do such a thing. Of course, we get a few people negligent with their licenses or who need better training to care for their familiars, but such blatant exploitation is unacceptable."

"We're going to rescue them, right?" I said.

"Of course. As soon as possible. We have Angel Forces' support?" Barney said.

"Cythera is eager to get the place shut," Zandra said. "She's loaned us two angels. Bertoli and Finn are scouting the warehouse area with Lucian and have identified the building they think the operation is running out of."

"It's the old artificial wing factory," I said.

"I know the place. Have they identified who's running the operation?" Barney said.

"They saw a couple of people come and go, but there's probably more. And it's busy. Finn saw two groups go in."

"The money made from this venture won't go to anything legal. And rainbow snail goo is addictive. Once you're hooked on it, you need more, so they have a captive audience who'll pay anything for their next hit."

"We're ready to go shut this place when you are," Zandra said. "You are coming with us?"

Barney looked at his paperwork. "I wish I could, but this report won't wait. I've got the paperwork in order and the warrant to search the warehouse, so you have nothing to worry about from our side. But I don't want you going alone. Oleander's out, but let me see if Glenda's free. She had a busy morning but should be back for lunch." He bustled out of his office and along the corridor to the small break room.

We followed him. My toe beans tingled with excitement and anticipation. Sometimes, animal control work was less than inspiring, but this mission would make a huge difference to the lives of vulnerable creatures, and I was determined it would succeed.

Glenda sat with her red high-heeled boots up on the table, her chair rocked back on two legs. She had three meatball subs in front of her and a large order of salted fries covered in ketchup. "Hey, boss. How's it hanging?"

"We have a snail situation. An illegal venture in town involving the rare rainbow giant snail."

"Shocking!" Glenda broke a meatball in half and tossed a piece to me.

"We're working with Angel Force to close the operation as soon as possible," Barney said. "Could you move around your appointments this afternoon to help?"

Glenda sank her teeth into one sub. "No can do. I've got Mrs. Bronski's estate to check. I'm convinced she's hiding a griffin, but she denies it. There's evidence, though. Droppings and scratch marks on the trees. She's been banned from keeping them after she trained one to eat her neighbor."

"How about after you've checked for the griffin?"

"Then I've got to go to the Lockley site on the opposite side of town. There have been more sightings of an unlicensed flame-throwing dingbat roaming loose. I figured I'd pay them a surprise visit, so they can't conceal evidence. Then I can fine them and take the animal away."

Barney scrubbed his chin. "I've had several complaints about the Lockley site. What about Randal?"

I didn't miss Zandra stiffen at the mention of her almost boyfriend's name.

"Randal's not equipped for the field," I said.

"He's trained, even though he prefers to work with his machines," Barney said. "I wouldn't ask him if this wasn't important. He'll understand."

"We could get him to confirm the site information remotely. He may be able to see how many people are inside the building. He can do amazing things without leaving the office," I said.

"Hmmm... we need more bodies on the ground for this task. What about Sammy? You two work well together, and he's always ready for a mission when you ask nicely." Barney looked around. "Although I've seen little of him. Has he found a new magic user to bond with?"

"He's busy doing other things," I hastily replied. "And he's busy today." I didn't want another rude encounter with Sammy. I'd yet to resolve the last one.

"That only leaves Randal," Barney said. "Zandra, could you check if he's free?"

"I'll do it." I bounded out of the room and dashed to the office Randal had taken over with his extensive bank of machines. "Greetings, Randal!"

He swiveled in his large black office chair and raised a hand, his gaze going past me for a second. He just about hid his disappointment when Zandra didn't appear behind me. "Hey. Haven't seen much of you lately."

"Oh, you know, spending time with my wonderful witch while saving the world, as always."

He chuckled and ran a hand through his floppy hair. "Glad to hear it. Someone needs to. Things are weird out there."

"About that weirdness. We need your help with a situation of the snail kind." I updated him on the illegal snail enterprise.

"Sounds sticky, if you'll pardon the pun. What do you need me for, though? I have zero experience with snails. Most animals, actually. Now, if there were a tech problem to solve, I'm your go-to guy."

"And you're top of the class with all tech, but we need you in the field."

Randal pulled off his glasses and cleaned them on his sweater. "Oh! I assumed you wanted me to run a scan of the site."

"That, too. Any information we can get before we go in is welcome. But no one else is free to help, and I don't want Zandra going in alone. Although we'll have two angels as backup and a feisty owl, they know nothing about the snails."

"Um... I don't know much about snails, either. But I don't want Zandra put at risk." Randal turned his seat to the bank of screens. "Let's start with the site. I'll get all the information I can. That could be enough to set you up. Maybe there's nobody home, so you and Zandra can sneak in, grab the snails, and get out."

I didn't continue the debate as Randal focused on his machines. I trotted back to the others, told them what he was doing, and then returned to sit by his side, watching as he weaved his tech magic.

Randal blew out a breath and tipped back in his seat. "There are a lot of people in that place. And I'm getting weird pulses of energy in a concentrated form. Huge globs of power."

"That must be the snails," I said. "Their slime is powerful. Whoever is running this could be harvesting the slime and storing it to use later."

"That could be it. I reckon there are at least thirty people in the main room."

"Then we need you with us," I said. "Bring your magical tech gadgets in case things get nasty and you need to zap anyone."

Randal rapid-tapped his fingers on the desk. "I could do that. It looks risky."

"Risk comes with the territory when you're dealing with misbehaving animals or people exploiting them. We aren't letting that stop us, though, are we?"

"Give me five minutes, and I'll meet you out front." He shoved away from his desk and strode out of the room.

"Everything good?" Zandra said as I rejoined her and Barney in his office.

"Randal is on board. He's gathering his equipment."

Zandra muttered something under her breath.

"Don't be down on him. Your second date will go much more smoothly. And just think, you'll have snail stories to share."

"Let's not get into that," she muttered. "Barney, as soon as we have any news, I'll let you know."

"You won't let the snails down. They'll need careful handling, though, and specific containment.

While you're gone, I'll get tanks set up so they have somewhere quiet to rest after their ordeal."

While we waited for Randal, Zandra paced the corridor. I wanted to reassure her everything would turn out fine between them, but the way they acted around each other, I was having doubts.

Romance could be tricky, but if people simply sat down and talked things through, none of these misunderstandings would happen. Everyone would get their happily ever afters.

I needed to take a leaf out of my own book and speak to Sammy about why he was running around with a strange female and ignoring me. I'd been evoking unpleasant scenarios in my head that did me no good.

But I trusted Sammy. He'd never betray me. As soon as we'd dealt with this snail investigation, I'd get together with him, and we'd sort things out. Even if he no longer wanted to be with me, at least I'd know and could move on.

Randal emerged from a storeroom. He wore an army style hat, a camera perched on the top. Strapped around his waist was a utility belt stuffed with gadgets.

He looked at me and shrugged. "You never know what you're dealing with when you go into these illegal operations."

"Of course. A tool for every takedown. This way." I trotted along the corridor, and we met Zandra at the entrance.

She nodded at Randal, her gaze moving over the equipment, but she didn't comment. "We can go in my van."

We climbed in after I'd allowed Randal to remove my comfy bed from the passenger seat and settle himself on it. I hopped onto his lap, not happy his utility belt stopped me from finding a comfortable position to make biscuits on his stomach.

"Any idea how many people in the building are customers?" Zandra said after Randal had given her a briefing on the numbers we'd be dealing with.

"It was impossible to tell from the scan," Randal said. "They were all spaced out evenly, though, with two smaller groups standing close by. Do we go straight in or watch first to see what's going on?"

"So long as there is no one outside to cause problems, I vote for going in straightaway. The longer we watch, the more there's a risk they'll figure out we're onto them."

"We've got angel backup, right?"

"Finn and Bertoli have been at the scene since it was identified, along with Lucian, the dead goblin's owl guardian. But they've not seen much," Zandra said. "Whoever is behind this is keeping it low-key. Maybe it's an invitation-only place."

"Eric tagged onto the back of a group and got inside with no trouble. They can't have great security if he did that. Or if it's invite-only, they don't bother checking the invites," I said.

"Which is a bonus for us," Zandra said.

"We could try that approach," Randal said. "Sneak in and look around."

Zandra glanced at his utility belt. "It would be hard for you to sneak in anywhere unnoticed. And what's with the hat?"

He blushed. "I wanted to try my latest thermic magic wave camera. I figured we may need a live recording, in case things get damaged or they destroy the site. Using this means we'll have evidence to present in court."

"Good thinking," I said. "Maybe we should all wear camera hats. Is it heavy? It looks heavy. Can you make one to fit me?"

Zandra wrinkled her nose. "I'm happy to use my eyes. But you use whatever you need to get the job done."

An awkward silence descended as we headed to the warehouse district. But at least they were keeping things professional.

Zandra pulled up before we reached the old artificial wing factory, and we sat quietly for a moment.

"There's no one around," she said. "You two ready?"

"Where are the angels and the owl?" Randal peered through the windscreen.

"On top of the building. I spotted wings a moment ago," I said. "They've seen us. If there were any problems, they'd let us know."

Randal adjusted his helmet and blew out a breath. "Let's go."

I hopped off his lap and climbed out of the van then jumped onto Zandra's shoulder. This position gave me an excellent viewpoint, so I could spot danger coming toward my wonderful witch and obliterate it before it touched her.

Until recently, the notorious Shadow gang had monopolized the warehouse district. No one had operated out of this site without their say-so. But since the gang got put away, it seemed other equally unpleasant individuals were taking advantage of its remote location.

"This could happen fast." Zandra stopped by the external door. "Don't be afraid to take down anyone who runs. We need to know who's behind this. But most importantly, we must protect those snails."

"Got it." Randal tapped his helmet.

"Juno, focus on locating the snails. I'll work with Randal to grab the people in charge."

I booped her cheek then crouched as she yanked open the door.

There was no one on the other side, but a pungent smell hit me as we entered the quiet, concrete floored corridor.

"It smells like a spa," Randal whispered. "Is that incense?"

"Could be," Zandra said. "Let's keep going."

We headed along the corridor, trying a couple of doors along the way. They were locked. We got to the third door on the right, and the incense smell intensified. There were also quiet voices.

"This is it," Zandra said. "Ready?"

We nodded.

She shoved open the door. A sweet-faced, red-haired receptionist greeted us with a smile.

"Welcome to Blissful Sanctuary. Are you the Magdelene party?"

"We're the party from animal control." Zandra flashed her credentials. "We've had reports rare snails are being exploited on this site."

The receptionist's eyes widened a fraction, but her smile remained in place. "There's been a mistake. Everyone is here freely. Customers and... snails."

"You won't mind if we look around, then?"

I lifted my booping snooter, attempting to see past the gauzy curtain separating the small reception area from the rest of the room.

"Be our guests. And if you'd like a treatment, you're welcome. On the house, of course, since you're from animal control." Her smile looked increasingly fake, but it didn't waver, although her knuckles were white as she gripped the table.

Zandra turned and pushed past the curtain, Randal behind her.

"What the... Are they being eaten?" Randal peered over Zandra's shoulder.

She choked out a noise of surprise. "Whatever those snails are doing to those people, it can't be good."

Massage beds were set in two rows in the large, open-plan room. Each bed contained one person, and giant rainbow snails covered their heads. And when I say giant, I mean each snail was the size of a fully grown yeti's hand. I couldn't see an inch of skin as the snails slowly slid over the people's faces and necks, leaving behind a sparkly trail of goo.

An alarm blasted, making us jump. Footsteps pounded away from us, and a glance at the desk behind me showed the receptionist had done a runner. She must have hit the alarm before escaping.

More people left through doors at the back of the room, feet scuffling and voices muffled as they abandoned the snail ship.

"Get them!" Zandra was off and running.

We slammed through the first door into a dark room with glowing tanks set along one wall. The tanks were full of snail slime, along with a few sad-looking snails with chains wrapped around them. They were being guarded by two shady-looking guys with skinheads, big fists, and scowls.

"Step away from the snails," Zandra said. "We're from animal control."

The tallest of the two skinheads lunged at Randal. He grabbed him by the front of his shirt and yanked him off his feet.

The other guy went for Zandra. I blasted a knockback spell that slammed into his shoulder, but he was strong, and after a brief stumble and a growl, kept coming for us.

"You good?" Zandra yelled to Randal.

"Having a blast. You?" He struggled with the other guy, his hands going to his belt as his helmet was shaken off and clattered to the floor.

"Couldn't be better." Zandra whacked her attacker with a couple more spells, but they only slowed him.

"He's unnaturally resilient to magic," I muttered.

"It's a bonus of the goo." The guy circled us, fingers flexing and teeth bared. "It makes you stronger and faster if you drink it."

I shuddered. "You need to get a better taste in beverages. Have you tried green tea with honey?"

A zap of magic shot through the air as Randal whacked his attacker with one of his fancy bits of tech.

The guy snarled, lifted Randal off his feet, and dumped him into a tank of snail slime then held him under as they tussled.

Zandra thumped our attacker with another spell before racing over to help Randal.

The guy holding Randal under lifted a hand and shot out a jagged lightning bolt.

I raised a deflection spell, and the magic ricocheted off it, but it was insanely strong and almost got through my defenses.

"Let's get out of here, Bo," the guy we'd been battling snarled.

"But the snails!"

"Not worth it. You can stay if you like. I'm outta here." He turned and raced off.

"Should I go after him?" I said.

"No. Finn and Bertoli will get him once he's outside. We need to help Randal." Zandra slammed spells into the other skinhead, and after a few seconds of fighting back, he dropped Randal, blasted a hole in the wall, and shot through it at inhuman speed.

I balanced on Zandra's shoulder as she reached into the tank of slime and yanked Randal out.

He wobbled on his feet as sparkling goo dripped off him. "Wow! That was amazing."

"I thought you were drowning." Zandra wiped slime off his face and flicked it onto the floor. "You hurt?"

"It was so weird. I couldn't breathe, but I didn't care. I felt so calm. You should try it." Randal grabbed a handful of slime and wiped it onto Zandra's face.

"Eugh! Gross. What's the matter with you?" She rubbed her sleeve across her face to remove the slime.

"Don't you feel good? It makes you feel that everything is right with the world. Juno, you should try some."

I curled against Zandra's neck to avoid being coated in goo. "Hard pass. We need to hose you down, or you'll keep spreading the goo love."

"I know exactly what I need." Randal caught hold of Zandra's shoulders and planted a huge, gooey kiss on her lips.

# Chapter 15

## P.S. I slimed you

Zandra shoved Randal away. "Why do that?"

"Because I love you."

"You what?" Her mouth dropped open.

He reached for her hand. "I've adored you ever since we met. Now, there's nothing stopping me from telling you."

"There's everything stopping you." Zandra shook her head, her cheeks pink with embarrassment. "It's the slime talking. Zip it until you've got your head on straight."

"The slime stopped me from being afraid. It's amazing stuff. Have more."

Zandra shoved Randal's hand away as he tried to coat her with more goo.

I gently hissed a warning at Randal. "As charming as this is, your declarations of affection for my wonderful witch have to wait. There are people and snails who need our help."

"They won't feel like they need help if they're covered in the same stuff as me." Randal gazed at Zandra. "We could share a goo bath."

"Go find a hose to wash yourself down. Let's go see how the others are doing." She turned and stalked away.

"Don't be too hard on Randal," I said. "He's a simple guy when it comes to matters of the heart."

"I'm not. And I know the goo has turned him moron. But did he have to do that? Where does that goo excrete from, anyway? No! Don't answer. I don't want to know. I got some in my mouth."

"It comes from their glands." I chuckled. "And it was a sweet declaration, even though it was slime-tinged."

"All I'm thinking about right now is the goo." Although she glanced back at Randal and half-smiled.

We stopped by the first table, and Zandra gingerly picked the snails off the face of a white-haired woman and placed them on a tray beside the massage table.

"I don't recognize her." I peered at the older lady. "She must be a visitor."

"Do you think she came to Crimson Cove for this goo treatment?" Zandra also inspected the woman as she checked her pulse.

"Hold on a moment." I jumped onto the woman's chest. "This can't be right."

"What are you sensing?"

I looked up at Zandra. "She doesn't have magic."

Her eyebrows bounced up. "She must! This kind of power could kill a non-magical."

"We'd better check the others and get those snails removed fast."

We quickly removed the rest of the snails. Well, Zandra removed the snails while I stayed clear of the goo. That stuff would be almost impossible to get out of my fur.

"I know this guy! It's the coach guy, Gus." I stared at Gus's slimy face. "We know for certain he has no magic."

Gus opened his eyes and stretched. "Oh! It's you two. We keep bumping into each other. You work here?"

"We definitely don't," Zandra said. "What are you doing covered in snails?"

He grinned. "Blame my wonderful old ladies for getting me into this stuff. They heard about a new snail serum treatment and convinced me to come with them for some gooey delight. I was hesitant, especially when those huge snails were presented to me, but as soon as the first one sat on my face and oozed, all my cares washed away. I became blissed out."

"He shouldn't even be breathing," I whispered in Zandra's ear.

She nodded. "Where did your ladies hear about this place?"

"I'm not sure." Gus sat up. "I don't have a single ache and pain. Those snails are miracle workers. I should have tried this years ago."

As Gus extolled the virtues of the magical snails and their slime, I slid off Zandra's shoulder. It should be impossible for anyone in the non-magical world to hear about the unique properties of these snails. Was someone leaking information into the non-magical community? And if they were, were they targeting Crimson Cove?

"You sure you feel okay?" Zandra said to Gus. "I hear some of these beauty treatments can be intense. Leave you feeling dizzy or light-headed. You have any odd side-effects?"

"I feel like a new man. Rita, how you doing?"

The old lady with the purple rinse on the table next to him lifted her hand and smiled. "Like I want to go dancing all night. Those snails were marvelous."

"I found a hose and buckets." Randal wandered in, dripping wet, but still gazing at Zandra with devotion in his eyes. "Who needs washing down?"

"Oooh! Is this part of the treatment?" Rita sat up. "Should I take my clothes off? Will you rub me down with a salt scrub before hosing me?"

"Um..." Randal's expression grew panicked. "All I got is a hose and water."

"I didn't realize being hosed down was part of the treatment," Gus said.

"You don't want to walk around with a slimy face all day, do you?" Zandra said.

"This is like no spa I've ever been to." Rita was already shrugging off her dress to reveal a satin slip and a robust bra. "It's basic but does the job. I'll put up a five-star recommendation."

While Zandra and Randal helped de-slime everyone, I settled next to a tray of snails and dabbed a paw on top of a rainbow shell. The connection was instant, and a deep wave of sadness pulsed through me.

"I'm so sorry you've been trapped and exploited," I whispered. "Nothing bad will happen to you from now on. We're getting you out of here."

The connection pulsed stronger and warmed my toe beans.

"Thank you. We've been so scared. Several of us died. They were not kind." The snail's voice was a wobbly whisper in my head.

"I'm sorry for your loss. We're with animal control, and whatever you need, we'll be here for you. We'll get you well and find you a safe home where you'll never be exploited again. You have my paw-felt word."

"Look at that! The adorable kitty is playing with the snails," Rita said.

I pretended I hadn't heard as I slowly removed my paw from the shell and broke the connection. I didn't want the slimy old ladies to realize I was communicating with these incredible creatures and get curious.

Zandra was in one corner, discreetly typing a message on her mobile snow globe. She must be letting Barney know the situation. When she was done, she collected me, settling me back on her shoulder, so I missed none of the conversations, even though I couldn't contribute.

"It's Gus, isn't it?" she said to the coach guy.

"Well remembered." He beamed at her. "If you don't work here, are you waiting for a treatment?"

"No. Is this your first time using this facility?"

"We've been in town for a few days and come every day. My ladies insisted we visit the spa as soon as we arrived."

"Did you bring everyone here? We're interested in one guy in particular, Eric Smith."

"I know Eric! He's with one of my new families. Yes, he's been here every day. Comes in early and stays until closing. Snuck in the first time, but I was happy to have him join us. He's a diehard slime convert."

"Every day?"

"Never misses his slot. Even if I don't get a treatment, I still come with my ladies because they like someone to hold their hands and reassure them. Sweet old things. Eric would talk to them sometimes. He even snuck Rita a sip from his flask. She hasn't had anything stronger than a sweet sherry in years, so she was happy."

"What about the morning Night Mare showed up in town?"

"The guy wearing the scary horse costume, you mean?" Gus whistled out a breath. "I almost had to get my heart restarted after meeting him the first time. I don't know who does the special effects around here, but, boy oh boy, are they talented."

Zandra shrugged. "Yeah. They're amazing. That day, did you see Eric here?"

"Yes. We had the tables next to each other and chatted before our treatments started," Gus said. "He's a curious guy. Talks a lot about magical fantasy games. It's not my thing, but I was happy to indulge him. He had to leave mid-treatment when he got an urgent message."

I leaned against Zandra's head. With Eric's alibi confirmed, we could finally rule out a suspect in Adam's murder.

"What do you want with Eric? He's not in any trouble, is he?" Gus said.

"No. I'm into fantasy games, too. Just looking for a role playing buddy."

Gus's smile flickered as if he sensed the lie. "He's always happy to talk about them. I can put you two together if you like. Or if you wait around long enough, he'll stop by. He never misses his slime slot."

"Another time. Mind if I talk to your ladies? See if they know anything more about this place."

"Um... sure. What do you need to know, though? Thinking of starting your own boutique? If so, I recommend more ambiance. It's basic here. I'd never pick a warehouse for such a serene experience."

"Nothing like that. I'm curious about where they heard about the snails. This treatment isn't your average twenty-minute facial."

He chuckled. "It's one of a kind. They'll help if they can. Rita, you were the first to tell me about the goo. Zandra wants a word." Gus beckoned her to join us.

Rita wandered over, her face pink from having just been hosed down. "What can I help you with, dear?"

Gus patted her arm. "Where did you hear about this snail spa?"

"Online. Some fancy site promoting alternative treatments. The robots must have seen me researching wrinkle erasers and thought I'd be interested." Rita patted her damp skin. "You can't fight time, though."

"You look amazing," Gus said. "The slime has taken years off you."

Rita smiled. "You old charmer."

"Do you remember the website's name?" Zandra said.

"Can't say I do. It was one of those funny pop-up thingies. At first, I thought it sounded disgusting, but the more I read about the benefits of snail slime, the more interested I became. This place was recommended at the bottom of the article."

I kept my expression neutral as my thoughts whirled. There was no doubt about it. Someone was targeting Crimson Cove to ensure non-magicals kept invading our little haven and messing with our magic. But why?

"Were there any names in the article about who runs this place?" Zandra said.

Rita shook her head. "Nothing like that. I wondered if it was a joke until we visited. I'll definitely come again."

"It might be a while before you can get an appointment. They're closing to renovate," Zandra said.

"Oh! That's a shame. Still, the place could do with a freshen-up. We'll have to watch out for the reopening. They might do special offers. It's not cheap getting covered in slime."

"But worth every penny. Let's get you back to your accommodation, ladies." Gus slid off the bed and stood. "We can talk about our plans for tomorrow. I'm thinking a walk and a tour of the cafes."

His ladies gathered around, all dripping wet but goo-free. After toilet breaks, collecting purses, and saying goodbye, they left.

A few minutes after Gus ferried his ladies out of the warehouse, Barney showed up.

He glanced around, disgust on his face. "Good work! I've got tanks in the back of the van. We can transport the snails in them."

Finn, Bertoli, and Lucian flew down and joined us by the entrance.

"Did you catch the guys who escaped? There were two of them," Zandra said.

"Got them. Although they fought back. I think I cracked a rib." Finn had a hand clasped against his right side.

"The goo super charged them," I said. "It has all kinds of interesting side-effects. It seems to make people lose their inhibitions."

Zandra's glower warned me not to reveal the kiss from Randal. "We'll take the snails back and process them. See if we can get any useful information."

"How are they doing?" Barney said. "When you sent the message, I knew we had no time to waste in getting them help."

"I've spoken to them," I said. "They're glad to be free."

"That's good. That's good." Barney scrubbed at his chin.

"Something wrong?" Zandra lifted the first batch of snails and carried them to the van.

Barney followed her. "While you've been dealing with this, I received half a dozen new reports of holes dug around town and half-eaten animal corpses laid beside them."

I'd been so involved in the snail rescue and Adam's murder, I'd forgotten our mission to discover who was snacking on critters around Crimson Cove.

"That's odd." Zandra tucked the snails into the van and ensured the tank was secure so it wouldn't slide around. "The previous holes were always made after dark."

"Whoever is doing this is growing bolder," Barney said. "I know you've got your hands full with this investigation, but when you get a minute, keep looking into it. I don't want residents unsettled by finding more bodies."

"Of course. We'll get on it as soon as we can," Zandra said.

Barney nodded. "I can always count on you and Juno. Now, let's get these snails safe."

An hour later, and after a few slimy encounters, the snails were safely stored in the back room at animal control. Several were weak and had needed intense amounts of healing magic, but they'd all pull through and make a full recovery.

I passed Randal's office and was surprised to see the door shut. Well, perhaps I wasn't surprised. He must be embarrassed after what happened at the spa. The slimy kiss hadn't been mentioned again.

I discovered Zandra putting things in her locker.

She glanced over her shoulder and smiled at me. "How about we grab some food at Sorcha's?"

"Sounds perfect. And then we can talk about Randal and that kiss."

Zandra slammed the locker door shut. "Or not. I don't want to think about work."

"Randal is more than work. He said he loved you."

"He was also spaced out on snail slime."

"The slime lowers inhibitions and reveals truths."

"And you know that how?"

"I've been talking to the snails."

"Less talking, more focusing on food. I'm too whacked to think about anything as complicated as a relationship."

It had been a busy day, so I didn't press my witch as we left animal control. She said goodbye to the others, although she didn't speak to Randal, and we headed outside.

"Fish for you?" Zandra said.

"Always." I paused and lifted my booping snooter. "Do you feel that?"

"I only feel my stomach growling. What are you sensing?"

I flattened to the ground. There was a faint rumble under my paws. "Something is coming. Something big."

"A coach?"

I twitched my tail. "Something much bigger than a coach."

# Chapter 16

## The bloody queen

A line of black, silver-horned stallions appeared at the end of the street, thundering toward us on enormous, shiny hooves. They all wore a green and gold star emblem on their tunics. Razia Obelong sat astride the largest stallion.

"It's a goblin horde!" Zandra said.

"And the goblin leading them is Razia." Although I wasn't a goblin fan, Razia made an impressive entrance. She sat tall, her black hair streaming behind her, along with a long, emblazoned cape. Her pale green neck and face were the only parts of her visible, her lean, muscular body encased in a form-fitting black body suit.

Zandra took a step back. "This can't be good. We need to tell Angel Force they're here. You watch them. I'll go grab the angels." She turned and sprinted away.

There were several groups of non-magicals lingering, all staring openmouthed at the arriving goblins. Their fragile brains must be scrambling as magic flickered off the horde in hot waves.

Under normal circumstances, it would be impossible for non-magicals to see the goblins, but with the way magic was misbehaving in Crimson Cove, I was certain some saw the truth, and it was green-tinged and covered in weapons.

Store owners peered out of their windows but quickly disappeared when they saw the new arrivals. A goblin horde was never a welcome sight.

I moved into the middle of the street, puffed my fur, and crackled magic around me.

Razia raised a hand, and her goblins slowed. She trotted forward, flanked by two burly female warriors, and peered down at me. "You're our greeting party?"

"Since your arrival was unexpected, I'll have to do." I briefly bowed my head to acknowledge her power. "Greetings. I'm Juno. Familiar to the powerful Crypt witch, Zandra Crypt."

Razia pursed her lips. "A Crypt witch familiar. Interesting. I didn't know they operated out this way."

"They base themselves in Willow Tree Falls, but my witch lives here."

"You're expanding the demon prison? Looking for a new base?"

"No, I keep my witch away from demons. All trouble, actually. I hope that's not what you're here to cause."

"If it is, do you plan on stopping me?"

Razia's horde chuckled.

"Never underestimate any magical creature you encounter, no matter its size." I exuded more power, causing her stallion to step back and whinny its concern.

"Calm yourself, Juno. I'm not here because I have issue with anyone in Crimson Cove." Her gaze lifted. "Here they come. I knew the angels wouldn't be far away when they learned of my arrival."

Cythera, Finn, and Bertoli thudded down on either side of me, landing with their fists on the ground and their wings splayed. It was a risk, given we were being watched by non-magicals, but they couldn't leave the goblins unattended for any longer than necessary.

Lucian arrived a few seconds later, landing with a thunk and fluttering his wings. He death-stared Razia, but she barely acknowledged him.

Zandra appeared in a blast of magic. She swiftly scooped me up and settled me on her shoulder, her warm hand pressed against my side. "Everything good? No trouble?"

"We were just getting to know each other," I said.

"This must be the witch whose virtues you extol," Razia said. "It's a pleasure to meet you, Zandra Crypt. You have a wise and loyal familiar."

"I agree. She's amazing." Zandra's eyes were narrowed as she assessed Razia.

"And who else do we have here?" Razia checked out the angels.

Cythera stepped forward. "Cythera. I'm in charge of the local branch of Angel Force. This is Finn and Bertoli."

"I'm Lucian. Owl guardian to Adam Smith." Lucian hopped forward, clacking his beak, looking like he wanted to take a chunk out of Razia.

I leaped down next to him and rested a paw on his side. "There's a time and place for conflict. Don't pick a fight in front of all these goblins, or the town will be turned to ash."

He grumbled and sniped but didn't attempt any eye gouging or biting. "I'll make her sorry."

Razia threw her leg over the giant stallion and slid off, her weapons jangling as she walked. "I received your messages."

"You did? I had no response." Cythera's wing fluttering revealed her nerves, but she stood firm as Razia stopped a few inches from her, leaning into her personal space.

"My retinue received them. We cut through the red tape and came to the source, rather than spending days in negotiation. Is there somewhere private we can discuss this matter?" Razia glanced around, her expression growing curious. "Are the locals without magic?"

"They're just visitors. Follow me." Cythera led the way to the main doors of Angel Force.

Razia's goblins followed and surrounded the building on their stallions. She stopped by one of her burly guards and muttered in her ear. The guard nodded and stationed herself by the door, her axe drawn.

"That's unnecessary. You're safe here," Cythera said.

"I'm aware of that. My guards ensure no harm comes to me. They stay. We don't want to be disturbed while we resolve this misunderstanding, do we?"

Cythera studied the goblins for several seconds. "I'll have my angels wait with them."

Razia nodded. "As you wish."

After much ruffling of feathers and stamping of hooves, the goblin guards were in place, and the angels were with them, not looking happy at being left with a bunch of potentially marauding goblins if this meeting went sideways.

Cythera took Razia into her office and went to close the door on me, Zandra, and Lucian.

Zandra stuck her foot in the gap. "This meeting involves us."

Cythera hissed out a breath. "How?"

"I need to be involved," Lucian said. "I must know what that deceitful goblin tells you so I can reveal her lies."

She regarded Lucian with alarm. "I thought Juno needed to act as a communicator between us? I just heard you."

"Oh, we made some tweaks to Lucian's magic. It's still unreliable, though. We all need to be in there. Just in case..." I hadn't factored in Cythera would remember the tiny white lie told so we could remain involved in this investigation.

"In case I need to be deceived again?" Cythera attempted to shut the door, but Zandra leaned against it.

Lucian shrieked, wriggled through the gap, and entered the office.

Cythera turned to reprimand him, but Zandra grabbed her arm.

"Accept help. We're going nowhere, and you know we can be useful. Someone needs to be in this meeting to keep Lucian calm. The owl gets vicious when he doesn't get what he wants. And he has issues with Razia. If he attacks, you need someone who knows how to handle a feisty owl."

"I might attack at any second." Lucian played up to his role of big, bad owl, stomping around the office and knocking things over with his wings.

"This is a sensitive situation," Cythera said.

"Which is why you need our support." I stood on her white-booted foot.

She sighed and shuffled back. "If you must. But observe only. This requires a professional touch."

"We're always professional," I said. "Shall we? We don't want to keep Razia waiting. I expect she has an evening of slaying planned."

After a few disgruntled huffs, Cythera let us in. She turned and froze. Razia had taken the seat behind the desk and was looking around as if she owned the place. She'd also discovered Cythera's cookie tin and was rifling through the contents.

When she noticed us watching, she licked chocolate off her fingers, set down the tin, and sat forward in the seat. "You believe I have something to do with a young goblin's death. Explain your reasoning."

Finn eased into the room behind us and nudged past Zandra with Gideon and Bertoli on his heels. Bertoli stopped, smiled, and tickled me under the chin.

Cythera didn't seem to know whether to stand or sit, but in the end, she remained upright, her shoulders back, pretending not to care that her favorite chair was occupied and her cookies had been molested. "As you know, Adam Smith recently died."

"Such a plain name for such a noble creature." Razia smirked.

"We know the true name of the Smith family."

"Of course you do." Razia tipped her head back then nodded. "Gideon. Always unpleasant to see you."

He displayed no emotion as he stood beside Finn. "Likewise."

Razia inspected a chocolate chip cookie then threw it at Lucian.

He ignored it and snapped his beak at her.

She chuckled, the sound a deep rumble in her muscled chest. "It's never a happy day when a young goblin dies. Death on the battle field would be mourned, but then celebrated for his worthy sacrifice. But this... slain by an unknown hand at a street party! The family must be mortified. What a blow to their already crumbling reputation."

"You're not happy a rival clan member is dead?" Cythera said.

"Losing someone so young will always be mourned, and I take no pleasure in Prince Lork, excuse me, Adam's, death. I'm sure his family won't want to see me—"

"You can't see them. They wouldn't survive the encounter," Gideon said.

Razia barked a laugh. "True. Perhaps. Although that would mean I must hold old grudges. Am I really that bitter?" She waved a hand as if dismissing any comments. "If you could pass on my sympathies and let them know I buried a moon stone in his honor, I'd appreciate it."

Cythera nodded. "Tell me about your involvement with the Wrunard family."

Razia leaned back and sighed. "How long have you got?"

"As long as it takes. You weren't friends?"

"There's a twisted history of struggles between the clans. To be truthful, despite looking back over the records, I'm uncertain why it started. But the hatred for them is buried deep in our psyche. We despise each other."

"It started because of gold greed," Lucian said. "That's what you goblins are obsessed with."

"Most likely, Guardian of Adam. It is our most precious resource. Without gold, a goblin is nothing. Whatever reason the feuding began, the fighting has always been intense between us." Razia removed an axe from her back strap and set it down. "There is a continual dispute over the Shining Pines mine. My ancestors claim it as theirs, but the Wrunards believe they have the right to mine it."

"So an encounter with any member of the Wrunard family wouldn't be welcome," Cythera said.

"I avoid them when I can and deal with them when I must." Razia slid lower in the seat. "But I tire of fighting."

"Goblins never tire of fighting," Lucian said. "You fight for fun."

She scraped something from under a fingernail and flicked it on the floor. "It's true, we get pleasure out of the bloodlust, but you must be aware of the alliance being formed."

"An alliance! That would never happen. I would know if the family planned a truce with you." Lucian fluffed his feathers and stomped several times.

"You're displaying your lack of skills, little one." Razia glanced at Gideon. "It's time to retire this creature from service. He misses too much."

Gideon grumbled under his breath, while Lucian sank to the ground in a heap of feathery defeat.

"Tell us about this alliance," I said. "How were you able to communicate with the Wrunard family when they were in witness protection?"

"Ah, you found me out." Razia smiled slowly. "I had time to think when I was behind bars. I was there for almost five years before the injustice was undone, and I figured out war isn't always the answer. The families could be stronger if they united."

"For how long?" Zandra said. "Clans only unite when they have a common enemy to defeat."

"That's what has happened in the past. I want things to be different."

"Would you compromise over sharing the gold in the Shining Pines mine?" Lucian said.

"That mine is a tiny part of the issue," Razia said. "There are bigger battles coming, and I need other clans to stand beside me so I can be assured success."

"You're facing a new rival?" Cythera said.

"Not from the goblin community, but something is coming for us. We won't survive if we don't stand together."

I swiveled my ears. "Who wants to attack you?" It must be a mighty enemy if the goblins were prepared to work together.

"The origin of this new threat isn't important. The resources I need to fight them off and defeat them is what matters. You should ask around in the goblin community. I've been in talks with dozens of clans, and we're forming an enormous army to ensure survival."

"And you've included the Wrunard family, even though they're in witness protection?" Cythera said. "They can only offer limited help in their current circumstances."

"I need every goblin I can get. And I didn't reach out to them. A member of the family approached me when they learned of the issues we were facing."

A sigh slid from Gideon's lips. "What's the point of us putting a family in witness protection when they speak directly to their enemy?"

"This individual had his own motives for coming to me. He learned of the troubles and asked if the family could assist. Initially, I was as shocked as you, but it makes sense. The Wrunard family is ancient and powerful. That power is deeply rooted, and if they could use it again properly, they'd be an enormous asset."

"Who was it?" Cythera said.

"One guess. Simon," I said. "It's the kind of smarmy thing he'd do."

"You're correct. Simon visited me," Razia said. "He amazed me by sneaking into my territory and entering my room without being captured. I should have chopped him into little pieces but was impressed by his audacity, so I listened to what he had to say."

"Bertoli, find Simon and bring him here," Cythera said. "I want to hear his side of this story."

Razia snorted, and her hand settled on the axe. "You don't believe me?"

Cythera flinched. "I don't want to miss any information that'll help solve this murder."

There was a second of silence. Were we about to battle this goblin? I was ready, but I didn't want Zandra anywhere near that wickedly sharp axe.

"Do what you have to do." Razia shrugged and gestured at Bertoli.

He dashed out of the room after pausing to give me another pet. He was hopelessly devoted to my joy. It was sweet.

"Simon wanted to make a deal with you?" Zandra said to Razia.

"He came with a proposal. Put old grudges to one side, so the family could ascend to glory."

"And in return, they'd fight alongside you in this upcoming battle?" I said.

"Correct again. We have yet to finalize the details, but in theory, I was willing to enter into a deal."

"So the Wrunard family could return, claim their land and titles, and you'd leave them alone?" Gideon said.

"While we were allies, they'd be at no risk from me."

"Once the battle was over, you'd attack them again," Lucian said. "You goblins never forget a grievance."

"Only if I got bored or they disrespected me." Razia chuckled, but it lasted less than a second. "I was concerned after my last meeting with Simon, though. I'd been leaning on him to finalize things, but he was stalling. I wondered if he was tricking me. Then this incident with Adam happened, and the talks halted."

"You must have despised Adam," Zandra said. "He was the reason you were put away for so long."

"I despise disloyalty. Young Prince Adam should have walked away when he saw what I did. I can't understand why he went to the authorities."

"Adam was raised correctly," Lucian said.

Razia's nostrils flared several times. "The individual who was dispatched was a known troublemaker. I did the community a favor by tossing him off that roof." Her gaze danced to the angels. "Allegedly."

"Tell us when you last saw Adam," Cythera said.

"It was too long ago to remember. Don't forget, they have only recently released me. When his family went into witness protection, it wasn't easy to track them down."

"But you managed," Gideon said. "How?"

"I put out feelers, and Simon grabbed one of them. It was just after I was released. We've met several times since then."

"You must have been eager to make Adam pay," I said. "Did he ever come to the meetings?"

Razia smirked again. "He came once. Must have followed Simon to see where he kept sneaking off to."

"Was it you who hit him?" Lucian jumped up and down. "Adam came home with bruises on his face a few weeks before he died. He sulked about it for days. Did you catch him and teach him a lesson? He escaped, but you hounded him until you got your revenge?"

Razia tilted her head from side to side. "I was curious about him and, frankly, stunned he thrived in a non-magical setting. I expected Adam to cower when I cornered him, but his time living with the non-magicals did him no favors. He was disrespectful."

"You attacked him when my back was turned, so I couldn't protect him," Lucian said.

"Your back was so often turned, it was no trouble to get to Adam. Where were you, when he was following Simon?"

Lucian puffed out his feathers but dropped his head in acknowledgement he'd been a lousy guardian.

"Adam hadn't been schooled in the goblin way. I expected his mother to have taught him to be respectful of goblin elders. When he wasn't, I educated him in the appropriate protocols. Any other goblin would have done the same."

No one spoke, and everyone looked uncomfortable. Lucian looked like he wanted a hole to open so he could dive inside and vanish for good.

Everything Razia had revealed so far didn't place her in the spotlight of innocence. But why would she come here if she feared Angel Force would arrest her for Adam's murder? Was the visit a bluff?

Or was she being honest, and she needed the family in this upcoming fight?

"We need your alibi for the time of Adam's murder," Cythera said.

"I know when it happened. I was with my clan warriors. We were discussing tactics for the upcoming skirmish. Check with them. They'll confirm I was nowhere near Crimson Cove. And I never stealth stab my enemies. It's a cowardly way to slay."

"These clan warriors are with you?" Cythera said.

"Several are outside. They're my most loyal subjects."

I swished my tail. All that meant was they'd be happy to supply Razia with a fake alibi.

"If you don't mind waiting, we'll check your alibi and speak to Simon about the alliance talks," Cythera said.

Razia lifted her hands. "I've done many things that bend the rules of acceptability, but murdering that young goblin wasn't one of them. My name must be cleared, so I can focus on a more important battle."

There was a knock on the door, and Bertoli appeared. "Cythera, we have a problem."

# Chapter 17

## Secret dalliance

I hopped off Zandra's shoulder as Cythera hurried out of the room to join Bertoli. Gideon came with us. Zandra, Lucian, and Finn remained with Razia.

Bertoli crouched and petted me, making kissy noises.

"Stop playing with that creature and focus on your work. What's the problem?" Cythera said.

Bertoli leaped to attention. "I spoke to Simon. He's in the interview room next door. He denies any alliance talks with Razia."

"Is Razia lying?" Cythera said. "She must know she'd be found out the second we spoke to Simon."

"We should interrogate Simon," I said. "I don't trust him. He's too smooth."

Cythera glanced down at me. "We will. Come along, Bertoli. Leave the small fluffy. Gideon, you may sit in with us if you wish."

"Mighty kind of you." Gideon winked at me as he sidled past.

"Don't worry, Juno. I'll sneak you in." Bertoli grabbed me and hid me under his wings.

I was too startled to process what was going on for a second then dove deeper under the feathers, surrounding myself in a warm cinnamon scent.

"Thank you for coming in so promptly." Cythera took a seat, while Bertoli remained standing, so I didn't get squashed and could have a good view of the questioning.

After greeting Simon, Gideon leaned against the wall.

"Of course," Simon said. "Anything to help. I had a scare when your angel said this has something to do with Razia Obelong. She's not planning an attack on us, is she?"

"The opposite. Razia claims you've been in negotiations over an alliance," Cythera said. "You want to return the family to its rightful place and are prepared to work with Razia to do so."

Simon blinked several times and smoothed a hand over his hair. "The lies she'll tell to get away with things stagger me."

"It's untrue?"

"I'd never befriend her. That clan is full of traitorous thugs. They're the reason we've lost five years of our lives. If she hadn't declared a blood feud against us after Adam informed on her, we'd still be at the top of our game."

"Given your history, I was surprised when she told us this information."

Simon turned a fake smile on Cythera. "I can tell you're a clever angel. You saw through Razia's lies. She's only saying these things to muddle the investigation. She wants nothing but misery for my family."

"Ask about his statement," I whispered around a mouthful of feathers.

Bertoli gently petted me through his wings.

"Ask him why Razia would risk coming here and lying to the angels."

Bertoli kept discreetly petting me but made no attempt to ask a question.

Cythera cleared her throat. "I'm sorry we wasted your time—"

I burst through a gap in Bertoli's wings and landed on the table. "When your statement was taken, you said Eric had issues with Adam. You wanted us to think he was the killer."

"Juno!" Cythera's glare flicked from me to Bertoli. "You don't need to be here. My apologies, Simon."

I focused on a surprised-looking Simon. "After speaking to Eric, we ruled him out as a suspect. He's got a concrete alibi. Well, a slimy one. He couldn't have killed his brother."

Simon had already recovered from his initial surprise, and his smooth smile was back in place. "I'm glad to hear that. It would have been distressing for Julie if Eric killed Adam."

"Thank you, Juno," Cythera snarled through clenched teeth. "Why don't you disappear again?"

I flicked my tail at her but didn't move. "Since we know Eric had nothing to do with Adam's murder, you now think Razia was involved? You're quick to change your mind."

Simon's forehead scrunched. "I thought Eric could be the killer, but perhaps it was that evil goblin wench. With their history, she wouldn't be friendly. How did she know we were visiting Crimson Cove?"

"Someone tipped her off." I glanced at Cythera. "There could be a leak."

"Not at Angel Force."

"Not at witness protection," Gideon said.

Simon's eyes narrowed. "Who would do such a thing?"

I licked a paw and swooped it over an ear. "Perhaps Razia is prepared to forgive if there's truth to these alliance rumors."

"There isn't! Julie would never agree to work with Razia."

"Even if there was a larger threat to the goblin community?" I said.

He hesitated. "I can't imagine what that would be. Even then, she'd be cautious. We know how cutthroat Razia is. We wouldn't be able to trust her."

"Isn't that how these temporary alliances work? You watch your back, so you don't get obliterated, dispatch a common enemy, then go back to warring with each other?"

Simon tugged at his shirt cuff. "It's not that simple."

"Enough, Juno. Simon already said Razia lied to us," Cythera said.

"Why visit us and be so bawdy about it? Razia would know we'd check what she told us about making nice with the Wrunard family."

"Goblins have big egos," Simon said.

If I had eyebrows, I'd have raised them. He should know all about egos and pumping up his over-inflated opinion of himself.

"You're certain about Eric being innocent?" Simon said after a few seconds of silence.

"He has the perfect alibi," I said.

"Well, then, it was Razia who killed Adam." Simon leaned back. "Even before we were placed in witness protection, I never trusted that clan. Razia was always up to something. She'd be smiling while one hand slid a blade from her belt to hurl at you the second your back was turned. And that clan of her are thieves. They steal from our mine."

"She mentioned you had an ongoing dispute over a goldmine," Cythera said.

Simon's sigh was tinged with regret. "We've fought for so many years. It was a relief to go into witness protection. We didn't have to worry about a goblin sneak attack or arguing about boundaries on some ancient map."

"You just had to worry about all those non-magicals," I said.

"There was that. The novelty wore off when we realized how restricted we were. But Julie believed it was the safest place for her offspring. And since Razia issued direct threats to all of us, we had no choice but to leave." Simon checked his hair was still perfect with a firm swipe of his hand. "We should have chosen a different disguise. The arrangements aren't ideal."

"You're still alive, aren't you?" Gideon said.

"Adam isn't," I said.

He grunted. "It's hardly my fault if family members expose themselves to attack."

"I didn't do that," Simon said. "Razia is lying. It's what she does best. She weaves in convincing untruths to get people to turn on each other. I would never work with such a monstrous creature."

The door slammed into the wall so hard it knocked out a chunk of plaster.

Razia strode in, her axe sparking with green magic. "Why don't you tell the truth for once in your rotten life?"

Simon lurched back in his seat, knocking it off balance and hitting the floor. He stared up at Razia. "You're here?"

"Didn't we mention that?" I kept an eye on the axe. "Razia stopped by to clear her name."

Razia loomed over Simon, one foot pressed against his heaving chest. "The angels reached out because of this murderous situation, so I came to resolve things. Then I heard your lying words from the other side of the door. What's wrong with you? Does deceit run through your veins as hot and sour as that bitter blood of yours?"

Simon slid out from under her boot, scrambled to his feet, and backed away, his hands raised. "I didn't think you'd come to Crimson Cove."

"I wanted to shut down the rumors, so I don't lose my freedom again." She swung the axe and took a step closer to Simon. "As you're aware, there are bigger issues in our community. One tired skirmish with your family won't distract me from that."

Simon gulped and glanced at Cythera. "I... I don't know what you mean."

"Lower the axe," Cythera said. "We'll have no trouble here."

"There'll be plenty of trouble if this spineless wonder doesn't start truth-talking," Razia said. "Simon, have you been using me the whole time?"

He stammered out a series of nonsensical words. "It's not what it looks like."

"Since you've lost all sense, I'll come clean and let the angels in on our dirty little secret." Razia rested the axe head on the table. "I withheld information about my whereabouts during Adam's murder."

"You weren't with your clan warriors?" Cythera said.

Razia curled back her top lip. "I was with Simon."

All eyes turned to Simon, who was sweating and shaking.

"You said you were alone, taking a walk around Crimson Cove," I said to him. "Why lie about that?"

He rubbed his palms together. "I can explain. I made a mistake."

"You're saying I was a mistake?" Razia's hand flexed around the axe handle.

"No! I mean that was just between us. No one else was supposed to know."

My eyes widened. "You two were together? As in, getting naked together?"

Razia lowered her head. "I'm ashamed to say we were."

"How did this happen?" Gideon's mouth was open.

"I was telling the truth when I said Simon reached out to me," Razia said. "He wanted the alliance and for old grudges to be erased. If it hadn't been for the situation I'm facing, I'd have denied him, but I was desperate."

"This threat must be serious," I said.

"If we don't get ahead of the fight, we could lose everything. I'm aware of the Wrunard power, so I allowed him to speak to me. We got talking, had a few drinks, and one thing led to another. I'm not proud of it."

"And you were so disgusted with yourself that you faked an alibi rather than revealing the truth," I said.

"Hey! I'm not exactly proud about bedding the enemy. I faked my alibi, too." Simon lurched back and squeaked as Razia swung the axe past his nose.

"I promised myself it was a one-time thing, but then it happened again. Unfortunately, I fell for Simon's fake charm and whispered promises."

I nodded. His charm was as slimy as those snails we'd rescued, but it sometimes stuck to those who were wooed by a big smile and a warm tone of voice.

"Simon, is there anything you wish to add to this statement?" Cythera said.

He kept his gaze on the axe. "Razia can tell the story. She knows best."

"At last, some sense." Razia glared at him. "We were negotiating the Wrunard family returning to the goblin fold, but the deeper we got into the negotiations, the more suspicious I became about Simon's motives. He talked less about the family's needs and more about his own desires."

"That's not true," he said. "I'll always be on my family's side. And I care deeply for Julie."

Not enough that he didn't mind engaging in a fling with her worst enemy.

"Did you mean anything you said to Razia?" I asked. "You wanted an alliance, or were you only looking out for yourself?"

"I thought, if I got myself established in Razia's household, I could bring in the rest of the family when the time was right."

"When you started talking like that, that's when I had doubts," Razia said. "You were messing with me and your family. That was unacceptable."

"I wanted the best for everyone." Simon cowered in the corner. "I was being cautious."

From the expressions on everyone's faces, no one believed him.

Razia slammed the axe onto the table, splintering the wood. "You were looking out for yourself. You had no plans to bring the family on board in this fight. All those honeyed words were fake. This means war!"

Cythera's wings flipped out. "No war! Keep your temper under control."

"This slimy goblin lied to me. I've taken him to my bed many times, and all the while, he deceived me. I won't stand for it."

I leaned against the axe, the magic tingling my toe beans. "I understand how much you despise Simon, but an innocent goblin has been murdered. That's a crime against the goblins. If you're not guilty, can't you unite over that?"

Simon clasped his hands together and trembled. "Yes! We should. It's the right thing to do."

"You always were pathetic." Lucian stood in the doorway with Zandra behind him. "These are your true colors. Lily liver green with a side order of puke yellow."

I looked into Razia's angry glare. "Do you have children?"

"I have thirty-one offspring."

"Congratulations! And you must want the best for them. You want them to grow up strong, happy, and successful."

"Of course. My offspring are warriors or have amassed gold fortunes. Any that struggle, I give a helping hand. Fortunately, few do."

"So, you understand how Julie feels after losing Adam. She has only two offspring, and her hopes were pinned on Adam to ensure the future of the Wrunard family. With him gone, their clan is in trouble."

Razia drew in a breath. "And while that is unfortunate, once the Wrunard family is gone, it'll be a toxic thorn removed from my side. I should celebrate his demise."

"But you won't because you have solid values and know when to do the right thing."

She hesitated, her breathing even. "The Wrunard family should be utterly destroyed."

"Be careful if you keep talking like that," Gideon said. "You've just given yourself an excellent motive for murder."

Razia bared her sharp teeth at him. "I'm aware I should be the prime suspect. Not only would murdering Adam remove a problem, it would end my grudge against him. But I didn't do it." She looked at me. "I also understand how difficult this must be for Julie."

"Then agree to a ceasefire until the family's trauma is resolved. We need to know who murdered Adam, but if you force them to run by attacking them because of Simon's stupid misstep, we may never figure out who did it."

She canted her head. "You believe it was a member of the family?"

"Of course it wasn't," Simon said.

Razia pointed a finger at him and snarled until he dropped his gaze. "Will you punish this goblin for lying to me?" She addressed the question to Cythera.

"I can make that happen. He's wasted our time by concealing important information."

"I did it for the good of my family," Simon said. "And we agreed to keep the negotiations quiet until we figured things out."

"Until you figured out how to make the most out of the situation and manipulate everyone," Razia said. "If Simon is appropriately punished, I'll agree to a ceasefire."

"You guarantee you won't attack the family?" Cythera said.

Razia nodded. "You have my word. But I want a say in Simon's punishment."

"I'm not sure—"

"Yes! Deal. We'll work something out," I said.

Razia pursed her lips, a sharp smile flickering. "Know this, Simon Slimy Smith. Once this issue is laid to rest, I'm coming for the family. I'll leave you until last. You will watch what's left of your family disintegrate, and then I'll destroy you, and I'll take my time doing it."

Although I should be appalled by the goblin's cruel words, it was delightful to watch Simon cower.

"We'll see about that," Cythera said.

"Yes, we will. Because I never forget a betrayal." Razia looked at me. "Since you appear to be in charge, what is our next move?"

# Chapter 18

## Obsessively yours

"I thought for a minute Razia was going to obliterate Simon on the spot." Zandra leaned against the kitchen worktop in the Angel Force staffroom, a mug in one hand.

"It was a close call." I was curled on her shoulder. Finn, Lucian, and Gideon were with us, while Bertoli and Cythera showed Razia and Simon out to make sure there was no trouble between them.

"This could still turn deadly," Gideon said. "I've seen it blow up among goblins over the smallest of insults. Nice idea to pull on Razia's heartstrings, Juno. I didn't think she had any, but she caved when you talked about her kids."

"Family is always the most important thing." I nuzzled Zandra's ear.

She petted my side. "Since Razia and Simon were together when Adam was killed, we can rule them out as suspects."

"And with Eric being at the snail spa, spaced out on glittery slime, he's also in the clear," I said.

"Cythera told me about that place," Gideon said. "Some people are into weird stuff."

"That only leaves us with Julie, the mother, or Edith, the grandmother," Finn said.

"I don't know how many times I need to say this, but it was Julie." Lucian sounded so certain he knew who the killer was.

I glanced at him. He'd never given me his alibi. He'd helped at every step of the investigation and seemed sincere in his grief over Adam's death, but I needed to get Lucian on his own and double-check he had nothing to do with this.

I was almost certain he wasn't involved, but what if Lucian had grown disillusioned about his role and worried he'd be stuck with the family, living a non-magical life forever? It would be enough to drive many creatures over the edge into killsville.

"We should focus on Julie," Zandra said. "She has no alibi, and she's hardly grief-stricken over her son's murder. And goblins can be prideful. Perhaps, Adam humiliated her."

"It must have been bad if she killed her best hope for continuing the family name," Gideon said. "It's the most important thing to her. Julie often talks about their heritage with Edith. When Edith had all of her marbles, she'd recite the rituals they had to follow back in the day. It was fascinating."

"What about the old lady?" Zandra said. "She was at the scene when Adam was stabbed."

"She's harmless." Gideon drained his coffee mug. "And I can't remember the last time I saw her get out of that chair. I don't think she's got much longer left. And why would she want her grandson dead?"

"I'll look into Julie's background some more," Finn said. "See if anything raises a red flag. But if no one saw her do it, we don't have the evidence to charge her. Or anyone."

"So the killer gets away with it." Lucian huffed and ruffled.

"I'd better keep an eye on those goblins," Gideon said. "I want no more murders on my watch. The big boss is already unhappy about this situation, so I'm stuck doing daily progress reports. I'll check back in with you all soon." He nodded at us and left the room.

"You ready to head out, too, Juno?" Zandra said.

"Give me a minute." I trotted out of the staff kitchen and over to Bertoli's desk. I nudged open the bottom drawer to retrieve my bracelet. It was gone.

I hopped into the drawer and kicked everything out, not caring if his paper got rumpled. It must be in here.

After a thorough search, I'd still not found the magic-laced bracelet.

I hopped out of the drawer and stared at the desk. Bertoli must have found it and moved it. He hadn't come back since escorting the goblins from the office, so I couldn't ask him about it.

My gaze narrowed as an inspection of his desk showed no files or paperwork waiting for his attention. He must have clocked off for the day.

"You ready?" Zandra looked at the mess. "Uh-oh. What's Bertoli done to annoy you this time?"

"I was looking for a fishy treat he'd promised me. I'm getting hungry."

"We can't have you hangry." Zandra grabbed the papers and stuffed them in the drawer before shutting it. "Let's get out of here and find food."

I glanced back at Bertoli's drawer. I needed that bracelet.

"Everything okay?" Zandra walked beside me as we left Angel Force.

"Still hungry. And thinking about this case." I was glad to see Razia and her stallion-riding warriors had disappeared.

"It's a weird one. If Julie killed Adam, that family is broken beyond repair. Maybe they deserve to fade away if this is how they treat each other."

"Although Julie needs to be our prime suspect, it does seem self-destructive. If her top priority is to ensure the family name continues, she should do everything to protect her sons."

"Julie seems cold. And she was open about writing off Eric because of his addiction issues. Why not Adam? Maybe she's planning on having more offspring and starting a clean slate."

"But she sacrificed so much by taking them into a non-magical community and suppressing their powers. That can't have been easy. It's not the actions of a female done with her offspring."

We reached Sorcha's café and headed inside. I checked the menu but already knew what I'd eat.

"Your usual?" Zandra headed to the counter.

"Of course."

"I'm getting cake. After the day we've had, I deserve a treat. And several slices of that treat."

I sent a message to Mack using Zandra's mobile snow globe to see if he wanted to join us for food then picked a table while Zandra placed the order.

The globe buzzed. *I was sleeping. Catch you later. Bring plenty of snacks.*

I was reassured my badger guest didn't feel too ignored. I wanted to hang out with Mack, but this murder was taking up my free time.

Zandra joined me, and a few minutes later, Sorcha arrived with a tray containing a plate of smoked salmon and cream cheese for me and three slices of cake. One carrot, one coffee and walnut, and the other red velvet.

"Tough day?" She handed around the treats.

"We've had easier. Have you heard about the goblins?" Zandra said.

"Heard! I saw them stampede past not so long ago. What are they doing in town?"

"We need to be careful what we say," I cautioned Zandra.

"You can trust me. Let me grab my drink." Sorcha dashed away. She returned a moment later with a mug that smelled of strong herbs and honey.

"What have you got in there?" I tentatively sniffed the steaming mug.

"I'm fighting off this flu thing that's going around. I can't shake it, though. I've felt exhausted all week, yet no matter how much sleep I have, I wake tired. I figured some virus got me, and it won't let go, so I mixed a huge batch of healing tonic and have been drinking it all day."

"You must have caught a bug from a non-magical," I said. "They can be lax with their hand washing. I saw one child with his finger so far up his nose, I wouldn't have been surprised to see it sticking out of the top of his head."

Sorcha poked out her tongue. "Maybe that's it. They keep coming in, so I could have gotten something gross from one of them. There are more arriving every day. Have you noticed?"

Zandra sliced off a chunk of coffee and walnut cake with a fork. "We've been too busy. But I'll keep my distance if they're making us sick."

"Good plan. You definitely don't want what I've got."

I paused from scarfing my food. Sorcha didn't look healthy. Her normally rosy color was gone, and she kept yawning behind one hand.

"Still not found any help?" Zandra said.

"Maybe I'm being picky, but the right person hasn't come in. I don't suppose you want a change of career? I can train you so you don't burn everything."

"Even though the animals aren't always easy to deal with, I've found my passion," Zandra said.

Sorcha grinned. "And it all started right here, with Barney's vacancy notice pinned to my board. I'm proud I introduced you two, and you found your perfect career."

"Cheers to that. I had doubts about joining animal control, but it's worked out well."

Sorcha cut off a small piece of red velvet cake and ate it. "So, the goblins? I promise, I won't breathe a word to anyone about the case, no matter how hard the customers beg."

Zandra ate more cake. "You already know about the murder."

"Of course. Do you know who did it?"

"We've narrowed down the suspects. There should be an arrest any day."

"You don't look happy about that," Sorcha said.

"That grouchy face has nothing to do with the murder investigation. Randal kissed Zandra," I said.

Zandra dropped her fork. "Juno! We're not talking about that."

Sorcha raised her eyebrows. "Oh! We so are. When did this happen? I thought you two were on a break."

"We were never together to go on a break," Zandra said. "It was nothing. A misunderstanding."

"It was something," I said. "Randal helped when we raided an illegal snail spa. He got covered in magical slime and let his feelings show. He planted a huge smacker on Zandra."

"Aww! He's such a sweetheart. You two are great together," Sorcha said.

"Not great enough, since life keeps getting in the way of anything actually happening."

"Oh, raspberries to life. You deserve to be happy. If Randal makes you happy, then go for it. You're both single, lonely—"

"I never said I was lonely," Zandra said.

"Your best friend is a cat."

"I see no problem with that," I said. "We make excellent best friends and are the most loyal of companions."

Zandra stabbed a fork into the chocolate cake.

"How was the kiss?" Sorcha said.

"Slimy."

She wrinkled her nose. "Not a great first kiss, then? It was your first kiss, right? Or have you been holding out on me with the smooching gossip?"

"No, yes, no." Zandra shoveled chocolate cake into her mouth. "This is good. Can I have more?"

Sorcha raised a hand and grinned. "I get it. Keep my nose out of your private life. But if you ever want to talk, I'm here. I may be a sad, lonely singleton myself, but it's always good to talk through any worries. If nothing else, I'll make noises of sympathy and feed you all the cake you desire."

"Thanks," Zandra mumbled around a mouthful of chocolate frosting. "I'm focusing on work, for now. Angry baby dragons and grumpy sloths are easier to handle than starting a relationship with someone I work with."

"Focusing on work is perfect, since Randal is there," I said. "You'll keep bumping into each other and will work things out."

"Maybe I should take a job here," Zandra said. "Although you'd be closed for good inside of a month, thanks to my lack of culinary skills."

"The offer is there if you get desperate. The pay's decent, and you can take home leftovers for free." Sorcha patted Zandra's hand. "Maybe stick to the angry animals, though. And Randal."

Zandra grumbled to herself. "Let's talk about murder, rather than romance."

"Always happy to discuss the latest scandal." Sorcha winked at me.

Zandra moved on to the carrot cake. "Finn's doing background checks on the remaining suspects."

"And I want to speak to Lucian," I said. "I don't think he did it, but he was negligent in his duty. Maybe there's more to that."

"Vorana mentioned a couple of suspects to me but remind me who Lucian is," Sorcha said.

"The dead goblin's guardian owl. Witness protection assigned him to the family. He got bored on the job and wasn't around when he should have been."

"Even if Lucian was keeping watch, I doubt he could have done anything to save Adam," Zandra said. "The attack happened so fast and in the middle of a crowd. No one saw what happened. We were the first to spot Adam on the ground after he'd been stabbed."

"I agree. Lucian has just had an unlucky run. But I want to make sure we've missed nothing."

"Poor bird. Must be tough on him. I expect he feels guilty," Sorcha said. "What'll he do now? Is he homeless?"

"No opening your home to a suspect," I said. "You're busy enough. And unwell."

She smiled. "An owl might be too stimulating for my foster cats. Elijah hates anything with feathers. And fur. Well, he pretends to hate everything. You know what he's like. What's your next move?"

"Nothing for the rest of the day. Tonight, we need a break. And cake." Zandra grabbed the final slice of cake.

I nodded. With everything that had been going on, I was ready to curl up on Zandra's bed and sleep for at least twenty hours.

But after my cat nap, I had plans to execute.

“I didn’t come stay with you so I could break into places.” Mack scurried beside me through the gloomy dawn morning.

I glanced around, grateful the low light made it easy to move without being seen by any early bird nosy neighbors. “You’d get bored if we didn’t have fun while you were here.”

Sage squeaked along beside us in her harness. “Juno hasn’t told you about our visit to the corpse with Archie, has she?”

“I’m not sure I want to know,” Mack said. “Did the corpse get up and start biting?”

“We got caught red-pawed. Juno was poking around the body and stealing things—”

“Hey! I took one thing, and it belonged to me, so it can’t be called stealing.”

“That’s your story,” Sage said. “We got trapped in a room with no escape route, a dead body behind us, angry angels, and a weirdo from witness protection. It wasn’t the best end to one of her kitten impossible missions. They rarely end well.”

“Maybe not. But this mission is simple.” I slid a glare toward Sage. “If you’re that grumpy about it, you can go back to bed.”

“I’m here now,” Sage said. “If I don’t stay, I’ll stress about you getting arrested or chased or stumbling into something you can’t control.”

“Then stop being a curmudgeon. All we need to do is get inside Bertoli’s apartment, find the bracelet he took from me, and leave. We'll be in and out before anyone notices."

"Didn't you say that when we broke in to snoop around the corpse?"

I grumbled at her. Sage was being particularly grouchy today.

"What's Bertoli doing with your jewelry, anyway?" Mack lumbered along, pausing now and again to sniff the dirt.

"It came off the corpse," Sage said. "Apparently, it's got some of Juno in it."

"Huh?"

"It's a long story. But I need that bracelet. Are you with me, or am I riding solo on this mission?"

"Sure. Since you promised me breakfast after we raid the angel's place, I'm in," Mack said.

Sage simply grunted, which I took to mean yes in grouch code.

We sat and watched the small apartment block Bertoli lived in. He had a place on the first floor, which would make it easy to get in.

And luck was on our side when someone came out of the entrance to the apartments a few moments later.

I hurried over, snuck through the gap, and held the door open for the others. Once inside, we located Bertoli's front door.

"What if he's awake?" Mack said.

"We all have magic if we need to slow him down, but he won't mind me being here. He adores me," I said. "If Bertoli discovers us, I'll say I came to spend time with him."

We stared at the front door.

"I'm surprised you didn't bring Sammy on this mission," Sage said. "Or aren't you friends anymore?"

My whiskers twitched. "Why say that?"

"He's been hanging out with Tinkerbell, and she hates everyone. I figured he was doing it because you'd had a fight and he wanted to make you jealous."

I huffed out a breath. That was another puzzle to solve. "Let's focus on this mission. Mack, if I may." I hopped onto his back so I could reach the lock, pulsed out an unlock spell, and hung off the handle to open the door. It was heavy and took our combined efforts to get it to move.

Once we were inside, I eased the door shut, and we stood in the hallway, taking a moment to get our bearings.

Bertoli's shoes were neatly stored underneath the tidy coat rack, and next to the coats, there was a small shelf with pictures of himself on it.

There were no sounds in the apartment. Not even faint snoring. Maybe angels didn't snore. I'd never spent the night with one, not even in my pre-cat days. There was just something about all those feathers that didn't sit well with me.

"You stay by the door and be ready to get it open in case Bertoli comes out," I whispered to Mack.

He nodded and stood sentry-like by the door, although he nosed the air as if searching for scents. He was probably sniffing for food. Mack was ruled by his stomach.

I beckoned Sage with my head to follow me.

We inched along the hallway and turned right into the open-plan lounge.

My gaze swept the room several times. "Am I in a dream?"

Sage sat back in her harness. "More like a nightmare. I thought I'd seen it all, but this is ridiculous."

"What is it?" Mack ambled in behind us.

"You're supposed to stay by the door to make sure we can get out fast," I said.

He ignored me as his jaw dropped. "Whoa! Juno! There are pictures of you everywhere."

# Chapter 19

## Goddess worship

"This is a shrine." Mack took several steps back to get a better look at the hundreds of pictures of me all over Bertoli's living room walls. And it wasn't just pictures. There were sketches and paintings too, showing me in various poses. Some were rather good. Although I looked plump in a few of them.

"Zandra mentioned Bertoli was being weird around you," Sage said, "but this is a different level of weird. Did you know about this?"

"Of course not. Although, it's not uncommon for people to worship me. This is a bit extreme." Before I'd turned into a cat, I'd received regular gifts from loyal subjects, often paintings or drawings, showing me in all my radiant glory. But I'd never come across anything like this.

"Why has he got a cage in the corner?" Sage said. "I didn't think Bertoli had any pets."

"He doesn't. At least, none I'm aware of." I inched closer to the cage. I'd yet to meet an animal who was fond of being behind bars. It was roomy enough, and there was soft bedding on the floor, but it was clear no animal had slept on it.

"It's sturdy. Once you got shoved in there, you'd struggle to get out," Mack said.

"There's no animal smell, so this must be a new purchase. Maybe he's got a furry friend arriving soon," I said.

"Or maybe those furry friends are us," Sage muttered. "I knew it was a mistake to come here."

I glanced at the cage again. "Ignore this. It's a distraction. Let's look for my bangle."

Before we started our search, a bedroom door snicked open, and soft footsteps sounded on the wooden floor.

"Hide!" Mack squeezed behind the couch, getting his rear end stuck, so his tail and butt were on display, his back legs flailing. "Someone push me in."

Sage and I were shoving Mack's coarsely furred rump when Bertoli appeared, dressed in a pair of white boxer shorts and nothing else. Did angels only own white clothing?

His concerned expression morphed into an enormous smile when he saw me. "Juno! When I heard noises, I thought someone was breaking in. But it's you!"

"Greetings, Bertoli. I hope you don't mind the intrusion." I yanked Mack out from behind the couch with my teeth. "We were passing and thought we'd say hello. I was telling my friends what a wonderful angel you are, and they were keen to meet you."

"You can stop by anytime. Would you like breakfast?" He smiled at us all. "Any friend of Juno's is a friend of mine. I always have salmon, just in case I get a surprise visit."

I was staring at his wrist and almost missed the salmon comment. He was wearing my bangle.

Bertoli caught me looking. "I'm right in thinking this is yours, isn't it?" He lifted his wrist and waved it around. "You left it for me in my desk drawer as a gift. I knew the second I touched it, it belonged to you. We're so connected. I know everything about you."

"It is mine," I said cautiously. "But I left it in your desk for safekeeping. When I went to find it, it wasn't there. I'm glad it's in safe hands, though."

He stroked the bangle. "It feels wonderful to wear it. It makes us even more connected. Especially since I now know how special it is to you and how you trusted me to look after it. I'm honored."

Mack nudged me. "This angel is being weird."

"No weirder than usual," Sage muttered. "He's been like this since Juno weaved her magic over him."

"Can I have the bangle back?" I ignored my friends' continual muttering. "It's important I have it."

"Oh! I'm keeping it forever." Bertoli dropped to his knees. "Juno, you must know, you consume my thoughts. You're all I care about. Having this bangle means the world to me. You wouldn't take that away, would you?"

"That's sweet of you to say, but I need it," I said. "I could give you something else of mine. I have lots of comfy beds in Zandra's basement—"

"You shouldn't be with that witch." He waved away my comment. "She's not good enough for you. Be with me."

"That's a generous offer, but I'm bonded to Zandra. We're meant to be together. I can't sever the bond and leave her unprotected."

"It can be done. I know it can. I've seen other familiars leave their magic users. Move in here. It's much more luxurious than that damp basement Zandra forces you to endure."

"I like my basement lifestyle. And it's not damp. Vorana looks after us."

Bertoli tutted. "That bookish witch has nothing on me. I'm offering you the chance to live with an angel. I have connections. I can take you places. We'll have fun together." He held out his arms as if expecting me to run into them and hug him. "Come live with me. Then I can paint you all day."

"We should leave," Sage whispered. "I'm getting bad vibes from this guy. Insane angel vibes."

"What did you do to him?" Mack said. "This isn't natural angel behavior."

"Nothing bad," I muttered out of the corner of my mouth. "Bertoli, your interest in me is delightful, but I must decline. I'm happy with my situation. Now, if I may—"

"You can't be happy chasing after that weird witch, keeping her out of trouble, and dealing with those miscreant animals. There's no joy in that. I could have you working by my side in Angel Force. We'd be a team."

"Cythera would hate me being in the office every day. She barely tolerates me."

"I'll work on her. Get her to see sense. And if she doesn't..." He passed a finger across his throat.

"You'd kill Cythera for me?" For a second, I was tempted to defect. Cythera could be a serious pain in my fluffy behind.

"I'll make sure she isn't a problem. I've had my eye on a promotion. I can see myself running this branch of Angel Force. And with you by my side, we'd be unstoppable."

"This dude needs to be stopped," Mack said. "Grab the bangle and let's get out of here."

Bertoli reared back, his cheerful expression hardening. "No! This bangle is mine. Juno gave it to me."

"Not exactly," I said. "I placed it in your drawer to retrieve at a later date. I didn't mean for you to find it. I'm sorry, Bertoli, it was never meant as a gift."

"It was!" He clutched the bangle to his bare chest. "It strengthens our bond. If you want it, you'll have to stay. There! How's that for a deal? You can have the bangle if you agree to live with me."

"No, it doesn't mean I have to do anything of the sort." I stood and fluffed my fur. Bertoli tried my patience. "I'll have my bangle, and we'll be leaving."

"Stay! I got a cage prepared for you. You live in there, and I'll pet you forever. You'll want for nothing."

"I'd want my freedom. I'm not living in a cage like some trapped tiger, pacing back and forth, waiting for my owner to return to spare me a scrap of comfort. Unacceptable. Bad form, Bertoli. Now, give me my bangle."

His piercing blue eyes narrowed. "Agree to stay here."

"Never going to happen."

"If I have to stuff and mount you to keep you forever, then that's what I'll do. Don't think I won't. You're mine."

"No one stuffs and mounts my friends." Mack lumbered in front of me, growling, magic sparking off his rough coat.

I petted his rump. "Bertoli didn't mean it. He's unwell and not making sense."

"Because of you," Sage grumbled.

"You're mine, Juno. I'm not letting you get away. Not now I have you here." Bertoli lunged at me.

We scattered in different directions, and he hit the floor, catching only air.

Mack jumped on Bertoli's legs while Sage grabbed an arm.

I leaped onto Bertoli's back and pinned him down. "Come to your senses. You don't want this. You don't want me in a cage or stuffed as an ornament on your shelf."

"I'll take what I can get," he growled. "I can't stop thinking about you. I dream about you. I know it's unnatural, but you're all I care about."

"Let me help with that. Hold still, and I'll remove the magic."

"What magic? You're making no sense. We're meant to be together."

I tried to get hold of Bertoli's head so I could extract my beguilement magic without doing harm, but he wriggled and bucked so much, it was all I could do to hang on.

"Will you behave?" I snapped.

Bertoli's wings shot out, and I flew through the air and hit the wall.

Mack growled and bit Bertoli's thigh, while Sage chewed on an ear, flooding magic all over the angel to subdue him.

"You alive over there?" Sage said around a mouthful of ear.

I was rattled, but nothing was broken. I dashed over, tore the bangle off Bertoli's wrist, and flipped it over my head. I'd need this power to deal with the angel. I gave it a few seconds to activate, but the magic refused to wake.

I tapped into it again and again, but whatever surrounded it was strong and wasn't giving up without a fight, and I didn't have time to puzzle through how to unlock the magic.

Mack lifted his head. "What should we do? We can't let him go, or he'll just keep coming after you."

"Hold him still. I need to take back my beguilement magic. That should be enough to stop the obsessional thoughts. The rest we'll figure out when he's calm."

"Juno! You're mine. Don't spoil things. I promise I won't stuff and mount you. And I can get you a bigger cage. Whatever you need. But you must be—"

I thumped a paw over his mouth and hunted for the threads of my magic that wrapped around him.

I'd beguiled Bertoli more strongly than I'd realized. It was no wonder this angel was so obsessed with me.

It took several minutes of wrangling before the last of my magical influence left Bertoli, leaving him slumped on the floor, sweating, his eyelids fluttering.

I stood back and stared at him. How had I made such a mess of this angel? I wasn't a Bertoli fan, but he didn't deserve this. Was I losing my touch? With my magic so scattered, I wasn't always in control, but this situation made me doubt myself. Should I even use magic if it did this to a powerful angel?

Sage finally let go of Bertoli's ear and joined me next to his sweaty face. "How will you fix this? You broke him."

"Bertoli just needs a few days' rest and relaxation. I'll need to remove the memories of us being here, but then I'm sending him to a special spa." I knew a place that helped traumatized magic users. And a witchy family who'd know how to help this guy.

"You'd better be paying for that special spa," Sage said. "It's the least you can do."

I nodded. The thermal spa in Willow Tree Falls was the perfect restorative retreat, and the Crypt witches would watch Bertoli to ensure he recovered. "He'll wake with no memories of us being here, no desire to obsess over me, and he won't remember discovering my bangle."

"That's what tipped him over the edge," Mack said. "There must be some power in that trinket."

"Of course there is. It's my power. Find his snow globe. I'll make the arrangements then translocate him there."

It took half an hour, a fair degree of effort to yank away all the inappropriate memories Bertoli had of me, and time to dress him and pack a bag, but he was finally gone.

"We should take down these pictures and drawings," I said. "We don't want him coming back and having his memory jogged."

Sage muttered as she wheeled around the room, yanking down sketches and paintings. "You don't know your own strength, sometimes."

I joined Mack on the other side of the room. "I used to. I wasn't always like this."

"Someone needs to go back to magic school," Mack said. "I had to go through a re-education program after my vampire was killed. They said I had anger issues. I'm better now. Well, less likely to go ballistic for no reason. I still get mean when someone needs to learn a lesson."

"I don't need re-education," I said. "I just need all my magic back. Once I have it—"

"Yeah, yeah. You'll be perfect. You'll rule the world again, and you'll forget about the little cats." Sage huffed and tore, huffed and ripped, as she worked her way across the wall.

"Like us?" Mack said. "Once you get important and famous, or whatever it is you're chasing, you won't want anything to do with us?"

I rested a paw on his side. "There'll always be a place in my court for such splendid individuals."

"You can keep your court and stuff your place where the sun doesn't shine," Sage said. "I'm happy in Crimson Cove with Vorana. I want nothing to change."

"Things are always changing," I said. "If you don't change, you die."

"Then I die! I'd rather that than become some highfalutin, fancy pants demi-beast who struts around because she owns the place."

"I never ruled like that. And I was never a demi-beast." Although now and again, I'd heard a few mutterings about me being full of myself, but that was just jealousy rearing its unpleasant head.

"Let's get this done," Sage said. "We can burn them out back."

"Thank you, Sage. I appreciate your help." Sage was just being grumpy, as usual. When she saw what I could offer, she'd change her mind and be happy to be one of my magical misfits.

"What we gonna do next?" Mack said.

"First, breakfast." I crumpled a pile of charcoal drawings. "Then I'm tackling a feisty owl."

# Chapter 20

## Military mice

After my eventful early morning adventure with Mack and Sage, I'd returned to bed and napped for hours beside Zandra. We were on the night shift again, so there was no hurry to get up.

When Zandra rose around noon, we ate then I left to find Lucian, who'd gone out while I was sleeping.

Mack was entertaining himself with some serious snoring and dream running, so I left him to his fun.

Before I went out, I hid my newly acquired bangle with the stone that contained another piece of my power. I'd tried to activate the bangle several times, but it still wouldn't work, so I left it to settle. Perhaps it was shocked after spending time with an angel and needed a period of readjustment before the power felt ready to emerge.

I knew how that felt.

It didn't take long to track down Lucian. Startled squeaks and crunching sounds led me straight to him.

"You're comfort eating." I sat on the small bench looking over an area of green grass close to the center of town.

"Maybe I am. You want one?" Lucian lobbed me a warm, soft rodent.

I never turned down quality food despite having just had lunch, so I ate with Lucian in silence for a moment.

"What's on your mind?" I said.

"Why should anything be on my mind?"

"If you're like me, I comfort eat when stressed. It takes the edge off and helps numb things. That peace rarely lasts long before the worries return, though. Then I need to face the issue or keep eating. And that second choice does nothing positive to my waistline."

"What have you got to be stressed about?"

"You'd be surprised. Perhaps sharing with me would help."

Lucian gulped down another mouse. He must have discovered a nest. "I can't stop thinking about Adam."

"It must be tough to lose someone on your watch."

"That's just it. I should have been watching him, but I wasn't. I was bored with my guardian role. No one hunted the family while they stayed in the non-magical world. It was the perfect disguise."

"Not so perfect, since Adam didn't make it," I said.

"That's his fault. He should have stayed where he was. If they hadn't kept dipping their toes into magic, Adam would be alive." Lucian spat out a small piece of rodent fur and inspected it for any nibbly bits.

"You can't know that for certain. If someone was intent on getting Adam, they could have killed him anywhere."

Lucian hung his head. "I should have been a better owl. I wanted to be, but I never signed up for this. The short-term assignments were easy. Go in, do the job, and get out again. But I was with that family for years. As irritating as Adam was, I liked the guy. He had potential. He was growing into a decent young man."

I picked rodent out from between my teeth then walked over and sat beside Lucian. "I sometimes mess up with my witch. I put her at risk, even though I promised I'd never do that. Even the best make errors."

"Your witch is still alive, though, isn't she? Adam's gone."

I gave Lucian a moment to ruminate on his thoughts. "What were you doing that was so important you had to leave Adam's side on the day he was killed?"

"That's where it gets worse. Nothing. I'd taken to the wing and was circling around. I'd found this place on the outskirts of Crimson Cove, where there are loads of animals. It's a refuge or sanctuary. I was flying over it, being nosy. There was no purpose other than to ease my boredom."

"You must mean Finn's animal sanctuary," I said.

"If you say so. There were a couple of ghouls wandering around. They looked like they worked there."

"That's Zandra's mother and Joel. They're an item."

He stared at me. "Zandra's mother is a ghoul?"

"Long story. It's a recent change, and we're all adapting. Did they see you?"

"Yeah. They waved at me."

That alibi would be easy to check. I was grateful. I'd grown to like this snappy owl, despite our less-than-ideal introduction.

Lucian rootled under his wings and pulled out a stray downy feather with his beak. "You asked because you think I killed Adam?"

"Don't be offended, but we must cover all the bases. I don't think you killed the young goblin. We've whittled down the suspects, and a quick check of your alibi will mean you're also off the list."

"I don't need to whittle anything to figure this out. It was Julie. When will you charge her? And before you do, can I have five minutes alone with her in a soundproofed room?"

"Not sure. And why?"

"To teach her a lesson."

"Bad idea."

"Three minutes?"

I shook my head.

"Thirty seconds? I could still get in some good nips. Give her a scar to remember Adam by."

I stroked a paw down his soft wing. "I understand your anger, but if Julie killed Adam, the angels will make her pay. We just need proof to get the murder charge to stick."

Lucian stamped his taloned foot on another mouse and squeezed. "It was her! She's got ice running through her veins. I don't think I've ever seen her cry."

"That doesn't mean she has no love for her family."

"Julie cares about her reputation and how soon she can get back on top. If that means killing a few relatives along the way, then she'll do it."

"Mind if I have that mouse?" I said.

Lucian belched. "Be my guest. This nest is repeating on me."

I caught the mouse with a paw and checked it was no longer alive. It would make the perfect gift for Zandra.

"I'm not giving up on showing everyone she's guilty," Lucian said. "Julie is the killer, and I'll figure out how she did it and get the proof I need to put her away for life."

"And you don't need to do it on your own. Working together, we can achieve anything."

Lucian huffed out a breath then nodded. "Agreed. We do this together."

⁂

Zandra yawned long and loud as she pulled the van up outside the front of animal control. "I'm glad this shift is over. Although I don't feel like we got much done. We spent most of the time chasing shadows or being ignored by people who were pretending they weren't home."

"We found more holes with dead creatures beside them," I said. "That's something."

"That news will only make Barney even more stressed. I wish we could figure out who is digging all those holes."

"We'll catch them in the act soon enough. We just haven't timed it right."

Zandra opened her door and slid off the seat. "I keep thinking about the shovel we found. Could it be a were creature? Maybe they're having trouble changing, so have to use a tool to capture their prey. It could be they're hiding their actions out of shame. They need to eat, but don't have the natural born weapons to do so."

"They're using the shovel as a club?"

"It's dual purpose. Actually, triple purpose. Club, disemboweling tool, and evidence hider."

"I get where you're going, but why dig a hole and not put the remains in it?"

Zandra lifted her hands. "You're right. I'm too tired to think straight. These night shifts suck."

I waited in the van while she headed inside, dropped off her paperwork, and then returned. We drove home in silence. We'd been quiet most of the night. I'd been thinking about Sammy, Adam, and my magic bangle that refused to work. And although Zandra hadn't mentioned it, I was certain she'd been thinking about Randal and how to fix the slimy kiss situation.

We'd just gotten inside as Vorana came down the stairs. Sage was clasped to her chest in her usual cozy papoose, looking half-asleep.

"Morning! Perfect timing. Who's for pancakes?"

"So long as there's salmon with them, I'm in," I said.

"There'll always be salmon when you're living here." Vorana tickled my head. "Will your friends be joining us?"

"Mack has a breakfast date with Archie and Remus. I'll give Lucian a shout." After I'd left Lucian yesterday, I'd checked with Adrienne and Joel to see if they'd seen him hovering around the animal sanctuary at the time of Adam's murder. They confirmed he'd been there, which ruled him out.

I called down to Lucian, and he flapped up the stairs a moment later. He landed in a feathery heap on the back of the chair and sagged.

"Bad night?" I said.

"I've been thinking about my future, and I came to no cheerful conclusion. The family won't want to keep me, since I've proven myself to be unreliable. And I'm about to get fired from witness protection. Where does that leave me?"

"Look at this change as a good thing," I said. "You don't enjoy your job. You signed up to do a certain kind of work, but they gave you this. If witness protection decides you're not right for them, it's a sign to move on and do something you're more suited to doing."

"Like..."

I nudged a breakfast roll toward him. "You'll figure something out."

Vorana opened the refrigerator door. She stared inside for a second, squeaked, then slammed it shut. She turned and pressed her back against the door.

"What's wrong?" Zandra said. "Moldy mushrooms?"

I hurried over. "I was keeping it in there as a treat for Zandra. It was warm, so I didn't want rot to set in."

Zandra narrowed her eyes. "Juno. What gross thing did you put in Vorana's fridge?"

Vorana stepped away from the refrigerator. "Please, get it out of there."

"If you wouldn't mind..." I nodded at the refrigerator door. I could open them, but the lack of opposable thumbs meant heavy doors were always a challenge.

"I'll do it." Zandra stomped over and yanked open the door. She looked inside and groaned.

"I forgot I put it in there!" I hopped up and knocked the chilled mouse off the shelf and onto the floor. "It was meant to be a surprise."

Zandra planted her hands on her hips. "I don't know why the words no mice as gifts never stick in your brain." She pointed at the back door. "Get that thing out of here and then apologize to Vorana."

"It's okay," Vorana said. "I was just startled. Although, Juno, I'd rather you didn't keep your food in the fridge. I can get you a mini fridge for the basement if you like your mice chilled."

"No! No vermin in any fridge. Ever!" Zandra kept pointing at the door.

"It looks tasty to me," Sage said. "You should all try mouse. You might be pleasantly surprised. It has a tangy flavor. Sort of gamey if you've ever had moose or deer."

Vorana and Zandra both poked out their tongues.

"We'll stick to pancakes." Zandra glared at me as I picked up the mouse, exited the house, quickly buried the creature in the back garden, and then returned.

"It's gone?"

"Never coming back. No more mice in the fridge. Got it," I said. "And I meant no harm. One day, you'll see what a wonderful gift a mouse can be."

After Vorana settled Sage in her chair and scrubbed the fridge, she got to work on the pancakes. As hungry as I was, I didn't dare ask her to hurry.

Lucian huffed and fluffed and seemed unable to settle on his perch on the back of my chair.

"Everything will work out," I said to him. "And every investigation hits a sticky patch. We just need to find a way to trip Julie up so she confesses. Then all of this will be over, and you can move on."

"You've found your killer?" Vorana poured pancake mix into a sizzling pan.

"Possibly," Zandra said.

"Lucian has convinced me it was Julie, Adam's mother. Based on the evidence, it can't be anyone else." I licked a muddy paw, which tasted faintly of mouse.

"She's a cold fish. But not everyone is great at displaying their emotions. And grief kicks in at different times," Zandra said.

Vorana puffed out a breath. "Goblins can be brutal. I kept reading that book on goblin history. It gets dark, and families turn on each other. The fights mainly involve disputes over gold."

"Julie feels nothing but relief that Adam is dead," Lucian said. "She only keeps people around if they're of value to her. It's why I need a new path to fly. If I stayed with them, she'd forcibly enroll me in military school like she planned to do with Adam."

"That was his career path?" I said.

"Not if he had any choice, which he didn't. Adam loved photography. He wanted to do that for a living, but Julie threatened to send him into the army, so he'd grow a backbone and become a warrior."

"How sweet of her." Vorana arched a brow as she placed a plate of croissants on the table while she waited for the pancakes to cook. Once they were done, she put salmon on Sage's plate and then mine before joining us at the table.

"Regular or magical army?" Zandra helped herself to three pancakes.

"Magical. The plan was to sneak him in undercover and ship him to some out-of-the-way place for a few years. They'd have to alter his disguise, so he'd fit in, but Julie figured no one would pay attention to one more no-name grunt."

"She really wanted that for Adam, or was it a threat so he'd grow a pair?" Sage said.

"Most goblins respond well to threats," Lucian said. "She wanted it, though."

"Did Adam know this was happening?" I said.

Lucian chewed on a breakfast roll. "Of course. They argued about it."

"How bad did the arguments get?" Zandra snagged a croissant.

"They got heated. Adam had courage but not in the way his mother wanted. She considered him undisciplined and was determined to get him into the army and teach him respect and obedience."

I sat back in my seat, forgetting my salmon. "You were often off doing your own thing, weren't you, when you should have been watching Adam?"

Lucian spat out a lump of soggy dough. "Jeez! Not all the time. Don't make me feel worse than I already do."

"I didn't mean that. But you could have missed some of their arguments? What if Adam stood up to Julie one too many times? She snapped and got rid of him."

Zandra nodded slowly as she chewed a mouthful of pancake. "Julie wanted Adam's death to look like a random killing, so it wouldn't be pinned on her. She knew they were coming to Crimson Cove for the festival, so she took the opportunity to get rid of a disobedient son."

"That's evil," Vorana said. "What kind of mother kills her own son?"

"The goblin kind," Lucian said. "You said yourself they have violent tendencies. Julie has traditional values and is determined to keep the family name relevant. And how many goblin photographers do you know? If Adam had followed that career path, their name would have been a laughingstock if they ever returned to the goblin community. Julie would never have allowed that."

"What if Adam refused to go to military school? Maybe he wouldn't sign the application, or show up for the tests. That would have made Julie angry," I said. "We need to find out if an application was ever made."

"Let's see if the angels can help with that. I remember Finn mentioning having friends in the military." Zandra pulled her mobile snow globe from her pocket and hit a button before shaking it. "Hey, Finn. We need information about a military school application for Adam." She set her globe in the center of the table and put it on loudspeaker.

"Aww. And there I was, thinking you were calling to take me to breakfast." He grinned and waved a piece of toast in the air. "Shouldn't be a problem. What's your thinking?"

"Julie threatened to send Adam to goblin military school. We're wondering if he refused to go, so she killed him to get rid of a misbehaving son."

"Interesting theory. I've got a buddy who works in military recruitment. He's a good guy. Let me set up a three-way link to see if he can help. Hang for five. I'll be back."

We continued eating while waiting for Finn to make contact. The mobile globe sprang to life, showing Finn and a dark-haired man with several days' worth of stubble on his chin.

Zandra opened the connection.

Finn raised a hand. "Everyone, this is Marlon Buckley. I've given him the background on the investigation and why we need to know about Adam."

There was a brief round of introductions.

"Hey, everyone," Marlon said. "Since this information could help in a murder investigation, I'm happy to assist."

"We appreciate that," I said. "Was an application made for Adam Smith or possibly Prince Lork Wrunard to join the goblin military academy?"

"Sure was. He came in under Adam Smith, with some bull story about a goblin disguise and needing a non-magical name. I didn't think it was so weird. You get all sorts applying to join. You often find teens with no support or those at risk of becoming homeless signing up in desperation."

"You mean, they have to risk death while fighting for a war they don't understand because they have no other option?" Vorana sipped on her coffee.

"Lady, I don't make the rules, and I don't start the wars. I just help the newbies not fall at the first hurdle. Those who aren't fit for duty don't get in." Marlon checked something in front of him. "What the Wrunard family weren't aware of is we have links with witness protection and state-of-the-art facial recognition magic. No one gets in under a fake name. I knew who I was dealing with."

"When was the application submitted?" I said.

"Eight weeks ago. Adam's mother was the main signatory."

"I knew it!" Lucian squawked. "Hateful woman. Not a kind bone in her body."

"I reckon not. She requested Adam enter our toughest academy and get fast-tracked, so he'd be on active duty as soon as possible. For a young guy of that age, it was risky."

"Almost like Julie was setting Adam up to fail," I said.

"More like setting him up to die. I always start my recruits off easy, get them used to the routine, give them skills and experience, so when they go up against an enemy in the field, they don't freeze. I advised against it, but she said they were from a military family, and fighting ran through their blood."

"Other Wrunard family members served in the military?" Zandra said.

Marlon turned away from the globe for a few seconds. "They did. It's a long list of names. I've got dead cousins, aunts, uncles. Even Adam's gran served. The mother wasn't lying when she said they had a long history of military service. Lots of medals got handed to this family."

"That doesn't mean Adam would be any good in the field," Lucian said. "He loved exploring nature. He wasn't into violence. Well, not to the level expected from goblin warriors."

"And it was definitely Julie who signed off on the application?" I said.

"Looks like she wrote the whole thing. Same neat, precise handwriting. And the same handwriting on the covering letter requesting the academy Adam go to and that his application be fast-tracked into active duty." Marlon leaned back in his seat, his expression thoughtful. "Interesting family. Anything else I can do you for?"

"That's it, thanks," I said.

After a few more words, we signed off with Marlon and Finn.

"Julie kept all that quiet," Zandra said.

"Once we've finished breakfast, we'll see what the mother has to say about trying to get her son killed on the front line," I said.

"We know the truth now. Julie never had any patience. She couldn't wait for Adam to die in military service, so she killed him herself." Lucian squawked and fluttered his wings.

I nodded. As uncomfortable as it was to accept a mother had murdered her son, it looked like we'd found our killer.

# Chapter 21

## Mother's love

We wasted no time finding Julie. Now we'd uncovered her desire to shove Adam into the military academy, it seemed even more likely she'd killed him. Something terrible must have happened between them to ensure she destroyed her only way of continuing the Wrunard family name.

After a visit to Angel Force to meet Finn and update Cythera, we were off again.

I accompanied Zandra, Finn, and Cythera to her apartment, where the Wrunards were still staying. Lucian had wanted to come with us to confront Julie, but in his agitated state, he'd have caused problems, so I sent him off to find Mack.

"I haven't seen Bertoli today," Finn said. "He's not called in sick, has he?"

Cythera shook her head. "He left me a curious message. Apparently, he's checked himself into a thermal spa. He said he was stressed. I wasn't aware Bertoli was having problems, were you?"

"Bertoli seemed his usual self to me." Finn glanced at me. "Mostly."

"His voice sounded odd, as if he had a head cold."

I focused on my paws. That would be because Mack had disguised his voice to sound like Bertoli when leaving the message.

"The last time I saw him, Bertoli seemed distressed." I didn't make eye contact with Zandra. She could always tell when I wasn't being entirely truthful. "The thermal spa will work wonders on him. He'll come back a new angel."

Cythera grunted. "Maybe he will, but it leaves us in the lurch. This is a busy time in Crimson Cove with the festival still going on. And those pesky non-magicals keep popping out of the woodwork like unwanted termites. I can't afford to be an angel down."

"You wouldn't want Bertoli to work while he's sick, though, would you?" I said.

Cythera grumbled a few times. "Of course not. But he could have given me more warning."

We reached the apartment, and Cythera knocked on the door.

"You could just let us in, since you must have a key," I said.

She shrugged. "We can't just barge in."

Julie opened the door. If she was surprised to see us, she didn't show it and nodded a greeting to the group. "Cythera. Has there been a development in the investigation?"

"There has. May we come in?"

Julie stepped back and allowed us inside. She led us into a tidy lounge. Edith sat in her wheelchair, her large purse stuffed beside her and a huge bundle of knitting on her lap. Simon ambled in from the kitchen.

His easy smile slipped when he saw us.

"Go get Eric," Julie snapped at him.

Simon sighed. "I won't be able to wake him. He never surfaces before noon."

"Do it! He'll want to know what happened to his brother."

Simon bowed his head. "Whatever you say." He turned and left the room.

"This information mainly concerns you," Cythera said to Julie. "We've discovered you made an application to enroll Adam into military academy."

A flicker of annoyance crossed her face. "Why should that matter? We're warriors. We all need training."

"Warriors kill and plunder." Edith jerked around in her seat.

Julie rested a hand on her mother's shoulder. "The Wrunard family has a long history of fighting for what we consider worthy. Why should Adam have been any different?"

"You fight for more resources, you mean," I said. "Your skirmishes revolve around the possession of gold and mining rights."

Irritation flashed across her face. "Sometimes. But not always. We're often painted as being obsessed with accumulating wealth. But everyone needs assets. You can't live on air."

Simon returned, Eric stumbling behind him, wearing a stained white T-shirt and boxer shorts. He rubbed his bleary eyes. "What's going on?"

"You didn't consider sending Eric into the military academy, too?" I said.

Eric blinked several times then focused on his mother. "Military academy? What's the cat talking about?"

"It's nothing," Julie said. "I was concerned about Adam's future. I wanted him on the right path."

"He wouldn't have been on much of a path if he'd been killed serving on the frontline," Zandra said. "That's where you wanted him."

"Julie, is this true?" Simon said.

Her eyes narrowed. "Playing the innocent doesn't suit you. We talked about it and agreed it was the best thing for Adam. You encouraged it."

"Why would that be?" Cythera jumped in with a question, cutting me off. "Serving frontline warriors in goblin battles have a high mortality rate. Death and glory, isn't that one of your battle cries?"

Simon looked shame-faced to be called out on his lie. "Adam showed some worrying behaviors. His attitude needed changing if he was ever to become a strong leader."

"Because he liked photography rather than fighting?" I said.

Julie pivoted her glare my way. "How do you know about that?"

"It's useful to know everything about a victim. It helps uncover the reason they were killed," I said. "Were you humiliated by his interest in creative pursuits rather than turning into a strapping goblin warrior and providing dozens of offspring?"

Julie hissed out a breath. "I thought it was a phase, but Adam didn't grow out of it. He asked for his first camera when he was barely a teenager. I foolishly indulged him, expecting the equipment to be ditched in a corner to gather dust, but he became obsessed. He'd go out at all times of the day and night and take photographs."

"He even won an award for one of his beach pictures," Simon said.

Julie dismissed his comment with a hand wave. "Adam was making a name for himself in the wrong thing. I couldn't allow that."

"So you taught him a lesson," I said. "You couldn't face the humiliation of having a son who was in touch with his emotions."

"The only emotion we should be in touch with is rage," Julie said. "Rage promotes action. It makes you fight for what you believe in. Adam gambling around talking about flowers and lighting, it was ungoblin-like. I was glad we lived among the non-magicals, so we couldn't be too humiliated."

"You were sending him to military academy to toughen him up?" Eric said. "He'd have hated that. Adam didn't even like to rough play with me. I always went easy on him because he'd cry and make me feel bad if I landed a hard blow."

"Which is another reason he needed discipline," Julie said. "It's my fault. I indulged him. I bought him whatever he desired and didn't pay enough attention to his education. And you were no help!" She jabbed a finger at Eric. "Acting up and seeking the next thrill."

"Such a gentle boy," Edith said. "Always taking my picture. Following me around and asking what I was doing."

"Yes, he was," Julie said. "Adam was too gentle. That had to stop. He shouldn't have focused on childish fantasies when the future of this family rested on his shoulders."

Eric grumbled to himself and tugged down his T-shirt.

Simon patted him on the shoulder. "You had your chance, and you blew it."

Eric glared at him. "Like you care about my future. You're only here for one thing."

"Less of that," Julie snapped. She focused on Cythera. "I'll admit I was ashamed of Adam, but I didn't want him dead. I wanted him stronger. Going to military academy would have transformed him."

"Adam didn't agree with you, did he? He didn't want a place at the military academy," I said. "You must have been angry when he went against your order to sign up."

"He'd have gone. We were still discussing it before... well, before he died."

"You applied on his behalf," I said. "You specifically requested Adam get fast-tracked and go into active duty as soon as possible. You were willing to put your son in an extremely dangerous situation to teach him a lesson."

"Adam didn't need that!" Eric said. "He was figuring things out. He'd have put down the camera and towed the line, eventually."

Julie's expression was stony. "There was nothing to figure out. I had a path planned for him. Whether or not he liked it, that was his future."

"It's clear to me Adam didn't like it," Cythera said. "And you have no alibi. You were ashamed of Adam and needed to protect the family name from being ruined by his artistic pursuits."

"You're talking as if you think I killed Adam. I didn't. I was at our rental."

"Yet no one saw you walking there or going inside," Finn said. "We checked with your neighbors. If you can find one eyewitness that puts you there when Adam was killed, we'll know you're innocent. Until then..."

"She was dancing," Edith said.

"What was that?" Cythera said.

"My daughter. She was dancing at the festival."

"Ignore her," Julie said. "Mother spat out her pills this morning. She babbles nonsense when her medication is off kilter."

Edith stared up at Julie, and for the first time since I'd been around her, her eyes were clear. "You were in the crowd, dancing in the parade. I saw you just before Adam went to photograph that beautiful horse beast."

"I wasn't there." Julie pinched the bridge of her nose. "You must have seen someone who looked like me. Your eyesight's not what it used to be."

Finn crouched beside Edith's chair. "You're sure it was Julie?"

Edith nodded. "I know my daughter. I waved at her, but she ignored me. She always does. No one ever listens to me. Always telling me what to eat and think. When to sleep. Pushing me around in this chair like a baby."

"Take Mother to her room," Julie said to Simon. "And make sure she takes her pills this time."

"Edith's going nowhere," Cythera said. "She just proved you lied to us."

"She's a crazy old lady who hasn't had a sensible thought in her head for over five years." Julie threw up her hands. "You must have checked her medical records. She received a head injury when fighting Razia during a skirmish. She hasn't been the same since. Mother has delusions. She sees things that aren't there. I wasn't dancing in the crowd while my son was being stabbed."

"I saw you," Edith said.

Simon stepped away from Julie. "Were you there? I believed you when you said you didn't do it. But... the threats you made to Adam. Even I was worried you could be involved when he was killed."

"Be quiet, you coward!" Julie snarled at him, her hands fisted and her chest heaving. "Don't try to make me look guilty."

This was bad for Julie. She had no alibi. There was proof she despised Adam. And the rage flickering in her eyes revealed she had anger issues.

Julie raised her hands and backed away. "It wasn't me. I'd never kill my son."

Cythera and Finn exchanged a look.

"I've heard enough." Cythera gestured at Finn.

He stepped forward. "Julie Smith, also known as Queen Dixia Wrunard, you're under arrest for murder."

"This is the best way to celebrate catching a killer." Zandra raised her piece of gooey, cheesy pizza into the air.

I sat opposite her, Lucian perched on the back of my chair. "It feels good to have things figured out."

"Once the angels get a confession from Julie, the case will be closed." Zandra bit into her pizza and grinned.

Lucian heaved out a sigh. "It's over for all of us."

"I figured you'd be pleased Julie has been arrested. You said from the start you thought it was her," I said.

"It's not that worrying me." Lucian sank lower until I could barely see his eyes.

"You'll get a new assignment from witness protection if you want one," I said. "Ask for short-term only, so you don't get so bored."

"I'm not sure I want another assignment, but I don't know what I'll do next if I give this up. I've got no home with the Wrunards, and if I resign from my job, I'll have no purpose. I'll be a missionless owl."

"Take some time out and think about your future." I chewed on a crust of cheesy, prawny pizza. "And it'll take the angels a while to process this case and bring Julie to trial. You'll need to be involved with that. You'll be called as a witness."

He fluffed out his feathers. "Maybe I should just leave. Disappear into the wilderness and let nature deal with me. I feel like a burden."

Voss wandered over, Sid the raven on his shoulder. "I heard you were celebrating. That young guy's killer got caught thanks to you."

"We were pivotal in the investigation," I said. "Angel Force couldn't have done it without us."

Zandra lifted her gaze to the ceiling. "They'd have figured things out. We just speeded things up."

He leaned closer. "Rumor has it they arrested the mother."

"Rumor would be right," I said. "No charges have been brought yet, but she's the only one who could have done it."

Voss shook his head. "It's a bad business, but it hasn't put people off attending the festival."

"Adam would be happy to know that," Lucian said. "He took loads of pictures while he was here. He wouldn't want the fun to end because Julie turned evil."

"Maybe we could do something with his photographs." Voss was inspecting the bare walls. "I've been meaning to put up decent artwork in here. We could get some images of the festival blown up and framed."

"Adam would approve of that. He was so proud of his pictures." Lucian pulled himself upright. "I like that idea. This could be my final mission for him. Make sure there's a permanent place for Adam's work to be displayed. Show people there is more to goblins than fighting over gold."

Voss nodded. "Bring in some photographs, and we can pick out the best ones." He hurried away when a group of non-magicals wandered in to order food.

I turned to Lucian. "You see. You're already finding new ways to occupy your time."

"It's the least I can do for Adam. If I'd done my job properly, we wouldn't be in this situation. I still can't figure out how Julie snuck into the crowd without me seeing her. She must have been wearing a costume."

"The angels are checking with other people who were in the crowd that day," Zandra said. "Someone will have seen her. She won't get away with it. You never know, maybe the guilt will kick in and she'll confess."

"I hope so, because we need a more reliable witness than Edith," Lucian said. "The family wasn't lying when they said she's not all there. She surprised me by how lucid she was when we confronted Julie."

"Does she take sedatives?" I said. "Maybe that's the problem. Julie said Edith didn't take her pills, so maybe she was remembering more if her head wasn't so fuzzy. That was why she was able to tell us about Julie being at the festival."

"She does. But she's got no choice but to take all those pills. Edith's in constant pain, thanks to Razia almost killing her in battle."

Finn dashed past the pizza parlor, a blur of white and feathers. He saw us and doubled back, yanking open the door. "Razia just tried to kill Edith!"

# Chapter 22

## Final battle

We were all on our feet, paws, or wing, dashing after Finn into the cool evening.

"What happened?" Zandra said.

"The details are fuzzy, but we just got reports of two women fighting in an alleyway. Someone was brave enough to look and discovered Razia had Edith out of her chair and in a headlock."

"Why would Razia want to kill Edith?" I said.

"You'd think it would be the other way around," Zandra said. "Razia is the reason Edith has to take all those pills and is confined to a wheelchair."

"Whatever went down between them, it sounds serious." Finn zoomed ahead, and we followed him to an alleyway close to Vorana's bookstore. There were two angels already at the scene when we arrived.

And what a scene. Edith's wheelchair lay on its side with one wheel bent. She gripped the frame with bony hands, her face pale as she muttered to herself, her gaze on the ground. Razia was on her back, out cold and bloody.

When Edith saw us, she raised a filthy hand. "It was her! Razia killed my grandson. Now she wants us all dead."

Lucian flew over the scene, squawking his distress as he wheeled around.

"Easy now." Finn crouched beside Edith, alongside another angel. "Can you tell me what happened?"

"Razia came for me because I'm the weakest. She plans on wiping us all out. I tried to stop her, but she's too strong."

"Have you got medical assistance coming?" Finn said to the other angel.

"On its way."

I kept my distance with Zandra as the angels worked on Edith and Razia. Blasts of magic had blackened the stonework, and chunks of brick lay scattered around. These magic users were powerful to do so much damage.

Lucian flapped down and landed beside me. "It's carnage! Razia is pure evil to do this to Edith."

"Razia doesn't look too good," Zandra whispered.

"I hope she doesn't make it." Lucian squawked again. "After everything she put this family through, she deserves a grim end."

"Her chest is moving," I said. "But that's an awful lot of blood leaking out of her."

A doctor and a nurse appeared in a sparkle of magic. They took a few seconds to assess the scene, get details from the angels, then got to work on Razia.

"Razia must have decided this was an opportunity not to be missed," Zandra said. "She still held a grudge against the family because of what Adam did. Now he's dead, she's going after the rest of them."

"And she attacked the family member she thought would be easiest to pick off," I said. "But Razia underestimated Edith."

Zandra glanced at the damage. "No kidding. That old goblin still has power, even if she is heavily medicated."

Lucian stomped his feet. "Edith is as ancient as the hills and as dippy as a fruit bat after gorging on fermented grapes, but she still has her moments. I see the proud, old warrior in her now and again. She holds a deep pride in her ancestors' achievements."

Finn strode over to the medics working on Razia. He talked to them for a moment and then headed our way.

"How are they doing?" Zandra said.

"Not good. They inflicted major damage on each other. Razia is in the worst shape, and they're not sure they can save her. They need to take them to the medical center for treatment. We can't patch them up with what we have here."

Edith groaned and slumped down, her eyes flickering shut.

Lucian leaped in the air. "Do something! She's dying."

The nurse hurried over, checked Edith, rested her hands on her, and they disappeared. A few seconds later, the doctor did the same to Razia.

"You want to come with us?" Finn said.

"Of course we do," I said. "We're seeing this through to the end. Razia can't go unpunished."

"I'll meet you there." Finn blasted into the air, leaving a few white feathers fluttering in the breeze.

"Translocation spell?" Zandra scooped me onto her shoulder.

"The sooner we get there, the better. I didn't like the look of either of them, and we need answers before they both expire." I glanced at Lucian. "You know the way to the medical center?"

"I'll be there before you." He swooped away into the darkness.

Zandra cast the spell, and we arrived outside the small medical center on the outskirts of Crimson Cove. We hurried inside and found Finn talking to the receptionist.

He turned to us when he was done, shook his head, and blew out a breath. "I've just given them all the information on who the Smith family really is. What a mess. Just when we thought this was over. Gideon was taking the rest of the family home tomorrow and figuring out their new relocation and identities. Doubt that'll happen now."

"Did Edith say much before she passed out?" Zandra said.

"Nothing useful. She was in shock and kept saying the same thing. Razia attacked her. She tried to kill her, and Edith defended herself."

"What was Edith doing out alone?" I said. "She usually has a member of the family watching her."

"She didn't say."

"Edith must have put her old military skills to use," Zandra said. "I'm impressed she survived. I wouldn't have thought she stood a chance against Razia."

"These old goblins are tough," I said. "What about Razia?"

"She's in a critical condition," Finn said. "They're doing what they can for her, but they're not hopeful. Edith blasted a spell directly into Razia's heart."

Zandra grimaced. "Nasty. She meant business."

"Why wouldn't she if she was jumped by Razia? Edith wasn't going down without a fight," I said. "We'd all do the same. If an enemy strikes, you don't sit there and allow her to do whatever she wants. You obliterate to the best of your ability."

The doors crashed open, and Simon and Eric charged through. Lucian was behind them. Finn headed them off then brought them back to meet us.

"We just heard," Simon gasped out. "How's Edith doing?"

"They're still assessing things," Finn said.

"Can we see her?" Eric's hair was messy and his shirt misbuttoned.

"Not yet. The doctors will tell you more soon."

Lucian hopped over and settled next to me. "Couldn't get the door open. I had to wait for these idiots to arrive and let me in."

I patted his wing. I'd offer to show him my trick with doors, but now didn't feel like an appropriate time.

Simon shook his head. "I never trusted Razia. I should have known she'd do something like this."

"You trusted her enough to sleep with her," I muttered.

A flush of pink rose up his neck and onto his cheeks. "That was a moment of weakness. It was one we both regretted."

"It was more than one moment."

Lucian squeaked an agreement and snapped his beak at Simon.

Simon's expression hardened. "We all make mistakes."

"Did you know what she had planned for Edith?" Finn said.

"No! I'd never have allowed her to go after Edith. Razia said she was here to clear her name, and I believed her."

"She changed her plans." Zandra's expression was filled with suspicion as she studied Simon. "You were definitely with Razia when Adam was stabbed?"

He sighed. "Unfortunately, yes. Why do you ask? What does Adam's death have to do with Edith being assaulted by Razia?"

I nodded approvingly at my witch. "The attacks could be related."

"But you think my mother killed Adam because of the whole military thing. You took her away," Eric said. "I'm confused. Didn't she do it? It was Razia?"

Finn glanced at me. "We're still investigating."

"As much as it pains me to say this, Edith was certain Julie was in the crowd when Adam was stabbed, so perhaps she did do it," Simon said. "I've always considered Julie to be an excellent female, but she's been under stress. With Eric's ongoing problems, Adam refusing to obey her, and Edith's poor health, maybe it all got too much for her."

"You fooling around with her mortal enemy can't have helped the stress levels," I said. Was Simon glad Julie had been arrested since it meant he was in the clear? He was quick to point the finger when he realized Angel Force suspected her.

"And as I've said, I deeply regret that. I've learned my lesson." Simon looked more angry than regretful. He probably only regretted being caught.

He turned his back on me and continued to discuss Edith's condition with Finn.

Lucian glowered at Simon. "I wish he was guilty. I never liked him."

"If Gran's not going to make it, I want to see her, so I can say goodbye," Eric said. "She can be weird, but I still like her."

"You can see her soon." Finn turned from Simon. "Let the experts do their work. The doctor will be out with a progress report as soon as possible."

We found seats and settled in, only having to wait half an hour until the doctor who'd appeared in the alleyway came and saw us.

Eric jumped to his feet and approached him. "How's my gran?"

"You're Razia Obelong's grandson?"

"No! I don't care about her. Edith Smith. She's my gran."

"Mrs. Smith is stable. But she'll need to stay here for monitoring," the doctor said. "We want to keep her overnight and possibly longer, depending on how she responds to treatment."

"Gran will recover, though?" Eric said. "She'll be okay?"

The doctor consulted his notes. "I believe so. She's remarkably strong for her age."

"Edith will need her medication while she's here," Simon said. "It's important she doesn't miss a dose."

"Come with me. I'll take down the details and make sure she gets what she needs."

"What about Razia?" Finn said. "I'll need to speak to her as soon as she's conscious."

"That could be awhile. She's stable, but her condition is serious. She suffered significant damage to her heart. We'll have to work on her overnight before we know her long-term outcome."

"Has she regained consciousness?" Finn said.

"No, and I don't expect her to. To give her a chance to heal, we put her in a hibernation spell to allow us to work on her without her feeling any discomfort. If you'll excuse me." The doctor led Simon away.

Eric watched the doctor go then turned to us. "Does this mean you think my mother is innocent?"

"Not necessarily. We'll continue to question her. And we're doing follow-ups with people who were in the crowd when Adam was attacked to see if anyone saw her," Finn said.

Eric tugged on his bottom lip. "She was always hard on Adam, but I never thought she'd do this. Maybe you've got the wrong person. It was Razia, after all."

"Unless Razia and your uncle were untruthful in their statements, it would have been impossible for her to have murdered Adam," Finn said.

"Oh! Yeah. Those two were at it when Adam died. Gross." Eric shuffled on the spot and tugged at his misbuttoned shirt. "I'd better go see how my uncle's doing."

Finn turned to us. "You don't have to stay, but I thought you'd be interested in this. It seems there are some loose ends to deal with."

"More than a few," I said.

He tilted his head. "You're doubting Julie's guilt?"

"I thought we had it figured out. Now, I'm not so sure. Is Razia behind all of this?"

"I wondered that, too," Zandra said. "But maybe we're just not used to the level of violence goblins live with every day."

Lucian grumbled his agreement. "At first, even I was shocked by how rough they can be, and I've been involved with shady characters for years."

Finn shrugged. "If you figure it out, let me know. Go. I'll be in touch if I get anything useful from Edith or Razia. And keep this quiet. The last thing we need is Razia's horde showing up, surrounding this place, and demanding Edith's head on a pole."

I left the hospital with Zandra and Lucian, and we walked home.

"Goblins sure know how to hold grudges," Zandra said. "I can't believe Razia thought she could get away with this."

"I'm not sure I believe it, either," I said.

Zandra raised an eyebrow. "You saw the scene. It must have been Razia who started the fight."

I nodded as I processed everything that had just happened. This unpleasantly murky mystery wasn't over yet.

As hard as I tried, I couldn't sleep. After our visit to the medical center, Zandra had showered and gone to bed. I'd joined her but had tossed and turned all evening as I'd thought through these worrying new events.

Admitting defeat, I quietly rolled off the bed. Mack's grumbling snores let me know I hadn't woken him. Lucian had his head tucked under one wing, and Zandra's deep breathing reassured me she was still slumbering.

I did a full body stretch, checked my fur was pristine, and then headed up the basement steps and outside.

I was halfway to my destination before I stopped in the middle of the street and my heart flip-flopped. I'd been going to see Sammy. He'd always been my sounding board, but it felt like I was losing him. He must know about the investigation but hadn't come to see me and ask how things were going.

Sammy used to be so concerned about my well-being, but we were becoming strangers, and my heart hurt as I realized, for whatever reason, Sammy no longer wanted to be in my life.

"Hey! Where are you going?" Lucian zoomed over my head and landed in front of me.

"To see a friend. But I've changed my mind, since I don't think he's my friend anymore."

"What's wrong? I heard you tossing and turning before you left." Lucian hopped beside me as I changed directions.

"It's this investigation. Razia's fight with Edith. Adam being stabbed."

"By Julie."

"Maybe. Maybe not. I understand how fiercely protective goblins are of their reputation and how they want to ensure their name inspires fear and respect. That could have happened through Adam, even if he hadn't followed the traditional goblin path."

"The Wrunard family are fighters. If you're not born a fighter, you don't stand a chance. And I never liked the look Julie would get in her eyes when Adam talked about his photography. It was a mix of hatred and shame. It was her."

"But with Adam dead, that leaves Eric. No one thinks he'll achieve anything. Is that really how the Wrunard name will snuff out?"

"I dunno. I'm just glad it's over and I don't have to deal with them anymore."

"That's the thing. I don't think it is over."

Lucian clacked his beak together. "Let this go. Julie will be put away, Razia will hopefully die a horribly painful death, and Edith will get back in her wheelchair with her crazy knitting patterns and imaginary friends. Slow down! Where are you going?"

"Nowhere. Just need to move. It helps me think." I slowed as we reached the pizza parlor. Half a dozen photos had been stuck in the window. "Did you choose these with Voss and Sid?"

"After we left the medical center yesterday, I needed something to do, so I took a load of pictures to Voss. I didn't know he'd get them enlarged so fast, though." Lucian waddle-hopped to the window.

"Adam was talented. He never stopped until he got the perfect shot."

"They're all from the festival." I peered closer at one picture.

"Yeah. Adam was excited to get loads of pictures of Night Mare and Skull Dugger. Seeing those ancient, magical beings made him feel more connected to his roots."

"This one has Edith in it." My fur bristled, and my toe beans heated.

"Huh! What's she doing?" Lucian hopped over.

"She's standing."

"That's not so weird. She can. I mean, Edith can't walk far, but if she has to, she can shuffle about."

My gaze went to Edith's hands, and my breath whooshed out of me. I turned and raced off. "I must see Finn. We need more information about Edith."

"Hold up. Why?"

"I have an idea about that scatty old goblin. Let's go drag an angel from his beauty slumber."

# Chapter 23

## Pride before a fall

"You're sure he's home? He could have stayed at the medical center." Lucian hop-waddled along the hallway outside Finn's apartment.

"He can't still be working. Finn must be a sound sleeper." I thumped on his front door again. I'd been trying to wake him for several minutes.

Dawn was just breaking outside, and Finn had been working late nights, so I understood him wanting to catch up on his sleep, but this matter couldn't wait.

"Here, let me. I have a trick that wakes the dead." Lucian hopped back to the door. He opened his beak and screeched.

I backed away, my ears lowered. "Some warning, next time! I almost lost both eardrums."

"You said you needed this angel's help, so we don't have time to mess around." He screeched and hollered some more.

There was shuffling on the other side of the door, and a few seconds later, Finn's face appeared in the crack. "Juno! Lucian! Why are you making that demon awful noise? I thought something was dying."

"Greetings. It's urgent we speak to you," I said. "I've got an idea about Adam's killer, but I need your help. Well, your contacts."

"Come in, come in! My neighbors won't be happy if you wake them." Finn ran a hand through his sandy brown hair and stepped back, opening the door wider.

"And we've not had breakfast," Lucian said. "Got any fresh rodents in the fridge?"

"I'm all out. This way." Finn stumbled to the kitchen, yawning. "This has something to do with Adam?"

"We need to speak to your military contact again." I hurried after him. "We need files on the rest of the family who served in the military."

Finn raised a finger. "Coffee first. Otherwise, the explanation won't make any sense, and you'll have to start again." He opened a cupboard, rifled around, and tossed a packet of dried jerky on the counter. "That's the closest I've got to rodent. From its color, it could have been some sort of rodent."

Lucian made short work of the packaging and scattered the jerky across the counter for us to share.

I chewed on a piece, masking my impatience as Finn brewed coffee, scratched himself, then headed off to put on a T-shirt.

Once we'd eaten several strips of jerky, and Finn was on his second mug of coffee, he settled in a seat. "Okay. Why do you need to speak to my military contact? We solved this case. We arrested Julie. No alibi, solid motive, and she lied about where she was. It all fits."

"Have you got a confession from her?" I said.

He scrubbed his fingers across his chin scruff. "Not yet. But who else could it be? Razia and Simon were together. Eric was at the snail spa getting gooed out, and the gran was stuck in her chair on the sidelines."

"Let's get the information first. But I have my suspicions. I need them confirmed before I go out on a limb."

Finn checked the time. "Marlon should be up by now. He always gets up early." He brought over his snow globe and made a connection.

Marlon appeared a few seconds later. He looked freshly showered and brighter-eyed than Finn. "Hey. I didn't expect to hear from you so soon. Problem?"

"Possibly. We need more information about the Wrunard family members who served in the military."

"This is for your case?"

I hopped onto the counter so Marlon could see me. "Greetings. It is. In particular, I need to know if any family member ran into difficulties while serving."

"What difficulties are we talking about?"

"Unscrupulous behavior. Reprimands on their record. Anything that would suggest their service was less than glowing."

"How far back do you want me to go? It could take time."

"Stick with the immediate family," I said. "Julie, Simon, and Edith. Eric never served."

"That's easy. Give me their full goblin names and a few minutes."

More coffee was drunk and jerky consumed while we waited for Marlon to work his magic.

He puffed out his cheeks and blew out a breath as he focused on us. "This family loves their military service. Unfortunately, few survive it. They sacrificed a lot to defend their assets. I had a quick scan over the decades, and there were thirty-nine recorded dead while serving."

"Did Julie serve?" Finn said.

"She did two tours. Got a commendation. No problems on her record."

"And Simon?" I said.

Marlon's top lip curled back. "He went through basic training, went on his first mission, and got injured. Although it was never confirmed, it appears he stabbed himself in the foot. He was honorably discharged before going into battle. He's what we call a toy soldier. He got the training and the uniform to impress then backed out of doing any work."

"No surprise there." I drew in a steadying breath. "And Edith?"

"This is where it gets interesting. The Queen Mother, or Edith as you call her, served twelve full tours of duty. Barely anyone makes it through that many tours without a scratch. Physical or mental. She must have had to retire when she got too old to serve."

"That's the interesting part?" Finn said. "Her long service?"

"No, the interesting part is that most of her file has been redacted. I can't read most of it."

"Which means what?" Lucian said.

"Edith either did something incredibly important and top-secret, or something bad, and the military covered it up because of her efficient reputation. And by efficient, I mean, bloodthirsty. She has an eye-wateringly high kill rate."

"Something to be proud of," Lucian muttered.

Finn turned to me. "Where are you going with this? Do you think Edith killed Adam? That's impossible. She's stuck in that chair and lives most of her life in a fantasy world. I've checked her medical records, and she's not faking it."

"She isn't," Lucian said. "I'm around her most days, and she spends most of the time sleeping, singing, or talking to shadows. She's no threat to anyone."

"Not in her current state, but the family gives her medication," I said to Lucian.

"Sure. She's on pain meds and a light sedative."

"Maybe that sedative isn't so light. Edith is unstable, and if she's not drugged up to the eyeballs, she gets frisky. Starts remembering her kill rate and wants to add to it."

Lucian tapped his beak on the table. "The family is always strict about giving her those meds. No matter what they're doing or where they are, they never miss a dose. I always assumed it was because they didn't want her to be in any pain."

"Or it's because they need to control Edith. If she's off her meds, she attacks them."

"I don't know about any of this," Finn said. "As Marlon said, she's ancient."

"Being old doesn't mean you can't have great power," I said. "And there's something else. Two somethings, actually. Lucian delivered some photographs Adam took to the pizza parlor. Voss got them enlarged, and one picture shows Edith standing."

"She can do that?" Finn looked at Lucian.

"Not very well but when she has to. She usually falls over."

"What's the other thing?" Finn said.

"Edith's fingernails. They're always dirty."

"How does that prove she killed Adam?"

"I'll explain when I see more of Adam's photographs. I believe they hold the answer to this puzzle."

Finn nodded slowly. "I'll roll with that for now, since we don't have enough evidence to charge Julie. Marlon, any chance you could get that file unsealed? It would be useful to see what's been concealed."

He tilted his head from side to side. "I'll see what I can do. But no promises. I'll get onto my contact and let her know this relates to a murder. It may be enough to sway her to reveal the details. Especially if lives are at risk."

"Thanks. I owe you," Finn said.

"Next time, the beers are on you."

Finn signed off and sat back in his seat. "Should we put a watch on Edith? You think she could be a risk to other family members?"

"If they get in her way. Edith is making plans, and she wants to get out of her wheelchair and out of this constrictive life." I paced the kitchen counter. "She needs resources to do it, though, and if her military experience is anything to go by, this woman lets nothing stand in her way."

"Edith can't have killed Adam," Lucian said. "Even if he annoyed her, that's not enough of a reason to kill him. It was Julie! Edith is a distraction we don't need."

"What do you mean by resources, Juno?" Finn said. "You think Edith wanted something from Adam and he refused to give it to her?"

I didn't have time for explanations. All evidence pointed to Edith's growing instability, and she needed to be stopped. "No, not that. Lucian, let's speak to the family, but keep it casual. We need to know how much they're controling her with her medication."

"You don't want any angels with you?" Finn said. "You might need backup."

"You need to be ready for when Marlon calls back," I said. "If my hunch is right, Edith's military career didn't end well. And find Gideon. He'll want to know about this development."

"It's not Edith!" Lucian said.

I ignored the fluttering owl. "We'll take Zandra with us. We're back on day shift at animal control, but she'll have time to help. We'll stop by Cythera's and ask the family a few questions."

"They're not there. They've moved back to their rental. I'll join you as soon as I've heard from Marlon." Finn pinched his chin between his finger and thumb. "With the lack of evidence against Julie, there were doubts we'd get a conviction to stick. She's probably been released on bail this morning."

"That's a good thing," I said.

"Not if she did it," Lucian grumbled.

Finn tapped his fingers on the counter then downed his coffee. "Try not to get into too much trouble."

I left the apartment with Lucian, and we dashed home. Zandra was just leaving.

She jumped when I leaped onto the porch, Lucian beside me. "Juno! Where did you two go so early? Mack wasn't happy to wake and learn you'd left him behind."

"We've got a lead on Adam's killer," I said. "Care to join us to see how it pans out?"

Zandra glanced at her watch. "Sure. I was heading in early to check on the snails. And I wanted to give Barney an update about the lack of progress on figuring out what's digging all those holes."

"Come with us, and we can figure out that problem, too," I said.

"You think the holes and the dead animals have something to do with Adam?"

"Almost certainly. Follow me."

I gave Zandra a quick update on our visit to Finn and my thoughts about Edith. She seemed as incredulous as Lucian that a harmless old goblin could be involved.

"I still think we should stick with Julie," Lucian said. "If the angels keep applying pressure, she'll give in."

I shook my head. I had all the puzzle pieces now, and I wasn't being diverted from this path. "Has there ever been a time when the family has seemed scared of Edith?"

Lucian didn't answer straightaway as he hop-walked beside me. "Not scared, exactly. I'd sometimes catch them huddled in a corner, talking. They never let me in on the conversations, so I figured it was private family stuff. Maybe they were discussing Edith. She can be kooky and says weird things."

"Do you think she's dangerous?" Zandra said.

"No! Even if she messed up her military career by blasting out a few too many killer spells, Razia injured her. That attack put her in the wheelchair and gave her a life of daily medication and delusions."

"I'm not suggesting Edith wasn't injured, but maybe she's been healing herself over time. Some injuries take longer to recover from than others, especially brain injuries. Now she's feeling strong enough to strike out on her own but needs everything in place before she can do that," I said.

"Like what?"

"Money, a place of her own, freedom from the family. It must be stifling to have no control over your life. Edith is done being pushed around and told what to do."

"She's not aware of what's going on most of the time. This is pointless." Lucian fluffed his feathers and snapped at a passing bug.

"If this doesn't work, we'll go back to Julie and look for more evidence. But I have a feeling this sweet little old goblin will be a sour candy once we've dug beneath the surface."

Lucian grumbled and ruffled his feather some more but stopped arguing.

We reached the rental and discovered Edith on the porch, singing to herself.

"They let her out of the hospital early. How do you want to play this now Edith is here?" Zandra said.

Lucian shuffled his talons in the dirt. "You marching over and asking if she killed Adam?"

My gaze went to the purse that was always on Edith's lap or wedged in beside her. "I've never seen her without that purse."

Lucian plucked at a feather. "So?"

"Maybe there's something in there she doesn't want us to see. When Julie tried to take it from her when she gave her the reveal potion, she slapped her hands and hissed."

"Because Edith's crazy."

"Maybe there's a hint of crazy mixed in, but we should look inside."

"You're suggesting we steal an old lady's purse?" Zandra whispered. "I don't feel good about that."

"Would your conscience be less troubled if you knew she killed Adam?"

She moved her jaw from side to side. "You'll have a lot of making up to do if this doesn't work out."

"Have I ever let you down?"

Zandra lifted her gaze to the sky. "Well, there was that one time..."

I swatted her calf with a soft murder mitten. "We'll distract Edith. Lucian, you swoop in and grab the purse."

He shrugged. "My career is over, anyway. If I'm arrested for attacking a defenseless old crone, it won't make my life any worse than it already is. Ready when you are."

Zandra plastered a smile on her face, and I hopped on her shoulder as we headed over to Edith.

She looked at us and waved. "Beautiful day. I was singing with the birds. They keep telling me they're hungry. Greedy, fat things. Catch them and put them in a pie."

"Sounds delicious. How are you feeling today, Edith?" I said. "No ill effects from your fight with Razia?"

"What fight? I'm as bright as a button. I'm going dancing later."

"That sounds fun," Zandra said. "Is anyone else home?"

"They're all in there." She gasped. "Was that a dragon?"

I ducked and squinted at the sky. "You mean that cloud?"

"Yes! It looks like a dragon. One of the spiny ones that spurts acid."

"I see no dragons, but is that a green-winged sun sandpiper? They're really rare and have a beautiful song." Zandra pointed into the distance, where a brown bird buzzed around.

Edith turned her head, and Lucian swooped and grabbed the purse. He heaved it away but then sagged under its weight.

"Bad owl!" Edith's hand shot out at an alarming speed. She grabbed Lucian's wing and the purse and tugged them into her lap.

He squawked and flapped his free wing to get away, but Edith wasn't letting go.

"I always knew you were bad. Didn't look after Adam, and he's dead. And now you're stealing from me." She raised a hand to strike Lucian.

I leaped off Zandra's shoulder and landed on the purse. I bit Edith's arm, and she screamed.

Magic sparkled off her fingers in gray, jagged waves. "Evil kitty! Put you both in a pie and make you sorry. Bad! Bad! Bad!"

Edith stopped tugging on Lucian's wing, formed a fist, and whacked me in the stomach.

Air whooshed from my lungs as I shot back, flipping booping snooter over tail several times. But my claws were dug deep into the leather purse, and it came with me as I spun through the air.

Edith shrieked and gripped the chair arms. "My purse! Give it back."

"What's going on out here?" Simon appeared with Eric. And behind them was Julie.

"Deceitful bird. Evil cat. Kill both of you," Edith said.

"Mother! Don't say things like that. What made you so angry?" Julie rushed to her side.

Edith shoved her away. "Hate you, too. Grandson killer."

"Shush!" Julie glanced at Zandra. "What are you doing here? Did you just attack my mother?"

"She attacked us," Zandra said. "She tried to pull Lucian's wing off and punched my familiar. Juno, are you hurt?"

Edith shrieked again. "Give me my purse. Thief!"

I rolled onto my paws and did a full body shake, my stomach sore. I grabbed the purse, upended it, and tipped out the contents.

Edith roared her disapproval and struggled to get out of the chair.

"Stop that!" Julie caught hold of her shoulders. "You'll hurt yourself. Your muscles are too weak, and you always get dizzy when you stand. Calm down!"

"Explain what's going on before we call Angel Force," Simon said. "Why are you here?"

"Because of this," I said.

Lying among Edith's things was a rusty knitting needle, a bloodstained scarf, and a bottle of pills.

# Chapter 24

## A purse of secrets

"My things! Give me back my things. You have no right to take them." Edith kept struggling against Julie, and Simon had to step in to restrain her before she fell out of the chair.

Julie was breathless as she tackled Edith. "Return my mother's purse and leave. You're upsetting her."

I sniffed the knitting needle. As I'd suspected, it wasn't rust coating it. "We had an interesting conversation with a military contact about Edith's career."

"Why does that matter?" Julie kept a restraining hand on her mother's shoulder as she writhed in her chair. "If you don't calm down, you'll have the restraints."

Edith snorted her anger but stilled, her bright gaze on me.

"Because we need to find out who killed your son," I said. "And since the angels let you out on bail, there's doubt over your guilt."

Julie glanced over her shoulder. "They kept me as long as they could, but they had to let me go, so I came back to my family."

"This is ridiculous," Simon said. "Julie is innocent, and so is Edith. None of us wanted Adam dead."

"Maybe that was never the plan, but Adam got in the way. He had to be silenced before he told everyone what was going on," I said.

"What is going on? You've accused just about all of us of murdering Adam," Julie said. "You clearly don't know what you're doing. And where are the angels? If this is about Adam, I want someone in charge here."

"They'll be here soon." I wandered over and checked on Lucian. His wing hung down at an unnatural angle. I rested a paw on it and healed him. "At one point or other, I thought all of you might be guilty, because you all had motives."

"Not me," Eric said. "I liked Adam."

"You considered him the annoying younger brother who held you back. Your life is one hedonistic party after another. Having a kid brother under your feet all the time cramped your style."

"That's not a reason to kill him."

"And you must have been envious Adam was the favored son. It's possible you made a drunken mistake that ended his life. Maybe he bragged about his future and mocked you because you had none."

"It wasn't me," Eric muttered. "Maybe I was jealous. She barely notices me." He glanced at Julie. "It's like I don't exist."

Julie blinked several times. "You don't need extra stress on your shoulders when you're fighting your addictions."

"He doesn't fight them that hard," Simon muttered.

"Why do you think I turn to those distractions?" Eric said. "You ignore me. Or make fun of me. You said I'd amount to nothing. I was living up to your low expectations."

"You sought comfort elsewhere when your emotionally repressed family couldn't give you what you needed. It was what you were doing when Adam was killed. Eric didn't kill his brother," I said.

"Told you," he mumbled.

I stood beside Lucian. "Everyone has to be scrutinized. Lucian included."

He fluttered his wings but didn't protest as the spotlight of suspicion landed on him.

"Lucian failed Adam. He was bored and looking for a challenge."

"Maybe deliberately," Simon said. "Were you bribed to look away while the killer struck?"

Lucian launched like a feathered rocket and smacked into Simon, taking him down. He jabbed and pecked at his face while Simon squealed.

I yanked the owl back by the tail. "Enough! Lucian admits to making a mistake. He cared for Adam, but he wanted more from his work than being a long-term bodyguard. Besides, Lucian has an alibi."

Lucian snapped at me then ducked his head and stopped fighting.

Simon scrambled to his feet. "I'll make sure you're fired after that outburst. Unprofessional."

Lucian hissed at him then stamped away.

"What about you, Julie?" I said. "Reputation is everything, and you'd do whatever it took to get back to glorious rule."

She calmly met my gaze. "There's nothing wrong with that desire. We had everything, but after Razia targeted us, we had no option but to retreat."

"You long for a return to power. Maybe you made a deal with Razia. You murdered Adam, and she allowed you back to rule."

"I'd never do that!" Julie said. "Without Adam, the family name dies. I have no one else I can rely upon to manage our power base."

"There you go again," Eric muttered.

Julie lifted a hand to him then lowered it. "I must do what's best for the clan. And you're not the best."

"I'm all you've got now, though. Maybe you should treat me better, in case I defect to Razia's side and tell her your secrets."

Julie's mouth opened and closed several times. "You've never been able to see the bigger picture. That's why you'll amount to nothing."

"I see what's important," he said. "Maybe you did kill Adam. He wasn't good enough for you, either, so you snuffed him out. You're sly enough to do it."

A glimmer of pain hit her face but was masked as she turned away from Eric.

"When we realized you were in disguise, and this wasn't a random attack on a non-magical, Julie was the prime suspect from the start," I said.

"So, charge me! If you're so certain it was me, put me behind bars," she said. "You've got no evidence."

"Julie is a good woman." Simon rested a hand on her shoulder. "She'd never do such a terrible thing."

She shoved him away. "That's not what you said when Angel Force took me. I've had enough of your silken words. I don't trust you. I never have."

"Simon is correct, though. You'd never do such a terrible thing. Julie is innocent." I kept watch on Edith, who looked like she wanted to obliterate us. "However, Simon, you might kill to get what you desire. Did you want the way clear so you could pursue Julie?"

"There's nothing like that between us." Julie slid a vicious glare toward Simon.

"He'd pursue any path to rejoin the goblins," I said. "Whether that means sleeping with Julie, Razia, or any willing goblin who promises him a way in, he'd do it."

"The cat's not wrong," Eric muttered.

"It is. I have morals," Simon said.

"I don't think you do. And you're not as smooth as you think. Razia realized you were playing her, and I'm certain Julie does. She keeps you around because you're family, and you'd cause trouble if she couldn't monitor you."

"And because I pity him." Julie shrugged. "There are so few of us, I can't toss him away, no matter how many times I've wanted to."

Simon sucked in a breath. "I thought we had an understanding?"

"She understands you're a creep and a user," Lucian said. "Julie's never been fooled by you."

He spluttered a few words. "My indiscretions aren't the focus. This is about Adam's killer. It was none of us, so it must have been Razia. And she was caught trying to kill Edith. If Razia survives, she must be charged with Adam's murder."

"The fight between Razia and Edith was the first big clue to revealing the killer," I said.

"There you go." Simon gave a firm nod. "Razia wants us dead. You can't let her go free."

"Who started that fight?" My gaze went to Edith. "Edith claimed it was Razia, but what if it wasn't?"

Julie bared her teeth at me. "My mother is a weak, old goblin. She can barely get out of this chair. It would have been impossible for her to go after Razia."

Edith burbled a few notes and waved a finger in the air.

"It was Razia," Simon said. "Why are you wasting time looking at dear old Edith?"

"Give me my purse." Edith had been quiet throughout the conversation, but she'd kept glaring at me and the scattered contents of her purse.

"I was fooled, like everyone else," I said. "Your frail act, pretending you can't get out of that chair, and obediently taking your medication so you're not seen as a threat to the family."

"Mother's a threat to no one." Julie glanced at the bottle of pills on the ground.

I rested a paw on the bottle. "This is the medication Edith hasn't been taking. She still needs pain relief, but she must have realized you've been sedating her. Why do that if she's no threat to you?"

Finn flew in and landed by the house with a feathery thud. He stood and nodded at me.

Gideon flashed into view a second later. He shoved back his long cloak and looked at the family. His gaze hardened when it settled on Edith.

"Did you get the information?" I asked Finn.

"Oh, yeah. The file provides quite a story. Want a look? I've highlighted the best bits. Well, the worst bits."

I dashed over and took a moment to scan the file, Zandra beside me.

"Whoa!" she whispered. "It's like reading a horror story."

"It makes perfect sense to me."

Finn raised an eyebrow. "Juno! No one could have imagined this would be in here."

Sadly, I could. History revealed two common traits among all intelligent creatures. They enjoyed violence, and they'd do anything to stay alive.

I trotted back to the family and paced the front of the rental. "There have been two investigations going on since your arrival in Crimson Cove. One of them concerns holes dug around the town and half-eaten animals left beside them."

Julie shot her mother a sharp look. "What's that got to do with us?"

"Adam discovered who was digging all those holes. They're very determined. There's something in this town they want to get their hands on." I stopped in front of the wheelchair. "You've been sneaking out with your shovel and grabbing furry midnight snacks, haven't you, Edith?"

No one spoke. Everyone stared at Edith.

Edith glared at me. "I still want my purse."

"I'm done listening to this fairytale." Julie grabbed the handles of the wheelchair. "Mother, let's go inside. You need a nap. And Gideon, we need to discuss our relocation. We can't return to our old home. And I was thinking a new disguise as orcs would be appropriate."

Gideon smirked and shook his head. "We can talk about that later. I have a feeling you'll be focused on family matters for quite some time."

"Edith's been desperate to escape the confines of this family." I jammed my murder mittens on the chair's footrests. If Julie wanted out of here with her murderous mother, she'd have to get past me. "She figured out what you were doing to her."

Julie looked at the bottle on the ground. "It was for her own good. She can be difficult."

"She's a lot more than difficult. Look at Edith's fingernails. They have dirt underneath them."

"Mother doesn't enjoy bathing. It's always a struggle to keep her clean. I do the best I can."

"You never wondered where it came from," I said. "How does she get so dirty if all she does is sit in that chair all day?"

Edith slid her hands underneath her thighs. "Crazy kitty. Steals my bag and accuses me of eating things I shouldn't. I'll eat you next if you don't stop talking."

Simon and Julie exchanged a worried look.

"I didn't link the clues at first, but her dirty nails made me wonder. Put them with the holes that appeared after Edith arrived in town, the nibbled-on animal corpses, and Adam's murder, and it all fits together." I focused on Julie. "It isn't the first time Edith's done this, is it?"

She pressed her lips together then sighed. "It's the reason we started sedating her. Mother began going out at night and digging holes. And... she'd sometimes catch small animals and eat them. She'd come home covered in dirt and blood. I was scared she was losing her mind. The pills keep her calm and stop that behavior."

"Finn, please share what you discovered in Edith's military file," I said. "It'll help everyone if they know what she went through."

His face was pale as he stepped forward. "Edith's file was redacted. I have a contact who pulled strings and sent me a copy of her full file."

Edith began singing again, although her eyes flamed with anger.

"Go on," I said.

"Edith's last tour of duty was a train wreck. She got stuck behind enemy lines and was abandoned. She was trapped with two injured goblins from her squad. They were stuck in the same place for months."

"That's all true," Julie said. "Mother's a war hero. She was the only one who survived that mission."

"She survived by eating the others," Finn said. "She murdered her squad and ate them."

Eric's mouth dropped open. Simon took a step back, and even Julie's expression tightened. Gideon simply shook his head and muttered 'goblins.'

"Maybe they were already dead," Julie said. "Mother had no choice. It was the only way she could survive."

"There were remains, which were recovered once Julie was found. The autopsies showed they were killed, dismembered, and eaten."

"After that mind-breaking experience, Edith got a taste for hunting and catching her prey," I said.

"I'm gonna be sick," Eric said.

"Once Edith recovered, the military did what they could for her," Finn said. "They put her on desk duty. They knew a broken warrior when they saw one but couldn't risk the scandal getting out. But Edith needed more. She'd spent her life in the field, so sitting behind a desk must have sent her stir crazy."

"Literally," Eric muttered. "My granny eats goblins!"

"They were tasty," Edith said. "And annoying. I was happy to do it."

"Be quiet!" Julie snapped. "You don't know what you're saying. You'd never eat another goblin."

Finn checked his notepad. "When Edith was assigned her desk job, she quickly got restless. Then she came across information about goblin gold taken in a heist. Apparently, it was buried until the heat died down and the thieves could dig it up. She requested a small troop attempt a retrieval, but the request was denied."

I nodded. "Crimson Cove was one place where the gold was rumored to be buried. And once Edith arrived for the family vacation, she must have remembered and begun searching, while taking a nibble from the local wildlife to keep her energy up."

Simon strode over to Finn. "This is an outrage. Edith can barely remember what she had for breakfast, let alone some rumors about buried gold from years ago."

"Why did you want that gold?" Julie said.

"Trust the goblin to focus on the gold first," Gideon murmured.

Edith hummed under her breath.

"She needs enough resources to escape the family who drugged her into obedience," I said.

Julie backed away from the chair. "Even if all of that is true, what does it have to do with Adam?"

"He found you, didn't he, Edith? Adam would go out at all hours to take photographs. He discovered you digging a hole while snacking on a fresh kill. Was he appalled? Did he tell you he'd speak to Julie? Or did he want a cut of the gold, and you decided not to share."

"Is that what happened?" Julie's tortured gaze rested on the back of Edith's head. "Adam said he wanted to talk to me about something the day he died, but I felt unwell, so told him it would have to wait."

Edith shuffled in her seat. "It was my gold. I needed it."

"You planned on keeping it, and you couldn't risk anyone in the family learning what you intended to do and stopping you," I said. "It was just you and Adam at the festival the morning Night Mare appeared. Did Adam lean down to speak to you, or you asked for help with something? While he was leaning over you, you used a metal knitting needle to stab him."

Everyone looked at the fallen bundle of knitting and the blood encrusted needle.

"The needle is so long and thin, there'd have been little blood to begin with," I said. "Adam may not have realized what had happened for a few seconds. He'd have felt pain but must have staggered into the crowd, and they bustled him away. He was trapped, in distress, and unsure what was going on."

"This murder was about greed." Lucian flapped his wings. "You killed your grandson for gold?"

I stamped on his tail to stop him from going after Edith.

"That's the knitting needle Edith used?" Finn moved closer and inspected the contents of the purse.

"I'm certain that's Adam's blood on the needle," I said. "And Edith must have used it to make that scarf. There's more blood on the wool."

"Tell me the cat is lying. You can't even walk properly." Julie's words wheezed out of her. "You wouldn't do this to Adam."

"Never have I ever killed someone." Edith giggled.

"Adam's photographs tell a different story," I said. "He was taking shots at the festival, and he caught Edith on the move. She can get around just fine. He even took a picture of her after she'd attacked him. Voss Black got the photograph enlarged, and it shows her holding a bloody knitting needle."

Edith peeled back her lips to reveal stubby teeth. "Adam was a snitch! He proved that by tattling on Razia. I've been planning my escape for such a long time, and nothing was standing in my way. I wanted my gold and my freedom, and that sniveling brat wasn't ruining things for me."

Julie wrapped her arms around herself. "No! How could you?"

"It took one thrust. He was such a weak creature. You should thank me. It reminded me of the good old days, when I got paid to kill. I want more!"

"I've heard enough," Finn said. "Edith Smith, you're under arrest for murder."

⚹⚹⚹⚹⚹ ⚹⚹⚹⚹⚹

"The next time you invite me to stay, make sure no one gets killed." Mack drooled on the pizza parlor floor as we waited for our order to arrive.

"That wasn't the plan. We were supposed to be dancing, eating, casting spells, and bobbing for candied treats. No one could have known a bunch of sneaky goblins would appear and cause such chaos." I sniffed the air and gently purred. The food was on its way.

After Edith's arrest, it had been back to business as usual. Angel Force had processed her. The remaining Smith family had slunk off with Gideon to figure out what to do next, and I'd accompanied Zandra to animal control for a day of dealing with misbehaving critters.

Voss walked over and set down a giant deep pan seafood medley pizza for me, Lucian, and Mack, and a mushroom cheese feast and a side order of garlic bread for Zandra. "I just heard from a customer that the little old lady in the wheelchair killed Adam. I'd never have figured that out."

"I don't think I would have either, but it was Juno who put the pieces together," Zandra said.

"Rumor has it she killed him so he wouldn't reveal the whereabouts of some goblin gold. Is there really buried treasure in Crimson Cove?"

Lucian squawked and ruffled his feathers. "If there is, it's not worth killing for."

"No, it's just a rumor," I said. "Don't start digging holes, or you'll find Angel Force on your doorstep asking questions."

Voss raised a hand. "I don't need any stolen gold in my life. Besides, I've got everything I want right here. Enjoy your food." He petted Sid, who was perched on his shoulder, then walked away.

Finn strode in a moment later with Gideon, and they pulled up seats and joined us.

"I'm done in. Thanks to Juno and Lucian's rude awakening, I've been working almost twelve hours straight," Finn said.

"Did the tests on the blood show it was Adam's?" I said.

He grabbed some garlic bread. "It was his. And we checked the medication Edith had in her purse. All sedatives. She knew what the family was doing, and she wanted out."

"And she was looking for the lost gold to pay her way to freedom." Gideon puffed out his cheeks. "I never thought their trip to Crimson Cove would end in murder. I have a pile of paperwork to slog through thanks to this."

"At least you're alive to do that paperwork," Lucian muttered.

Gideon gave a half-hearted shrug. "Yeah. Good point. I'll stop complaining about the paperwork."

"I'm happy the investigation is over, but I wish Edith hadn't chewed on all those poor animals while she searched for her gold." Zandra shuddered.

"I heard about that. Must be something seriously wrong with the old broad." The two pieces of pizza jammed in Mack's mouth muffled his words. There was another slice resting under one chunky paw. My honey badger friend loved his food.

"That last tour of duty broke her," Finn said. "It's not uncommon for long-term military personnel to come back changed. They see terrible things."

"And they don't always get the support they need when they return," Gideon said. "Edith had her family, but Julie was all about keeping up appearances and making them seem perfect. Her crazy mother running around eating things shattered that illusion."

"And Adam was just in the wrong place at the wrong time." Zandra sighed. "He was trying to live his life, and his unhinged gran stabbed him because he saw something he shouldn't."

"Some people have no luck," Finn said.

"And that lack of luck has been passed to me. I'm homeless, and I have no job." Lucian dropped the piece of pizza he'd taken.

"You're giving up on witness protection?" Gideon said.

"Of course! You don't want me, not after my failure."

Gideon rocked back in his seat. "You couldn't have stopped what happened. Even if you'd seen Adam with Edith, why would you suspect that evil old goblin of stabbing him with a knitting needle? Even I'd have missed that."

"So... I'm not fired?"

"You still have a job, if you want it."

Lucian glanced at me. "Yeah, maybe. But I need a long, paid vacation first. Then we're talking. I want more of a say in my assignments."

Gideon grinned. "I can work with that. You have skills, and I don't want to lose them."

Lucian picked up his fallen pizza slice and gave a cheerful chirrup. After everything he'd been through, it was good to see him happy.

"What about the rest of the Smith family?" Zandra said.

"Simon is still groveling around Julie, trying to earn her forgiveness."

"He doesn't stand a chance after his betrayal," Lucian said. "Once her trust is lost, it's gone forever. Look how she treats Eric."

Gideon nodded. "Eric is talking to someone about rehab. And they're all in negotiation with Razia."

"They're really considering allying with her?" Zandra said. "Even after she drove them into witness protection?"

"The desire for power and the need to keep the goblins from losing their next battle has won out over all previous grievances." Gideon snagged a slice of pizza.

The news didn't surprise me. Goblin bloodlust overruled everything else, although I wouldn't be surprised to learn of a new feud between them once the latest threat had been vanquished.

The door to the pizza parlor was shoved open, and a bundle of chattering non-magicals crowded in. Many of them wore Night Mare or Skull Dugger costumes.

If they knew the truth about those ancient creatures, they'd run for the hills, not canter around in fake ragged manes and impersonate them.

"Adam was much like those non-magicals," I said. "They're just in the wrong place and have no clue what's going on around them."

"They give me the chills," Mack said. "That's another thing I don't expect to see on my next visit."

"You won't get another invite to visit if you keep being so snippy," I said.

Mack growled at me then grinned as he gulped more pizza. Curmudgeonly old honey badger.

"Now things are quieter at Angel Force, we're making it our priority to see what's going on," Finn said. "We've got the Blood Moon event coming up, so we can't risk having them around then."

"I'm happy to help you clear them out," Zandra said. "It's hard to work when we're looking over our shoulders to ensure there are no non-magicals watching. They can't encounter us casting spells or trapping an animal that would blow their heads off if they looked at it the wrong way."

"What are they doing here, anyway?" Gideon said.

While everyone discussed theories about the non-magical invasion, I studied the photo prints Voss planned to hang around the pizza parlor. Adam had been a talented photographer, and these were a fitting memorial. He could even have become the first successful goblin photographer, if his family hadn't suffocated him with their lust for reputation and protocol.

My attention diverted from the photo prints as Sammy and Tinkerbell sauntered past the pizza parlor. My appetite faded as they leaned in close while they talked.

"Something up?" Mack said.

"Nothing I can't handle." I lifted my booping snooter and ignored the stinging in my eyes. I'd lost Sammy, and I didn't know why.

The goblin problem was solved, but things felt adrift in Crimson Cove. The non-magical issue was growing, my relationship problems seemed never-ending, and my newly found magic wouldn't cooperate.

I was unsure how to resolve any of it.

"You don't like your pizza?" Zandra leaned over and tickled me under my chin. She glanced out the window at Sammy. "Or is something else bothering you?"

"I have things to fix, but I'll figure them out with you beside me." I hopped onto her lap and curled into a ball.

"You always do, Juno. And whatever you need, I'm here for you." Zandra kept one hand on my side as she ate her pizza and chatted to everyone.

Although things weren't perfect, we'd solved the murder and uncovered a mystery in Crimson Cove. It was a good day to celebrate. But, right now, I planned on taking a long nap in my favorite place and forgetting all my worries.

# About Author

K.E. O'Connor (Karen) is a mystery author living in the beautiful British countryside. She loves all things mystery, animals, and cake.

If you want to practice spells, solve a few murders, and spend time with amazing witches and their talking familiars, join her weekly newsletter.

Sign up today.

**Newsletter:** https://BookHip.com/GXDVFRA

**Website:** www.keoconnor.com/writing

**Facebook:** www.facebook.com/keoconnorauthor

# Also By

**Witch Haven:** Welcome to Witch Haven, where nothing is what it seems. Meet four fabulous witches as they struggle with their destinies, deal with misfiring magic, murder, and the irksome Magic Council.

**Crypt Witches:** Meet Tempest Crypt, a witch who swallows demons, and Wiggles, her talking hellhound, while you enjoy magical murder and intrigue.

**Lorna Shadow:** A cozy mystery series set in the fun world of a personal assistant who sees ghosts. Meet Lorna, her ditzy sidekick, Helen, and Flipper, the dog who senses ghosts, as they solve crimes and save the day.

**Holly Holmes:** An adorable cozy culinary mystery series set in the beautiful English village of Audley St. Mary. Each book is full of treats, murder, and twists. Join Holly and Meatball, her clue-hunting dog, as they solve murders and eat cake.